THE
EMERALD

OTHER BOOKS AND AUDIO BOOKS
BY JENNIE HANSEN:

Abandoned

All I Hold Dear

Beyond Summer Dreams

The Bracelet

Breaking Point

Chance Encounter

Code Red

Coming Home

High Stakes

Macady

Some Sweet Day

Wild Card

THE EMERALD

a novel by

Jennie Hansen

Covenant Communications, Inc.

Cover image copyrighted, William Whitaker 2006

Cover design copyrighted 2006 by Covenant Communications, Inc.

Published by Covenant Communications, Inc.
American Fork, Utah

Printed in Canada
First Printing: August 2006

11 10 09 08 07 06   10 9 8 7 6 5 4 3 2 1

ISBN 978-1-59811-151-4

This book is dedicated to my granddaughters, McKayla and Alena, with all the love and hope I feel for these precious spirits as they embark on life's journey. It is my prayer that they will grow in truth and honor, develop their many talents, marry in the Lord's House, and become valiant mothers in Zion. May they love and be loved eternally.

PROLOGUE

The man with pale skin pointed to himself and made a strange sound. Then he smiled and pointed to her. He seemed to want to know what she was called. She leaned her head to one side, watching the motions he made with his hands and listening to his strange words. This man wasn't like the others. He'd come to her father's house alone twice. Before her father could hide the green stones the strangers coveted, the pale one had discovered him fashioning a ceremonial band liberally adorned with the sacred stones. The pale one admired the stones and her father's workmanship, but he hadn't grabbed them or struck her father as the others had. Now he sat on a large boulder in the clearing where she'd run when she'd first seen the men approaching the village. She didn't run from him because she had nowhere else to go. The others were surely in the village by now, and they would have blocked the paths leading to the mountains. Besides, she was curious about this man who was different from his companions. He asked for nothing, unlike the others who stole from the villagers, abused women they found alone, and demanded to be taken to the place where the green stones were mined.

Hesitantly, she whispered the name her mother had used to summon her in childhood. He repeated the name, which sounded strange on his tongue. He smiled again as he repeated the sound he'd made earlier and pointed to his chest.

After a moment, he held out his hand. Nestled in his palm was something bright and pretty. He motioned her closer, but she took a step back. After a moment, he set the shiny object on the rock, then backed away. Curious, she moved closer. Beads, looking like tiny, gleaming black flowers, were separated by bits of gold as finely worked as any piece of jewelry worked by her father's people in the mountains. Two intersected sticks of the fine gold dangled from one end of the chain. She almost touched the place where the sticks crossed each other, but caution brought her eyes up in a hasty, defensive motion. She was surprised that the man had made no move toward her while she was engrossed in examining the strange item. He motioned for her to pick it up. Afraid the curious piece held some dangerous enchantment, she retreated a step.

Angry shouts reached her ears through the trees, followed by a volley of thunderclaps. She knew the sound hadn't come from the sky. The strangers with hair on their faces carried fire sticks, and when the sticks roared, her people fell to the ground, dead from gaping wounds in their bodies. Running feet sounded on the path that led to the clearing, and the fire sticks roared again. Screams and angry shouts came closer. Frightened, she glanced about for a hiding place.

Arms encircled her, and when she would have screamed, a hand closed over her mouth. The stranger carried her into the jungle, easily subduing her struggles. He crouched with her in his arms behind a rotted log. Hanging vines provided complete concealment from the men who pursued the villagers into the clearing. When two of the strangers rushed past the hiding place, she thought the one who held her would join them and she would die, but he didn't call out. Time passed slowly, but eventually the shouts and thunder ceased. Many of her people lay still in the clearing and along the path. For a space, there was silence, then began the high, keening wail of a woman who had lost her husband and children. Her mourning stopped abruptly.

The man straightened, carefully placing her on her feet. He didn't hold her, but she made no attempt to run away. He lifted his hand, and she saw the gleaming black and shining gold of the chain he'd shown her in the clearing. With solemn deliberation, he passed it over her head and settled the chain about her neck. Looking into his eyes, she saw sadness. For a reason she did not understand, he had saved her life, then had given her a gift.

Reaching into a small pouch she carried on a thong about her neck, her fingers touched the stone she'd been given at her naming ceremony. Some impulse suggested that reciprocating the man's gift was more important than keeping the sacred stone as the wise man had instructed her to do. Her small hand thrust the stone into the man's pale hand, and then she fled from the place on feet as nimble as the sheeplike animals that leaped among the rocks high above the jungle. She would go to her mother's people high in their hidden valley.

* * *

Among the valuables confiscated by pirates from a Spanish galleon, but four days short of reaching the Strait of Gibraltar, was an incredible emerald. The young Spanish priest, who had resisted yielding the stone to the pirate, lay at the bottom of the Atlantic Ocean. The gem became a fitting tribute for the pirate's royal liege lord whose good graces kept the pirate from dangling from a yardarm. In time, it struck the fancy of a prince who'd had it set in a cravat pin to adorn the folds of the dandy's intricately woven neck-piece. It was his favorite jewel until the day a soldier, a second son from a respectable family, had come to the aid of his inebriated future king. The prince had fallen from his horse and was about to be trampled underfoot by his startled mount. Out of gratitude for the gift of his life, the prince awarded the jewel to the soldier. The soldier wore the gem proudly, even after circumstances had made him heir to an honored title along with one of the greatest fortunes in all of England.

* * *

"Help us, Miss! They've killed Papa!"

"Footpads attacked the coach," the Countess of Wellington shouted. "They've taken our jewelry and killed poor Wellington."

None of the party showed any sign of having recognized her, so Georgiana knelt beside Wellington, who lay facedown on the grassy verge of the road. She attempted to turn him over to examine his wound, but he was a heavy man, and she only succeeded in turning him to his side. Blood was flowing quite freely from a wound beneath his shirt. She leaned forward to check the wound and caught the faint rasp of his breathing.

"He's alive," she called. "Help me turn him to his back, and bring me something to stanch the blood." No one moved. They stared at her blankly while she flipped up the hem of her skirt and ripped off a strip of petticoat. Folding the cloth in a pad, she pressed it against the wound. As she did so, her eyes were drawn to a green stone shining brilliantly amid the folds of the man's cravat.

After sending the earl's daughters to fetch water, Georgiana found herself alone with the titled man who had once been a soldier. She had no quarrel with him, but someday his fortune would fall to the man who had betrayed her. Quick as a flash, she produced a small knife from the pocket of her gown. The soft gold prongs holding the emerald in place succumbed to her deft hands, and the green stone dropped into her hand. She pried loose the bit of green window glass from her bracelet and fastened it in the cravat pin. Later, the emerald would replace the glass in her bracelet.

1 ↷

October 1844

Momentarily forgetting her son clinging to her skirts and the heavy bag hanging from her arm, Margarette began to run, desperate to reach her baby. She wove her way through the crowd that separated her from the woman in a gray cloak who was walking away with her tiny daughter. Despair threatened to overwhelm her. She'd taken every precaution she could think of, and still they'd been found. A surge of strength lengthened her stride. She wouldn't give up—not ever. She was a good mother and her children needed *her,* not the bitter, cruel old man who claimed it was his right to raise his son's children and discipline them as he saw fit. She had no intention of allowing her children to be punched and whipped as their father had been until he'd lost all hope of a better life.

The woman stopped, and Margarette rushed toward her, determined to reclaim her daughter. A cry behind her was a reminder that Jens was clinging to her skirts, struggling to keep up. She stopped abruptly. What was she going to do? The strange woman had Annelise, but if she pursued her, would she be giving someone an opportunity to steal Jens too?

The woman carrying Annelise turned abruptly, retracing her steps and closing the gap between them with a couple of swift strides. Dropping the bag she still carried, Margarette grasped her son's hand in a protective grip and then straightened to face the beautiful, dark-haired woman rushing toward them. She briefly noted the gray cloak's bright Scottish plaid lining that framed the woman's face, before she centered on the woman's fierce facial expression.

Margarette lifted a hand as though she would somehow defend herself and her son, but instead of reaching for Jens, the woman thrust the baby girl hard against Margarette's chest. Margarette clutched at the infant with one hand and staggered back a step from the force of the abrupt gesture. She heard Jens's cry as she stumbled against him. Frantically, she struggled to regain her hold on him and to stay erect without dropping the baby.

She feared the woman's action was some kind of trick to distract her, but no matter what the woman did, Margarette was determined not to release her hold on her children. God had entrusted Jens and Annelise to her, and she would not relinquish them to anyone. The baby began to wail, and Margarette clutched her children tighter, watching as the fashionably dressed woman, without speaking a word, gathered up her skirts, turned, and raced with her gray cloak streaming behind her toward the plank linking the *Carolina* to its sister ship, the *Nightingale.* The bridge, she had been told, provided the passengers and crew of the other ship with access to the wharf via the *Carolina.*

"Mamma," the little boy sobbed against her hip. "You hurted me."

"I'm sorry, dear. Hold on tight to my skirt. We must get to our quarters quickly." She retrieved her bag with the hand that had held Jens's small hand, clutched the crying baby with the other, and with little Jens obediently clinging to her skirt though sniffling, she made her way to the stairs that led below. She wanted to run, to get her children out of sight as rapidly as possible, but she forced herself to move slowly, accommodating Jens's short legs as she threaded her way through the crowd that seemed oblivious to the short drama that had just taken place. She skirted the deck filled with passenger cabins and continued her descent toward the lower deck where the poorer emigrants crowded together in steerage.

Her heart was still beating rapidly as she found the bunk, two levels below the main deck, that she had claimed during the voyage from Denmark to England. The bunk was marked by a worn quilt her mother had stitched when Margarette was a child. It was among the few items she'd managed to bring with her from her former home.

She had claimed the lower bunk because she feared her children might tumble from one of the upper bunks and because it seemed the lower bunks were reserved for families. She noticed that in most cases, single men claimed bunks on one side of the aisle and single women on the other. Her closest neighbors, across the narrow aisle, the Pedersens, were an older couple from Copenhagen she'd met at a gathering of Saints preparing to emigrate to America. They tended to be polite and didn't seem to mind if her children were sometimes noisy. At times, they played with little Jens and entertained him while she nursed the baby, a kind gesture she appreciated. She suspected they knew more of her situation than she'd told them, having likely overheard the many explanations and cautions she'd given Jens, who resented his confinement to limited quarters.

She could see several bags and a strap of books on the bunk above the older couple, signifying that it had been spoken for while she'd strolled about the wharf with her children. The space had gone unclaimed on the trip from Copenhagen. She'd have to be more careful of her words now that the ship had taken on more passengers. She let her gaze wander down the long row of bunks. Nearly all of the spaces that had been empty before reaching London were now filled with baskets, bags, and piles of personal belongings. The ship would be filled to capacity for the remainder of the journey.

Seeking to reassure herself that she and the children were safe, she noted that the small pile of clothing she'd brought for her children still lay undisturbed on her quilt. She settled herself on the quilt and delved into her bag with one hand for a roll to keep Jens occupied while she attended to baby Annelise's screams. She wished they'd never left their small space, but after the cramped journey from Denmark, she'd decided to chance a stroll along the wharf and had discovered a bakery. She couldn't regret that the delightful aroma of baking bread had tempted her to buy two penny worth of the fragrant bread. The food offered passengers in the lower deck quarters was already growing tiresome, and she feared it would be truly unpalatable by journey's end. While the little boy munched on the fresh bread, she leaned against one of the posts supporting the bunk bed, tossed a small quilt over her shoulder, and began nursing Annelise.

"Come rest beside Mamma," she spoke to Jens, patting a spot beside her once the baby's cries subsided. She needed his sturdy little body next to her as reassurance that both her children were safe. She looked around to be certain the woman who had taken Annelise and then changed her mind hadn't followed them.

"Want to play with boys." Jens pouted.

"You scared me when you ran away to play. That was naughty."

"I sorry." Jens hung his head for a moment, then bounced back with a question. "That lady took Annelise. Is she one of the bad people?"

"I don't know if she's bad, but she gave Annelise back. Maybe she was sorry she took her." Margarette attempted to examine the question calmly. She really didn't know what had happened or why the woman had returned Annelise to her, but she was grateful to have her back. The whole upsetting incident had happened so quickly. They'd been returning from their short expedition ashore when she'd become aware that Jens no longer clutched her skirts. She'd turned to see him hurrying after some older boys who were chasing a barrel hoop across the ship's deck. Fearful he'd fall overboard or become lost, she'd placed the sleeping baby and the heavy bag of food between two thick coils of rope to keep them safe while she hurried after her son. In moments, she'd caught her wayward boy and returned for the baby, Jens in tow, to find the dark-haired young woman walking away with Annelise.

Margarette couldn't help wondering that if the woman had been sent by Lars and Maria, why she had given up so easily. She wondered too, if the woman would return, perhaps with someone stronger who could wrestle the children away from their mother.

Margarette decided she wouldn't go topside again until the ship left port. They were due to sail shortly after the moon came up and the tide turned. Until then, she'd keep the children below deck and watch for anything suspicious.

Jens, tired from their excursion, drifted to sleep, his arms flung wide, reminding Margarette of Jory and the way he'd flung himself on their bed to sleep, exhausted, during those brief months they'd lived in Copenhagen. That was before his parents, Lars and Maria, had found them and insisted their son and Margarette return to the farm to live with them. She wouldn't think about that unhappy time and the husband who became a tyrant once they arrived at his father's farm. In the weeks following his death, she'd come to understand that

Jory hadn't been prepared to live in the city and wasn't strong enough to continue working on the docks loading and unloading cargo indefinitely. His return to his father and his tyranny had been inevitable.

She couldn't bear to see Jens follow in his father's and grandfather's steps, becoming a cruel and bitter man. She'd promised on Jory's grave that she'd keep the children safe and give them a new life where Jens could grow to be a man without the fear of his grandfather's brutality and where baby Annelise could avoid the slavery imposed on the women in Lars Jorgensen's household.

The only way to keep that promise was to take them far away.

"Hello," a cheery voice greeted her. Startled, she looked up to see a tall, thin young man who appeared to be in his early twenties, smiling down at her with a slightly crooked grin. His head was bent to avoid brushing the low ceiling, and his dark curls fell across his brow, threatening to hide his deep blue eyes.

"Hallo," she responded in a tentative voice, trying to be civil. She felt self-conscious in a way she hadn't felt around a man in a long time as his eager gaze passed over the coiled braids that formed a pale crown atop her head and slid lower to her plain black serviceable dress and heavy peasant shoes. She knew she was taller than the average European woman and that hard work, unfashionable clothing, and the bearing of two children made her look older than her twenty years. She'd been told enough times that she was ugly— with her pale skin and eyes the color of the stormy North Sea, yet she sensed approval in his voice as he said something else. She shook her head, trying to let him know she didn't speak English.

He grinned and pointed to himself. "Matthew Holmes." Then he pointed in her direction.

"Margarette Jorgensen." She responded politely, not wanting to get off to a bad start with the young man who would be living mere feet from her and her children during the long voyage to America. She smiled tentatively. As he placed his belongings in the second-row bunk near the Pedersens', she glanced to the side, wondering if he were traveling alone or with friends or family. She didn't see anyone else, but the remainder of his party might be boarding later. The top, third tier bunks were so narrow that it was difficult to squeeze in more than one traveler, let alone a tall one like this young man.

"Jens." Her small son leaped to his feet and pointed to himself. "Annelise." He pointed to his sleeping little sister, who still lay in Margarette's arms.

The young man's grin grew broader, and he carefully repeated each name, pointing to the individual named. Once he was satisfied that he knew their names, he held out his hand to Jens as though the little boy were his equal. A rare smile erupted across Jens's small face as he shook the man's hand.

Margarette's breath caught for just a moment, and she struggled to keep tears from forming in her suddenly moist eyes. Seeing Jens and little Annelise laugh and smile was one of her greatest joys. She'd hated seeing her son cower before his father and grandfather. The old man had expected Jory to control his wife and children with a heavy hand. She and her son had seldom had cause to smile.

Memories crowded out the stranger's bright smile, and her thoughts drifted to the dock where she often went to watch the ships come and go—the place where, as a little girl, she'd waited with her mother for her father's ship to return laden with fish. One day word came that the fishing boat carrying her father had capsized in a storm and that all aboard had been lost. She and her mother had grieved, then her mother had found employment in a shop near the waterfront and Margarette attended a nearby school. In time, they'd learned to smile again, and when two missionaries from the Church of Jesus Christ of Latter-day Saints approached them, they'd eagerly accepted the message the missionaries taught and were baptized.

When Margarette was sixteen, her mother had become ill and passed away quickly, leaving Margarette afraid and on her own. On the second day of her search for employment, she'd walked to the dock. As she stood watching the ships, one of the men unloading a ship noticed her, and in a shy, hesitant manner, struck up a conversation with her. Their meeting had turned to courtship, and three weeks later, she and Jory were wed.

Jory had grown up on his father's small farm. The only thing he knew was hard work and severe punishment until, in desperation, he had run away. Jory's freedom hadn't lasted long; only long enough to acquire a wife and to learn that his minimal education and lack of training and social graces left him unprepared for city life. When his father had found him, he reverted back to the fearful, obedient but temperamental youth he had been before his desperate bid for freedom. But now instead of dreaming of escape, he had a wife and son on which to vent his frustration.

Margarette had been barely tolerated by her husband's parents, and any mention of her religious beliefs was forbidden, but after Jory's death in an unfortunate farm accident, she found herself needing her faith more each day. Her son became the focus of his grandfather's attention, and he was treated to a constant barrage of harsh discipline and expectations beyond the toddler's ability. He never smiled or played. She began to pray for a more normal life for him.

Heavy with a second child, Margarette could do little to protect her son. When she gave birth, Lars and Maria berated her for producing a worthless female for them to feed. Maria took over Annelise's care, and Margarette was relegated to the role of wet nurse, kitchen drudge, and farmhand.

Margarette had moved through each day numb with exhaustion, feeling she had not only lost her husband, but her children as well. Each night before she fell into exhausted sleep as she knelt to pray, her anger simmered beneath the surface—until the day Lars had viciously beaten Jens for some small infraction. When Lars refused to allow her to comfort the small boy or treat his cuts and bruises, she vowed she wouldn't give up the way Jory had. Kneeling in the darkness in the middle of the night, she prayed for help, and a plan began to form in her mind. She had her mother's wedding ring and felt certain that Mor would forgive her for selling it to aid in her escape plans. Stealing her children from their beds one night, she'd crept away in the darkness, hiding in ditches and walking until she had reached Copenhagen.

A small giggle ended Margarette's musing. Startled, she returned her attention to Jens. No longer was he snuggled against her side. The young man who had greeted her minutes earlier was seated on the floor between the two rows of bunks, facing her small son. He pointed to Jens's shoe and said, "Shoe." Jens repeated the word, then Matthew wiggled his fingers and said, "Fingers." Dutifully, Jens echoed the English word, held up his own fingers, and giggled.

Margarette was torn. She didn't want her son to bother the other passengers, nor did she want him to speak to strangers, but he'd had so few moments of pleasure in his young life, and he'd spent most of the voyage thus far healing from the harsh beating his grandfather had given him. She knew how he longed to play like other children, and sooner or later he must learn English, since that was the language that would be prevalent in America. She couldn't bring herself to deny him an opportunity to learn English, and if she listened carefully, perhaps she would learn a few words as well. She made up her mind to allow Jens this small pleasure.

"Ma'am."

Startled, she looked up to see one of the ship's officers. He held a paper in his hand and seemed to be asking a question of her. She shook her head, trying to signal her lack of understanding.

"No, no." The old man who shared the opposite lower bunk with his wife stood beside the officer, gravely shaking his head. She hadn't seen him and his wife return. The older couple had also taken advantage of the day in port to walk about the docks. She had been too caught up in her musings to be aware of her surroundings, a situation she must not allow to happen again.

The elderly gentleman said something more, his words sounding slow and unsure, in a language she didn't understand, then he turned to her, speaking rapidly in Danish. Margarette's puzzlement turned to fear as the old man attempted to explain the officer's question to her. "This man said he has been ordered to search the ship for a woman with two small children she stole from their guardian, the children's grandfather. He is asking if you are that woman. He wants you and the children to accompany him to the wharf where a magistrate will settle the matter. I told him he has made a mistake." She sensed he suspected there had been no mistake.

Margarette tightened her hold on her baby, and her panicked gaze flew to the little boy facing the Englishman on the floor. There was no doubt in her mind that she was the woman being sought. But she was also Jens and Annelise's mother and, to her way of thinking, she had every right granted by God, if not by man, to claim her own children.

Something about the situation triggered a reaction from the man playing with her son. He stood in one easy motion, then reaching down, picked up Jens and while holding the boy in his arms, strolled toward the officer. Soren Pedersen was struggling to interpret for her, but she couldn't concentrate on his words. A dark storm cloud seemed to be roaring toward her, drowning out her ability to think. Margarette's heart pounded, and she debated snatching Jens from the stranger's arms and fleeing.

Her eyes met Matthew Holmes's eyes, and she felt he was trying to tell her something. They'd only just met and didn't even speak the same language, so she had no reason to expect support from him, but she found herself searching his face for something and sensing some gossamer connection she couldn't explain. Her son, who was generally wary of adult males, reached a small arm about Matthew's neck. It seemed to become the deciding factor for the man.

"Is there a problem, officer?" he asked. He casually shifted Jens to his other arm and placed his free hand on Margarette's shoulder. She flinched slightly, but didn't shake it off. "Has my family wrongfully claimed space belonging to someone else?" Anna, Soren's wife was now beside her, whispering a rough translation. She didn't know why the Englishman was pretending to be her husband, but she didn't attempt to refute the implication that they were wed.

Looking confused, the officer glanced at him, then about the rapidly filling space. He shook his head. "I'm not aware of any other claim," he told the Englishman. "But the woman . . . and the children . . ."

"I came to London to work a year ago," Matthew spoke with casual ease. "She and the children have just arrived. Together we shall travel to America where there are better opportunities for the children. The bunk she claimed on the voyage from Scandinavia seemed to fit our needs, but of course, we will be happy to seek other space if someone else has a greater claim." She noticed from Anna's whispered translation that he was careful not to actually lie, but perhaps the implication he was planting in the officer's mind was just as wrong. She suspected her silence was also a lie. When the opportunity arose, she would ask the missionaries their thoughts on the matter, but for now she felt a compelling need to protect her children any way she could.

Anna's movements were spry in spite of the knot of gray hair on top of her head and the deep wrinkles carved in her face. She moved closer to Mr. Holmes, but seemed to be still translating for

Margarette. She spoke softly, words she knew the young man could not understand, though he nodded his head as though he did. Jens's small body stiffened, warning Margarette the boy heard and did not like whatever Anna had said. He leaned toward his mother as though eager to go to her. Before she could stretch her arms to take him, the old woman said something more. Though Anna faced Margarette, Jens seemed to know her words were meant for him.

"Far," Jens patted Matthew's cheek as though trying to gain his attention, then leaned forward to whisper loudly in his ear. The Danish words meant nothing to Matthew, but they told Margarette that the old woman understood Matthew was playing a desperate game to keep Margarette and her children from being removed from the ship and that Anna was instructing Jens on how to continue the game. She prayed her son would understand and play his part. She had an uncomfortable feeling that if her family left the ship, they would be in grave danger.

"The little one," the old man grinned sheepishly, joining in the charade, "seeks to relieve himself. He wishes for his papa to . . . Perhaps I could assist . . ."

Matthew almost grinned as the older man reached for Jens, who went to him willingly. The officer appeared flustered and began to apologize. He turned about and lost no time leaving the now-crowded area. Jens, it seemed, had provided the final convincing touch.

Matthew crouched before Margarette, who was now clutching her children to her and sobbing. The elderly woman patted her shoulder and made soothing sounds. He seemed to want to reassure her too, but unfortunately, she couldn't understand anything he said. She wasn't even sure she knew exactly what had just happened. Extending a hand, Matthew patted Jens's head. Margarette lifted her head, and her eyes met his. No words were exchanged, but she hoped he could read the gratitude in hers.

After a few minutes, Margarette asked Soren to translate for her. He listened to her jumble of words, then turned to Matthew and spoke slowly, stumbling over his words. "She wishes to thank you for coming to her aid. She loves her children and does not wish for them to be returned to Denmark. Her husband is dead and his parents beat the boy and do not allow them to meet with other members of Church."

"Church of Jesus Christ of Latter-day Saints? Mormons?" Matthew asked, a hopeful grin on his face. All three of the adults he faced nodded their heads, understanding his question. He grinned and pointed to himself. "I am a member too. I was baptized a little over a year ago. Tell her I am happy I could help, but it was little Jens who convinced the officer Margarette is not the woman for whom he is searching."

"Anna," the old man beamed with pride at his wife. "She whisper to boy. He smart boy, do as she say." The two men chuckled, then the older one extended his hand. "I am Soren Pedersen. We belong Church two years. I study English with missionaries to help other members they journey to Zion." Matthew shook the man's hand. Brother Pedersen waved his arm at the other Scandinavian passengers around them. "Sweden, Norway, Finland, Denmark. All baptized. All Mormon."

"I think many of the English passengers are members of the Church too. And there are six missionaries returning to Nauvoo." The old man nodded, signifying he was pleased with the information, then turned to share the news with the two women.

"Brother Pedersen," Matthew looked hesitant. He glanced at Margarette, then began speaking in an earnest manner to the older man. "My father was a brutal man who spent his meager wages on drink. My younger brother died at his hands during a drunken rage. My mother was everything to me, and when she passed on a year ago, I made up my mind to go to Zion. I know what a mother means to a boy, and I give my word of honor that I shall do all I can to keep young Jens from being separated from his mum."

When Soren translated Matthew's words, Margarette was deeply touched. She offered her gratitude, then sat down, feeling awkward.

After a few moments, with the baby still in her arms, Margarette rummaged in a bag that had been shoved under her bunk. She was aware that the Englishman watched her covertly with quick sideways glances. His scrutiny made her conscious of all her shortcomings, especially her rough hands, which revealed her familiarity with hard work. She withdrew a square of cloth from the bag. Placing the baby on the quilt, she proceeded to unfasten Annelise's gown. Matthew resumed his conversation with Brother Pedersen and Anna. Breathing easier with Matthew's attention directed elsewhere, Margarette continued to remove the baby's wet nappy.

Something that had been inside the nappy fell to the floor with a soft clunk. Margarette stared at the object in disbelief. Her gasp of astonishment attracted the attention of the Pedersens and their newfound friend. They turned as she knelt beside the bunk while keeping one hand on the squirming baby. All three stared at the object on the floor.

Matthew moved closer, his eyes following hers. There on the rough planks, half hidden by the hem of Margarette's quilt, lay a small black bag. He reached for it, and as Soren, Anna, and Jens crowded around, he released the cord that held it closed and gently shook the bag's contents onto Margarette's bunk.

A glittering bracelet dropped onto a quilt square. All four adults gaped in astonishment. The metal chain appeared to be of inferior quality, but five large stones, each a different color, gleamed almost as though they were hungry to claim the small amount of light in the ship's gloomy interior.

2

Margarette stared at the bracelet. Perhaps it was only her imagination, but the gems were both frightening and compelling, hinting at both good and evil. They were large and like nothing she'd ever seen before. She had no idea how long she stared without daring to touch the strange piece of jewelry, but at length, she pulled herself together. She couldn't leave the bracelet lying on her bunk to arouse questions and draw attention to her and her children. Stretching forth her hand, she touched it, then gathered it into her hand. She couldn't help staring as the gems spread across her palm. Shaking off the jewels' mesmerizing hold on her fancy, she found speech difficult, but she felt a need to say something.

"It fell from Annelise's nappy." They knew that, but she couldn't think of anything else to say. The others crowded closer, staring at the glittering band of color. Baby Annelise waved her tiny arm, catching the bracelet in her small fist.

Finally moving, Matthew freed the object from the baby's grasp. As he did so, he touched the large green stone her little hand had covered. "They're not real, are they?"

Margarette had seen few jewels in her life, and it was unbelievable that the brightly colored stones she held in her hand could be genuine. Yet their luster was startling, even in the dim surroundings of steerage. Surely glass or paste would not be so brilliant. She couldn't resist running her finger across the same large green stone Matthew and Annelise had touched. It seemed to almost hypnotize her.

"How did it get there?" Soren asked while his wife merely shook her head in disbelief.

"I don't know," Margarette began, then she remembered the dark-haired woman who had taken Annelise. "There was a woman," she began in a low, hesitant voice, taking care not to be overheard beyond their small group. She poured out the story to Soren and Anna while Matthew looked on in puzzlement. When she paused to take a breath, Soren repeated the details to the best of his ability in English.

"What if the woman you spoke of put the bracelet in your baby's nappy so she might call a policeman and have you charged with theft?" Anna asked, her eyes round and full of worry.

"I shall throw it in the sea." Margarette started toward the stairs that led to the deck.

"Where are you going?" Matthew stopped her by grasping her arm. They both turned to Soren, who carefully explained his wife's theory and Margarette's decision to throw the bracelet into the sea.

"No." Matthew shook his head. "If someone expected a policeman to find the bracelet in Margarette's possession and have her arrested, the ship's officer who was here moments ago would have insisted she be searched. I suspect those jewels are worth a lot of money, and she should keep them safe until we know to whom the bracelet belongs."

When Matthew's words were explained to her, Margarette sat back down. She didn't know what to do. She didn't want to keep the bracelet if it might bring a false arrest, but she couldn't throw it away if the woman who placed it in Annelise's nappy hid it there for safe-keeping and might return to claim it.

"Perhaps she was seeking a hiding place for the bracelet and had no connection to your husband's parents," Matthew speculated.

"I am thinking the same thing," Soren spoke with careful deliberation. He touched the stones with a gnarled finger. "Did you know there are legends attached to almost all of the precious gems?" His finger paused as it brushed the large green stone. He launched hastily into a story in his own tongue, directed to Margarette. "Emeralds are supposed to give their wearer the ability to think clearly, to quicken intelligence, and to provide protection. They are among the most valuable of jewels. It might be well to keep the bracelet out of sight until we learn if it belongs to the woman or if it was stolen." Anna picked up the small bag, and Margarette thrust the bracelet back inside it. She held it a moment, appearing uncertain, then turned her back to hide the velvet bag among her petticoats.

The small group huddled together, talking softly while little Annelise slept. Margarette glanced around at frequent intervals as though she expected the woman to return to claim her property. Nothing would suit Margarette better than to be able to return the black bag to the strange woman. She also wanted to make certain no one else got close enough to take her children or accuse her of stealing the piece of jewelry.

The large area under the second deck was filling rapidly with those who couldn't afford cabins. Some carried trunks, but many kept their few possessions in various bags or tied in cloths. Most spread quilts and bags on various bunks to mark the areas where entire families would live and sleep for the six weeks or more it would take to cross the Atlantic. With the passenger area filled to capacity, Margarette expected the trip would be noisy and smelly. A few passengers had been ill on the trip from Copenhagen, so she knew how unpleasant the lower deck could become, and she'd heard the Atlantic crossing was far rougher, and with winter coming on, it could be rough indeed, with so many people sharing the cramped space. Still, she wished they would get underway. She and the children would be safer once they were at sea.

A woman moved toward them with quiet determination. Margarette stiffened until she saw three children—two little girls and an adolescent boy—following her. They stopped several times to look at various bunks, then moved on. It was clear they were searching for an unclaimed bunk. Seeing them, Matthew waved his arms to attract their attention.

"Matthew Holmes!" The woman seemed excited and terribly relieved to see him. The smallest girl shook off her mother's hand and ran, whooping with delight toward Matthew, who picked her up and bumped her head softly against the low ceiling, bringing a squeal of laughter from the child. He directed the woman to the bunk above Margarette and helped the boy to store his bag beside his own on the bunk above the one claimed by the Pedersens. When they finished stowing their few possessions, Matthew turned to Soren to make introductions. Margarette wondered if the family were relatives of

Matthew's. Soren soon explained that the woman was the widow Mary Bacon, who was traveling to America with her children, and though they weren't kin to Matthew, he knew them because he and Mary's boy, Darren, had worked at the same mill and had listened to the missionaries together. Margarette thought the boy much too young to have worked in the mills. He appeared to be only about thirteen and was small for his age. She learned that Matthew and the Bacons had arranged to travel together to America. They shook hands all around, then after a short time, the widow and her children announced their intention of watching from the upper deck as the ship left their homeland behind.

Shortly after the Bacon family left, Jens grew restless, and Matthew reached up to his own bunk. After rummaging in a bag, he produced a large, red apple, which he proceeded to divide. Margarette contributed a few of the rolls she'd purchased from the bakery near the wharf, and Anna opened a small crock packed tightly with pickled fish. Once they were at sea, they would be provided with simple meals, but while docked, they were on their own. The dried fruit and rolls she'd purchased wouldn't last long.

Following their repast, Matthew suggested they go topside to observe the sailors readying the ship for departure. Margarette declined the invitation, wishing to stay out of sight until the ship left London.

"Me go with Far," Jens pleaded.

Margarette shook her head. "The baby is asleep. We must stay here." She wondered how to explain to Jens that he shouldn't continue calling Matthew *Far*.

"I will accompany them," Soren volunteered. His look told her he assumed she was reluctant to entrust her son to a man whom she'd known such a brief time. It occurred to her that their brief acquaintance had nothing to do with her reluctance to allow Jens to accompany Matthew to the open deck. Indeed, she felt a surprising amount of confidence in the young man. Her fear was that someone might recognize her son.

"He'll be safe," Anna assured her and wrapped a warm shawl about the little boy. "If the young man carries him and keeps him wrapped, he will not occasion notice."

Reluctantly, Margarette let Jens go. She felt a tug of sadness at seeing Jens perched on Matthew's shoulder and hearing him call the man *Far* again. They were both turned, listening to Soren Pedersen. A smile lit her little boy's face, and she wished her son could be sharing a happy moment with his own far and bedstefar.

Anna returned to her bunk, where she curled herself beneath a thick quilt and was soon asleep. Margarette took advantage of the relative peace to again feed Annelise and ready her for bed. The bustling noise of earlier in the day had diminished, and few people remained in the cramped and crowded space. She supposed that like Matthew, Soren, and Jens, most had made their way topside to watch the shoreline recede, then disappear, as the *Carolina* moved away from the river's mouth into the strait.

The sound of hurrying footsteps had her peering down the long corridor lined with bunks to see if Matthew and Jens were returning. Instead of Matthew or any of the Scandinavian passengers she'd become acquainted with, she saw a man who appeared greatly out of place. Dressed in cream britches, a mauve vest, and a fine velvet coat, the man looked to be a gentleman who had strayed onto the wrong deck. He appeared to be a little older than her, in a hurry, and not happy about his present errand. Occasionally, he paused to peer into a shadowy bunk. Her heart beat faster. As the elegantly dressed gentleman neared her bunk, she withdrew into the deep shadows and pulled her quilt over herself and her sleeping baby. She heard his steps pause nearby, then hurry on. She didn't dare raise the quilt from over her head until the sound of his footsteps died away.

She sat up and looked around. Anna was still sleeping, her soft snores reaching across the narrow space between their bunks. A Swedish courting couple stood beside her bunk with their belongings. Perhaps they were the reason the well-dressed gentleman had hurriedly left the steerage deck. Clearly, the pair was claiming the narrow third tier of bunks above the Bacons and the young Englishmen. They were each traveling alone. He had been rejected by his family when he joined the Church, and she was on her way to Nauvoo to make her home with an uncle and his wife. She noted with amusement their delight in discovering two empty bunks directly across from each other. They were pleasant young people, and she was pleased they would be close by.

After they wandered away, she heard an occasional voice from farther down the long row of bunks, a baby crying, and the heavy timbers of the ship creaking as it rocked at anchor. From far away she heard raised voices, then silence. Several sharp explosions broke the silence, followed by screams and the sound of stampeding feet.

Wondering what was happening, she backed out of her bunk, pulled the quilt closer around her sleeping daughter, then stood, peering down the long aisle. A man and a woman started down the aisle first, then ducked into a bunk. A group of girls who had become friends on the first leg of their journey came squealing into the steerage area as though fleeing from something that had frightened them. They were followed by a throng of running people.

"What is it?" she asked the first person who came close enough to ask. He dived beneath a blanket without answering.

"Gun," was the one word she could understand. It was repeated over and over. Turning her head from side to side, she looked for anyone bearing a gun, then climbed partway up the rail leading to the upper bunk for a better view. Over the heads of the milling crowd, she searched first for anyone posing a threat, then for Matthew, Soren, and her son.

"Has something happened?" She felt Anna tug on her dress. "Have pirates attacked the ship?"

"I'm sure it's not pirates," Margarette protested. "Pirates only attack merchant ships at sea, but I heard several people shouting something about a gun."

"Oh, dear. Where is Soren?"

"And Jens . . . and Matthew?"

"I see Matthew's friends, the lady and her children who claimed the middle bunk on your side," Anna pointed toward the woman and her children, who were attempting to push their way through the crowd.

Margarette was pleased to see familiar faces coming toward them. They greeted each other like old friends even though they couldn't understand each other's rapid-fire questions until the boy asked, "Matthew?"

Margarette shook her head. The small, blonde daughter pointed a finger and made shooting sounds. Her heart pounding with fear,

Margarette looked for any familiar face, someone who had traveled from Denmark and could explain to her what was happening. Spotting the Danish girls she'd seen earlier, she struggled against the crowd to reach them. Putting out her arm, she grasped one of the girls by her sleeve.

"What is it? Has someone been hurt?" She shouted to be heard over the tumult.

"Oh! Sister Jorgensen, it was so exciting at first. A passenger who had been delayed jumped from the wharf to the gangplank just as the sailors were withdrawing it. She barely made it, and we were all cheering, then someone began shooting at her. Everyone ran."

"Was the shooter on the wharf?" she asked, aghast that anyone would shoot toward a crowded ship deck.

"No, he was on the ship."

"Someone was shooting a gun on the deck of this ship?" Margarette gasped. Her gaze flew back toward her sleeping daughter.

"Yes!" Another girl responded. "He was hiding behind some barrels that are lashed near the companionway leading to the first-deck cabins. He stepped out from behind them and didn't seem to care that the deck was crowded and he might kill someone."

"Or be recognized," a third girl added.

"Was . . . was anyone hurt?"

"I don't know," the first young lady answered. "We rushed down the stairs at once. We knew our parents would be worried."

"And we were afraid he might shoot us."

"Did you see a man—a young man—and Broder Pedersen with my little boy?"

The girls shook their heads and looked concerned.

"I must find them."

"It's too dangerous," the girls protested.

Margarette turned toward the doorway that led to the stairs, shaking off their attempts to restrain her. The walkway was filled with milling people, speaking in frightened tones, and she found it difficult to push her way between them. Her progress was slow, but she had almost reached the doorway when she heard a child's voice call, "Mor, Mor," followed by Soren's shout, "Margarette, you are going the wrong way."

She took another step and found herself face-to-face with Matthew. Perched on his shoulders, safely above the crowd, rode Jens. As he entered the long, low-ceilinged area, Matthew swung Jens down from his shoulder to his arm and ducked his own head. Something inside her seemed to melt, leaving tears trickling down her face. She had remained strong and determined until she actually saw Jens, and she wished she never needed to let him out of her sight again.

Pushing their way toward their bunks was easier than going against the flow had been. When they finally reached the bunk where Annelise still slept, Matthew set Jens down on the edge of the bunk. Margarette sank down beside him and attempted to gather him into her arms, but it was evident he was more excited than scared.

"Bad man come. Swoosh. Lady jump in water. Bang! Bang!" He leaped from the bunk to demonstrate. Little Alice Bacon swooped from the bunk above, eager to join his game.

"Get back on this bunk," Mary Bacon ordered.

"Hush, my little one." Margarette gathered Jens back in her arms and turned to Soren for an explanation.

"A woman almost missed the ship. Just as some of the sailors started to help her aboard, shots were fired toward her. After she gained the deck, a well-dressed gentleman threatened her with a gun. She was rescued by the captain of the *Nightingale,* our sister ship. He wounded the villain, then caught her up and leaped overboard with her. The man fired into the water several times, then was subdued by a swarm of sailors and some of the passengers. He broke free, and the captain had no choice but to shoot him. The captain sent his first mate ashore to seek out a magistrate to take charge of the body."

"Why didn't Matthew bring Jens back here at once?" she demanded, casting a dark look toward the young man.

"The man with the gun was between us and the entrance to the stairs. We thought it best to take refuge beneath the canvas covering the cargo that is lashed to the deck. We made certain your boy was surrounded by heavy objects. Matthew stayed between him and the shooter every minute."

Margarette felt somewhat mollified. She turned to thank Matthew for protecting Jens and discovered that he'd gone to inform the missionaries of all he and Soren had witnessed so the missionaries could make an announcement that the shooter was no longer a threat.

"I feel certain our departure will be delayed," Soren confided. "The ship won't be able to clear port until the magistrate gives his approval. There will be an investigation, which will cause delay."

Delayed! Margarette sank slowly to the bunk where her children lay. Each minute's delay increased the risk that her children could be taken from her. She bowed her head, and her lips moved in silent supplication. A curtain of hair, pulled free from her coronet of braids, hid her face as she prayed.

Surely God hadn't allowed them to get this far only to be forced back to Denmark to lives of drudgery and abuse. A measure of calm filled her heart, and she raised her head, brushing her hair back with her hands. Slowly she released the remainder of her hair, then withdrew her brush from her bag. She swept it through the long, nearly white strands, and then with nimble fingers, she re-plaited her hair and coiled the braid atop her head. As she finished, her eyes caught those of the young Englishman watching her. Chagrined, she crept beneath her quilt.

Long after Jens fell asleep on the far side of his baby sister, Margarette lay awake. At first, the steady buzz of whispering voices told her she wasn't the only one unable to sleep—the day had been too filled with turmoil to find slumber easily. Not only was the risk that Lars's representative might catch up to them increased by the ship's delay, but most of the Saints, including herself, were traveling with meager funds. Rations provided by the ship for steerage passengers were inadequate at best, and those who could brought a few supplies of their own, but each hour's delay in London increased the risk they would run out of food before reaching America, especially should they meet stormy weather.

* * *

Annelise's hungry cry awoke Margarette from the restless slumber she finally succumbed to as a pale gray light seeped into the long, narrow room. The cries of children and the grumbles of their parents replaced the whispers and snores of the night. Those who had only been able to secure hammocks stretched across the aisle took them down. A new day had arrived, filled with uncertainty and the gentle rocking of the ship—which was announcement enough that they were still in port.

Matthew again engaged her restless son in a game of giving English names to various items in their cramped quarters. She found herself listening and committing the strange sounds to memory. While Jens repeated the words aloud, she spoke them silently in her mind.

The day passed slowly, and Margarette was grateful for the short trips Matthew or Soren made topside in search of news of a new departure time. No one seemed to know whether the couple who jumped overboard the night before had survived or not, though a sailor informed Matthew that he had heard the creak of oars approaching and then receding from the deep shadows of the *Carolina* and that the *Nightingale* had sailed, presumably with her captain aboard. Another claimed the shooter was a wealthy, titled lord and his demise was stirring great speculation throughout the city. His description brought to mind the gentleman who had seemed to be searching for someone or something in steerage the previous evening. Margarette thought of the bracelet and wondered if it was somehow connected to the two strangers she'd encountered.

She considered turning the bracelet over to the ship's captain, but felt reluctant to draw attention to herself. Besides, with each passing day, she became more convinced that the bracelet had been entrusted to her for safekeeping and that she must not give it up lightly.

Their hopes that they were about to sail were raised when the ship was loosed from its moorings and withdrawn to deeper water shortly after noon. When the anchor was again lowered, the passengers were uniformly disappointed. One of the ship's officers confided to Elder Adams that a magistrate had ordered their removal from the dock area to prevent anyone from leaving the ship while he conducted his investigation. Elder Adams passed the information on to the Saints. Margarette was pleased by the news because if no one could leave the ship, anyone with connections to her in-laws couldn't board the ship either.

By evening of the second day, she was feeling restless herself, and as though sensing her need to breathe fresh air and take a turn on deck, Matthew persuaded the Pedersens to watch her children while he escorted her to the main deck. She took care to wrap her shawl over her hair partially concealing her face. Despite feeling self-conscious, she allowed the young Englishman to take her arm as he guided her to a spot beside the rail some distance from the few first-class passengers who were also taking air on deck. A breeze blew off the water, bringing a respite from the stench of the docks and the close quarters of the crowded steerage. Breathing deeply, she surveyed the lights flickering along the shoreline and wondered how much longer they must wait to continue their journey. The light faded, and a few stars began to dot the sky. The breeze seemed to shift, and the ship rocked with the beginning of the outgoing tide.

Matthew touched the arm he had released when they reached the rail and pointed. She followed his outstretched arm with her eyes and was surprised to see the dark shape of a small skiff approaching the *Carolina*. There was no lantern aboard the small vessel, but when it came alongside and its occupants were brought aboard, they were met by the first mate, who emerged from the wheelhouse. Her eyes having become adjusted to the near darkness, she recognized the captain and the second mate who had approached her two days earlier. Two other sailors whom she'd also seen about the ship accompanied them. The sailors and the second mate slipped away, as though in a great hurry, while the captain paused to speak with the first mate.

Matthew sidled closer to the pair, and she found herself wishing she could do the same, though she was well aware that she wouldn't understand their words even if they stood right beside her. She vowed to take advantage of Matthew's willingness to pass his time with her and her children by encouraging him to teach them to speak English. It was becoming increasingly evident that she must learn the language of her new country as soon as possible.

A hand grasped her wrist, and she started to pull away before she recognized Matthew, who had returned to her side. Placing a finger on her lips, he signaled for her not to speak. He led her at a rapid pace to the stairs leading below.

Once they reached steerage, Matthew spoke quietly to Soren, who quickly translated for her. "We're sailing tonight. It seems the dead man's widow and an old peer, the Earl of Dorchester, appeared in court this afternoon, anxious to have the matter resolved as quickly

and quietly as possible. They met with the magistrate privately, and
then the bailiff conducted the captain to his private chambers, where
he was instructed to sail immediately and without attracting attention. We sail before we lose the tide."

The rattle of a heavy chain signaled the raising of the anchor. No
lanterns were lit, and a shiver of excitement slid down Margarette's
spine as the ship began to glide like a gray ghost toward the open
channel. Her hand brushed over the slight bump beneath her skirt,
where she'd pinned the small, cloth bag.

3 ✑

There was a monotonous sameness to the days that followed. Matthew experienced a slight queasiness for several days, but the ship's motion never seemed to bother Margarette or her children. She wondered if that might be because she was a seafaring man's daughter. Soren too seemed to suffer little, but poor Anna took to her bed and kept Soren busy emptying slop pails. It had been the same the first few days after leaving Copenhagen.

The stench of sickness made steerage almost unbearable. Still, Matthew and the youth who shared his bunk volunteered to empty slops while Margarette spent hours entertaining small children whose parents were too ill to care for them. Mary and her older daughter, Nancy, lay as though at death's door, but little Alice bounced cheerfully from one adventure to another while complaining loudly about smelling "stink" in her nose. At least she kept Jens entertained, freeing Margarette to care for those who were too ill to help themselves. After the first week, all but a few passengers were on their feet again, and some of the crew provided the steerage passengers with strong lye soap to scrub away the last vestiges of illness.

Beginning the first Sunday, the missionaries aboard the ship conducted church services on deck in the open air. Soren translated for the Danish passengers. Passengers, both those with cabins and those in steerage, intermingled, discussing the gospel afterward, while those passengers who were not Latter-day Saint émigrés, tended to stay to themselves, and the captain conducted a brief service for them.

As soon as the demands of sick passengers lessened, Matthew resumed teaching English to Jens, and when he discovered Margarette

silently mouthing the English words that he assigned the boy to practice, he insisted she join them. Margarette practiced diligently to learn
the words and simple phrases he taught. Though Matthew was an
excellent teacher, Margarette credited her many prayers with her rapid
assimilation of the language skills he taught. The little English girls
who shared the bunk above hers proved helpful too in her struggle to
learn English. Nancy had a school slate, which she was more than
willing to share, and Matthew borrowed a Book of Mormon from the
missionaries for a text. His class grew to include the Swedish man,
Olaf Kjelstrom, his sweetheart, Katrina, and the Danish girls
Margarette had befriended earlier.

Little Jens's vocabulary expanded at a rapid pace, well beyond the
words Matthew taught him, as he played with the other children, and
Margarette envied him his easy affinity for the strange language.
Margarette wasn't far behind him though and she soon found herself
able to understand simple statements or questions if the speaker
didn't rush the words, but learning to speak proved more difficult.
Her determination to communicate with others who spoke English
and prepare herself to find work in America kept her studying and
praying in spite of the difficulty involved.

Sudden squalls always brought a return of seasickness for many of
the passengers, and it became impossible to completely eradicate the
stench of sickness from steerage, so it became one of Margarette's
greatest pleasures to stroll on deck with Matthew and her children for
a short time each evening. Her gratitude for his willingness to
befriend her and her family grew each day.

They had been at sea almost five weeks and were anticipating
reaching New Orleans in less than two weeks when a rumor spread
through the company that the ship was slowly shifting direction.
Some said they were sailing in a wide circle. This was cause for great
concern to the passengers who had already spent many weeks in the
trying conditions of steerage. The portions of hard biscuits and gruel
were becoming smaller, and Margarette feared she would become
unable to nurse Annelise. Jens ate little of what was offered him and
was growing thinner. There had already been several deaths among
the hapless group, and she worried that her children might be next if
the trip were prolonged.

One day, after spending a couple of hours stitching and mending clothing with a group of Scandinavian women, she returned to her bunk where she had left Jens napping, to find him across the aisle, sitting on Matthew's bunk. He was chewing on a small, shriveled apple. She didn't see Matthew anywhere around. A jumble of feelings assailed her—joy that her son was eating something, fear that he had stolen the apple, concern that the three-year-old had climbed to an upper bunk, and concern for Anna, who had promised to watch him. Margarette lay the baby on the quilt that she kept spread across her bunk. As she did so, she watched Jens's dangling feet, fearing he might fall from the higher bunk.

"Jens," Margarette straightened, placing a hand on either side of her son. "Where did you get the apple?"

"Matthew say," he spoke in careful English. She understood his words, but reverted to Danish.

"Did Matthew give you the apple?"

"No," the small boy persisted in using English. "He say, 'More apple. Jens eat.'"

Margarette knew no more than when she started. She didn't wish to punish her son if he'd done nothing wrong, but if he'd stolen the apple from Matthew, she would have to make certain he understood that taking what didn't belong to him was wrong. The bag pinned to her underskirt brushed her leg, and for a moment, she wondered if she were wrong to hang on to the jeweled bracelet that had fallen into her hands but wasn't hers. Her case was different, she assured herself, as she reached for Jens. She was only holding on to the bracelet until its owner appeared to claim it. She hadn't stolen it.

Holding her son in her arms, she watched him stuff the last of the apple in his mouth.

"No, no," she laughed. "Do not eat the seeds. Give them to Mamma." Jens had begun calling her by the English term, and liking the word, she had begun using it herself. With Jens's persistent use of English instead of Danish, she could see she needed to speak to him more often in the new language.

With obvious reluctance, he spit three seeds into his hand and held them out to her. She took them, though they were wet and slimy. She looked at the seeds with uncertainty. They were probably too small to cause Jens to choke, but her mother had always told her she shouldn't eat apple seeds. An idea came to her.

"We'll put them in the little bag with the pretty bracelet we found in Annelise's nappy and someday, when we have a home of our own, we'll plant the seeds in our garden. We'll water them, and they'll grow into big trees with many apples."

Jens grinned his approval. She sat him on the floor, then sank down beside him to check on Anna, who still seemed to be asleep. The old woman's breath sounded harsh to Margarette's ears. She reached out a hand to touch her brow and was shocked by the heat that emanated from her skin.

"Anna . . . Anna." She tried to rouse the sleeping woman. When that failed, she grabbed a kerchief and ran to the water barrel to dampen it. Returning, she bathed the wrinkled skin. Anna moaned a couple of times, and Margarette continued her ministrations. "Jens, climb onto the bed and watch the baby. Don't let her roll off," she said before running to moisten the cloth again. She repeated the action over and over until she heard footsteps behind her.

"Anna! Is my Anna ill again?" Soren knelt beside her, worry in his voice.

"Here, let me wring that out for you." Matthew reached for the cloth she held in her hands, and though she didn't really understand all of his words, she understood his offer to help and surrendered the cloth to him.

Later, she stood, placing her hands on the back of her waist, stretching slightly to relieve the ache from leaning over so long. The ship lurched, and she grasped a bunk for support. *This is a bad time to run into a squall.* They'd encountered a few storms with rough seas during the past weeks, and each time the ship had changed its rhythm, poor Anna had taken to her bed. She hadn't run a fever those times, and this time her flushed cheeks and inability to stay awake caused Margarette to worry about the older woman.

Matthew returned with a freshly moistened cloth. Before she could accept it, Soren took it from her hand to bathe his wife's fevered brow himself. Margarette felt an ache of longing in her breast as she watched the old man tenderly minister to his wife. Through the remainder of the afternoon and on into the evening, Soren and

Margarette took turns bathing the fevered woman's skin while Matthew and the girls who slept in the bunk over Margarette's played with Jens and held little Annelise. By mid-afternoon, Nancy complained that she didn't feel well. She crawled into her bunk to lie beside her mother, who was suffering from a return of seasickness.

The ship's rocking motion grew more extreme, and it became difficult to walk without hanging onto the bunks. As one passenger after another became ill, the close quarters took on the foul odor that had permeated the air on the first days of their voyage, and the deck became slick and disgusting. Matthew lifted Alice to the bunk she shared with her mother and sister to keep her from slipping on the fouled deck that rose and fell in a frightening fashion. Jens used his small body to keep his smaller sister from being tossed from their bunk.

While Margarette cared for her sick friend, Soren went in search of the missionaries. When he returned, two of the English missionaries accompanied him. They placed their hands on Anna's head to anoint and bless her. Margarette was amazed that she could understand much of the blessing given Anna, and when Matthew, using simplified words, told her, "Anna will get well. She has work God wants her to do," she nodded her head in understanding.

The missionaries didn't linger as they were much in demand. They spoke quietly to Matthew, then lunged and staggered their way along the narrow passage to the next person who wished a blessing. Soon, even those who were not of their faith were requesting blessings.

Matthew urged Margarette to her feet. He led her a short distance away to where Soren stood wringing out a fresh cloth.

"Elder White said the storm is getting worse," Matthew said. She turned to Soren for confirmation that she had understood correctly. Matthew continued, "He spoke with the captain, who said his crew noticed the storm two days ago. It is moving into the gulf through which we must pass to reach New Orleans. He attempted to retreat out of the storm's path to wait it out, but it has grown so large that its outer winds are buffeting the *Carolina* and drawing us into its grasp." Soren clarified the terms she didn't understand.

The ship tilted precariously, sending unsecured items pelting to the opposite side of the deck, and the few lanterns that had been lit were snuffed out, plunging the steerage into total darkness. The ship seemed to hover on a ledge as though making up its mind whether or not to turn completely over. Deathly silence followed as everyone held their breaths collectively. Then the ship slowly righted itself, and a relieved sigh drifted through the darkness.

Margarette was surprised to find she was clasping Matthew about his waist. With one hand, he held to a pillar, and with the other he held her to him. When the ship settled back in place, she freed herself and felt her way to her bunk to check on the children.

"Jens," she whispered. "Are you all right?"

"Yes," his voice trembled. "I'm not scared. Only Annelise is scared."

"It's all right. You are safe and I am here." She picked up the crying baby and felt Jens's little hands grasp her skirt. "Soren," she called out in the dark. "How is Anna?"

"About the same," came his answer.

She felt someone perch on the bunk beside her, then Matthew whispered, "Jens, I've got you." She was aware of Matthew drawing Jens onto his lap, and she heard her son's quiet sobs and Matthew's gentle murmurs.

"Will we tip over and drown like Bedstefar Christensen?" Margarette heard Jens's frightened whisper, but before she could think of an answer, Matthew spoke. He may not have understood the mixture of English and Danish that Jens used, but he seemed to understand her son's fear.

"We have a good captain and crew, but Elder White suggested we all pray."

"Me too?"

"Yes, we all pray," Margarette answered. "Kneel on our bunk." She heard a rustle of movement, then Jens began his simple prayer. He was followed by Matthew, then she added her own fervent petition for their safety. She began in English, then reverted to Danish midway through. A small voice from the bunk above added her prayer. Margarette heard murmurs all along the aisle and knew others were praying also.

A sudden lurch of the ship brought her forehead up short against the wooden box of the overhead bunk. Blinking back tears, she hugged her baby daughter to her and felt nausea in the pit of her stomach. As the ship bucked and tossed, she prayed not only for safety for everyone aboard the ship, but that she wouldn't become too ill to comfort her children.

A lull in the storm brought silence, then someone lit a lantern. Moans sounded up and down the aisle. People sat on the floor, drenched in foul refuse, among blankets and personal items that had broken free.

Suddenly, she remembered the apple. "Matthew," she said. "You give Jens apple?"

He blinked his eyes and gave his head a slight shake. "What?"

She repeated the question. He gave her a strange look and climbed to his bunk. When he climbed back down, he held a shriveled apple in his hand. He held it out to Jens.

"No, no." She closed his fingers around the fruit and shook her head. "You keep." They looked at each other, and Margarette sensed he was as frustrated as she was by their failure to communicate as well as they wished.

"Soren," she turned to the old man who lay beside his wife across the aisle. "Please ask Matthew if he gave my son an apple earlier today." The old man dutifully repeated the question in English. Matthew answered promptly, though he appeared slightly embarrassed.

"Ja, he noticed the boy wasn't eating the gruel any more. He was worried that Jens might become ill, so he told him that each day that he eats all of his gruel, he can help himself to an apple until the apples are gone."

Margarette remembered how Jens had doggedly swallowed each bite of the tasteless mixture in his small bowl that morning. She didn't approve of bribery, but she felt as though a weight had slipped from her shoulders, knowing her child hadn't stolen the apple.

"T'ank you," she turned to Matthew, touching a finger to her head. "I t'ink he take, not ask."

Matthew smiled in understanding. "He's a good boy."

She smiled in response, her lips forming a wavering curve.

A sudden lurch would have sent her tumbling to the floor with Annelise except for Matthew's quick reaction. Steadying her with one hand, he reached for a secure hold on a bedpost. Once she felt steady, she reached for the post with one hand and clutched the blanket-wrapped baby with the other. After a few minutes, Matthew released his hold on her, but she kept an arm wrapped around the post. She pushed back the tangled quilt from Annelise's face. Her cheeks were wet, and Margarette became aware that the roar of the storm had drowned out the baby's renewed cries.

Matthew lifted the infant from her arms, holding her secure in the crook of his arm, while Jens snuggled against his mother, once more grasping her skirt in his clenched fists to maintain his balance. They again took turns praying that the storm would abate and that Anna would recover. Jens added his prayer, first in Danish, then in English.

A low moan brought up their heads, and they turned toward Anna. Darkness had descended again, and since it was considered unsafe to relight a lantern or candle, Margarette could not see the other woman's face.

"Water," Anna mumbled, and she heard Soren fumble for the small flask he'd filled earlier from the water cask at the far end of the communal sleeping quarters.

"Stay here, hold onto Matthew," Margarette told Jens. Calculating in her mind where a post should be, she flung herself across the aisle to help Soren. She grasped the post, then crouched to lift Anna's head as Soren felt for Anna's mouth. He trickled a few drops past her lips, then paused. "Water," Anna repeated the request, and he doled out a few more drops. Even that small amount was too much as the ship lurched and suddenly seemed to drop.

"Oh no," Anna moaned, and Margarette reached for the bucket tucked under the edge of the bunk.

* * *

Two days passed in a seemingly endless repetition of moaning, groaning, and retching. The wind howled unceasingly, and the ship rocked and lurched from side to side. Each time the ship rolled far to one side, Margarette feared it wouldn't right itself and they would all drown. Then the two missionaries who were still able to stand and walk among the people made their rounds, assuring everyone they would be safe if they kept faith. They secured a hurricane lantern from a sailor, and those who were not ill traveled the length of the rows of bunks by its feeble light, tending to the ill.

Once Matthew and the young Swede, Olaf, carried a barrel of slops up the stairs, tied themselves together with a rope that was attached to a heavy cleat near the door, and endeavored to empty the barrel. Olaf braced himself and made a half turn with the rope around a mast while Matthew pushed the barrel toward the railing. He tipped the barrel, and the fierce wind caught it, carrying it away. It would have carried Matthew away too, but for Olaf and the sturdy rope that towed him back to safety. He told Margarette about it upon his return, and she reached out to touch him, needing the assurance that he was safe.

Toward morning of the third day, Margarette fell asleep feeding Annelise. She didn't know how long she slept or what awakened her. She lay still, listening, for several minutes before she realized what had awakened her. It was the silence. The wind no longer roared like an approaching train, and the whimpering and retching had ceased. Slowly she raised herself and looked around, surprised that a faint light was turning the blackness to gray. She checked her children and found them both sleeping soundly. Carefully, she slipped from her bed. As though hypnotized by the faint light, she made her way to the stairway and crept up two flights to where a stream of light entered the open door. There, Matthew waited as though he'd known she would come. Greeting each other, they exchanged a few stilted sentences and smiled with enjoyment at the end of the storm. They stood at the rail for a long time, glorying in the bright sunlight and breathing the sweet, clean air.

A scream rose from below. They looked at each other, questions and dread in their eyes, before racing back to the gloom and stench of the steerage.

"What is it?" Matthew asked a man who stood on the edge of a small crowd gathered around a bunk.

"Brother Fanchon didn't make it. His wife awoke this morning to find he wasn't breathing. She called the elders, but there was nothing that could be done."

Margarette felt frustrated at her inability to understand every word, but she gleaned enough to draw a correct conclusion. This propelled her to squeeze past the crowd and hurry down the aisle to check on Anna. She found her looking tired and disheveled but accepting a few sips of thin gruel from Soren.

"Good morning," she crouched to speak to the woman in careful English. "You are looking more good, and the sun is shining. Today be better day."

Anna smiled weakly, then closed her eyes. Soren set the bowl he'd been using aside. He smiled tenderly at his wife and placed a gnarled hand atop hers where it rested on her quilt. Margarette turned away, swallowing a lump in her throat. Her parents had loved each other like that, and the Pedersens lent her hope that such love still existed. Though her own marriage had been a disappointment, she was grateful for her children and had lately begun to consider the possibility she might someday remarry if she discovered a man like Soren or her father who would treat her kindly and help Jens grow to be a good man.

Stooping beside her bunk, she discovered both children were awake. Jens tickled his little sister, and she giggled and held out her arms to him. Margarette gave Jens a change of clothing, wishing to air and refresh everything her family had worn through the past stormy days, though she knew it would take more than a change of clothing to begin to air out the rank stench of their wretched quarters. When the last button was fastened and his shirt straightened, she stood him on the floor with the admonishment to stay at their end of the row of bunks. He grinned at being allowed some freedom.

Annelise began to whimper. Seating herself, Margarette changed the little girl and proceeded to nurse her, feeling relief that the child was receiving some nourishment, though she suspected there wouldn't be enough milk to satisfy her. Not having eaten for two days, Margarette feared there would be little to satiate Annelise's hunger. If they didn't reach land soon so they could obtain supplies, she worried that her supply of milk would completely disappear and her baby would starve.

"I hungry," Jens announced, bringing pain to Margarette's heart and a rush of doubt to her mind. Had she done what was best for her children by bringing them on this voyage? At least they had had adequate food on their grandfather's farm.

"We'll take our bowls to get breakfast as soon as Annelise finishes hers," Margarette promised.

A dark scowl clouded her son's face.

"I'll take him." Matthew stood beside Jens, holding out a hand, which the boy eagerly accepted.

"Thank you," she said, acknowledging to herself that Matthew was proving better than she at persuading Jens to eat the tasteless porridge two sailors delivered in buckets to the steerage passengers each morning. Though there had been none for two days.

When Matthew and Jens returned, Jens was smiling and carrying a bowl carefully cradled in his small hands.

"For you, Mamma." He spoke English more than Danish now.

Annelise had finished eating and now lay atop their bunk kicking her small legs and blowing bubbles. Margarette reached for the bowl.

"Thank you," she said. She smiled, including Matthew in her gratitude. She looked down at her bowl and gasped. The gruel was thicker than it had been for more than a week, and it contained dark spots.

"It's all right," Soren assured her from across the aisle. "When I went for gruel for Anna, the sailors were just arriving with it. They told me the captain had ordered dried fruit added to the porridge this morning because we are but two days from reaching New Orleans and he believes the fruit will help everyone regain their strength."

"Two days?" Her voice held excitement mingled with gratitude for the small amount of additional nourishment. She had been wrong to doubt for even a moment that her Heavenly Father wanted her to take her children to Zion where they could grow up in the faith.

"It seems the storm crippled a mast, took two lives, and washed away some cargo that was lashed to the deck, but it also pushed us closer to land," Soren finished.

* * *

It was almost dusk when as many of the passengers as were able crowded on deck for the funeral service. Elder White stood at their head, the long, shrouded body of Brother Fanchon nearby. A slight breeze fluttered the pages of the open book he held in his hands.

Elder Hughes and Elder Adams, still looking unsteady, stood near. Four or five women gathered around the new widow and her children. They stood tight-lipped, waiting. A woman from one of the cabins held a canvas-wrapped bundle, refusing to relinquish it to other arms. Her husband, with their five-year-old twin daughters in his arms, stood behind her. Tears glistened on all their cheeks.

The service was brief, but held out hope that the families would one day be reunited. Sailors solemnly lifted first the larger bundle, then the smaller, and consigned them to the sea. It wasn't the first sea burial witnessed by the passengers, but coming on the heels of the terrifying storm and the hunger pangs that were never quite eased, a numbness pervaded the crowd, interrupted only by the quiet sobs of the bereaved.

4

With her bundles around her, Annelise wrapped in her shawl, and
Jens clinging to her skirt, Margarette looked around the wooden
wharf. Noise assaulted her ears from every side. Carriages dashed
about, and black men hustled cargo to and fro. Strange odors
assaulted her nose, and the sun bore down with unceasing intensity,
though the month was November. Nearby, Soren stood beside Anna,
who sagged against their trunk. A little way off, Matthew stood with
a group of young men who had been aboard the *Carolina* and a small
man who carried a buggy whip in the back pocket of his baggy
trousers. The missionaries dashed about, going from group to group.

Margarette examined every face on the dock, but she caught sight
of no one resembling the woman who had left the bracelet in
Annelise's nappy, and there was no sign of the ship that had anchored
behind the *Carolina* at the mouth of the Thames.

Moving closer to Anna, she whispered, "I do not see her."

"Who, dear?" Anna lifted her head.

"The woman who left her bracelet. How shall I find her?"

"If the Lord means for you to return the bracelet to her, He shall
place her in your path. If He has another purpose for it, He shall let
you know in His own time." Anna's head dropped toward her chest.
She was too ill and weary to worry about the bracelet, and Margarette
regretted bothering her with the problem.

At length, she understood the missionaries were encouraging the
scattered group to move toward another part of the wharf where
several stern-wheelers were unloading cargo and passengers. She
looked to Soren, who urged her to go ahead, but she couldn't help

worrying about how he would get the large trunk and poor Anna aboard. If Anna were well, she would no doubt offer to take Annelise while Margarette helped Soren with the trunk.

A shrill whistle sounded, and a small cart driven by a black man and laden with trunks turned toward the man with the buggy whip. He pointed with the whip toward the Pedersens. Seeing Matthew and Olaf hurry toward them also, she chided herself for not realizing Matthew would have already taken the matter in hand. She gathered up her bundles, admonished Jens to hold on tightly, and began moving toward the strangelooking boats some distance away.

Once the entire group was assembled in one place, Elder Adams spoke to them, then asked Soren to come forward to translate for the Scandinavian passengers. Margarette was pleased that she understood most of the instructions the first time. Drawing her few coins from a deep pocket of her skirt, she counted them twice. There would be just enough to secure passage with little left over. Once she reached Nauvoo, she would need to find a place to stay and seek employment at once.

Her hand brushed the familiar lump beneath her skirt, and she again wondered if the gems were real. If the stones were truly jewels, surely one would be enough to secure her passage, leaving her those few coins to purchase food and lodging for her children while she searched for work after their arrival. *They're not mine. I must be ready to hand them over when the bracelet's owner comes for them.*

But what if she never comes? she argued with herself.

The words Anna had spoken moments ago echoed in her mind. *He shall let you know in His own time.*

* * *

Life was easier aboard the paddleboat. She wasn't certain how it happened, but she and her children shared a cabin with Anna, Katrina, and Matthew's English friends. Matthew, Soren, Olaf, and the young English boy, Darren Bacon, along with most of the other men and a few families, slept on the deck in the open air. At first, this arrangement worked well, but as the boat moved north, the nights grew colder, and it became necessary for those on deck to construct shelters using blankets and canvas to ward off the cold night air.

Soren appeared at their door each morning to spend time with Anna. She didn't seem to be as bothered by the motion of the river-boat as she had been by the rolling waves of the ocean and was gradually able to manage short strolls across the crowded deck, holding onto her husband's arm.

Margarette bundled her children in their warmest clothes each day before leaving the small cabin to wander about the deck and peer in at an opulent lounge where the more affluent passengers assembled. She took special delight in just breathing the air, which was free of the stench of sickness. She availed herself of the use of a bucket and water drawn from the river to wash their soiled and salty clothing.

Matthew joined her most days for an English lesson and a turn about the deck. Jens always greeted Matthew with a shout of joy and a leap into his arms. From there, he soon perched atop the young man's shoulder for a ride about the deck. Occasionally, Jens chose to run on his own sturdy legs, and Matthew would snuggle Annelise in the crook of one arm while offering the other to Margarette. At those times, she found it difficult not to see them as others must see them, a small, devoted family. She took pains to erase such thoughts. Matthew was kind to them, but she would never trust another man as she had trusted Jory before she'd learned of his weakness and temper. Besides, a good-looking young man like Matthew would soon make the acquaintance of girls who both spoke English and were far more attractive than Margarette.

Better food and fresher air brought roses to the children's cheeks, and even Anna proclaimed herself much improved. She insisted on spending a short time each day on deck watching the villages and forests as they passed by. A general air of peace and optimism prevailed. A kindly black man brought Anna a rug to place across her lap as she sat in a sheltered spot on deck. Each time this happened, she turned to Soren or Margarette to exclaim over the courtesy and kindness of the colored staff aboard the boat. Neither she nor Margarette had seen black people before and at first found it difficult not to stare as many of the children aboard the boat tended to do.

One morning, when they had been on the Mississippi River for almost two weeks, a shout went up and someone pointed to a small city on the eastern banks of the mighty river. Smoke spewed from the riverboat's stacks, and the vessel began to slow. There were several sharp blasts from its whistle as it crept closer to shore, and Margarette realized their journey was at an end. But their new life in the Mormon city, Nauvoo, was just beginning.

She gathered her children close and breathed an inaudible prayer. Surely here they would be safe and she would be able to find work.

On a bluff above the city, she noticed a large uncompleted structure. Pointing to it, she asked, "Is that the temple?"

One of the missionaries heard her question and nodded yes. "It was begun before I left for England, and now it is nearing completion," he said. "It is my understanding the Twelve have made its rapid completion a priority."

Soren placed an arm around Anna where they leaned against the rail. She saw them both wipe at their eyes, and she felt a small measure of all that the magnificent edifice represented. The pair had never been blessed with children. Hearing that those who entered the temple would be blessed with eternal marriage and would be together for eternity, they had sold their few possessions and their home in Denmark to make the long journey. A longing filled her heart, and she wondered if she would ever, being without a husband, be able to enter the temple and receive the blessings promised the faithful there. There was so much she did not yet know about the temple, and she had heard that the Prophet had said there would be more revealed after it was completed. She vowed to learn everything she could.

The boat nudged against the sturdy planks of the wharf, and Margarette became caught up in the bustle and confusion of passengers gathering their belongings and departing from the ship. Black porters took care of depositing larger pieces of luggage on the wharf, but she carried Annelise and her own bag. At last she stood on the wharf, surveying the place that was to be her new home. Jens gazed around as eagerly as she did.

"Are we going to live here, Mamma?" he asked.

"Yes, dear." She wished she could assure him they would stay for the rest of their lives, but already she had heard rumors that the Saints were being pressed to move on. At least if she had to leave this place, she would be with others who faced the same trial.

A cheer went up from the crowd that had gathered to meet the newcomers. An important appearing man made a speech of welcome, and a committee passed quickly through the throng, assigning the newcomers to accompany various people to temporary quarters that had been made available for the emigrants.

She lost sight of the Pedersens and Matthew when a well-dressed couple stopped to speak to her. They asked her if she might be looking for employment. In her stumbling English, she let them know she was in need of work and a place to live. Minutes later, Margarette, with Jens clutching her skirts and her arms filled with Annelise and her heavy bag, found herself following the stout, middle-aged man and a woman dressed in black bombazine who twittered and turned frequently as though assuring herself that Margarette was still following behind them. Each time, Margarette smiled, hoping to assure the woman that she was following. She wished they would walk slower to accommodate her son's short legs and the heavy load she carried, but no matter how difficult the task might be, she would make every effort to keep up. She could hardly believe her incredible luck to be offered employment and a place to stay so soon after their arrival. Surely Heavenly Father was watching over her.

Margarette turned once, searching for Matthew and the Pedersens. Everything had happened so quickly that there had been no opportunity to say good-bye to them. She hoped she would see them again. They had become like family, and she would miss them sorely. Perhaps when they attended services on Sunday, she consoled herself. She heard a sniffle from behind her and knew Jens was missing his friends, too, and that the rapid walk had tired his little legs. Her hands and nose were chilled, and she feared for the children's comfort, but still she pressed on.

Margarette lost track of the number of blocks they traveled before reaching a red brick, two-story house that sat on a large wooded lot, a little distance from any of its neighbors. She caught a glimpse of a pasture with a few horses behind the house. The couple she followed turned in at the gate and led the way to a tidy porch and a freshly painted white door, which the man opened, then ushered the women through.

Margarette turned her head, carefully examining the parlor where she found herself. Beside the door, an ornately carved tree held hats and umbrellas. The ceiling was high, with intricately carved moldings. Heavy curtains were drawn over the room's single window. The floor gleamed with polish, and a rose-colored settee stood beside a handsomely carved table. A spinet graced one wall. The opposite wall was highlighted by a brick fireplace and a long, carved mantle, holding an array of curiosities from various parts of the world. Two chairs were drawn up before a cozy fire, and a woven rug filled the center of the room. It was the most elegant room she had ever seen.

The man bowed and left the room, leaving the two women alone. The woman's hands fluttered, and she cleared her throat several times before signaling that Margarette should follow her into the next room. They passed through a nicely appointed dining room with a heavy oak table and at least a dozen chairs to a room where Margarette surmised that meals were prepared. This room was nearly as large as the parlor and contained a generous supply of cupboards, a large black stove, and an immense, round oak table. Again the woman fluttered her hands, and Margarette guessed she was being invited to be seated at the table. She was glad to set down her bag and boost Jens to one of the chairs.

"Oh, dear. Do you speak any English at all?" The woman didn't appear to expect an answer but busied herself setting a teakettle on the stove.

Jens's small face lit up, and he responded. "I talk English. Matthew teach me good."

The woman's kettle clattered to the floor, and water ran in streams across the brick hearth of a mammoth fireplace.

"I'm sorry." Margarette set Annelise on the floor, well away from the spilled water, and took the cloth the woman was reaching for. Stooping, she mopped up the spilled water. "My English not good, but I speak little."

"Goodness!" The woman seated herself and fanned her face with her hand. "I didn't expect . . . I was told . . . But this is wonderful."

When Margarette finished the task of wiping up the water, she gathered up her wide-eyed baby and seated herself again at the table. The woman's hands fluttered again, and she pointed to herself. "Miss Jane Saunders." So the woman wasn't the gentleman's wife.

"I am Margarette Jorgensen. My children are Jens and Annelise," she carefully enunciated the sentences Matthew had taught her.

"My brother, Mr. Isaac Saunders, is in need of a housekeeper, as I will be returning to the East shortly. If you meet his standards, you will receive the use of the cottage and a small salary. Oh, dear, I do not know if you understand at all. If only he had chosen an English widow with references, as I urged him to do."

Margarette wasn't certain of all Miss Jane Saunders's words, but from the stilted conversation she'd had earlier with Mr. Saunders, it seemed his sister had mixed feelings about his choice of a house-keeper.

"You want I cook, clean?" She waved her arm to encompass the large house.

"Yes, yes." Miss Saunders beamed her relief that Margarette understood her.

"I start today?" Margarette sought clarification.

"No. Today you rest. Tomorrow I'll show you the house and teach you your duties."

Margarette's heart felt lighter. Surely, tending to such a lovely house and cooking for Mr. Saunders would not be as difficult as keeping her mother-in-law's house spotless and cooking to suit Lars's picky tastes. She wondered why Mr. Saunders's sister, rather than his wife, was handling the arrangements.

Another flutter of the black-clad arms signaled that Margarette should follow the woman again. This time, they left the house by a side door, and Miss Saunders led the way through a well-tended herb garden to a path that disappeared into a grove of trees.

A few more steps brought them to a small structure that Miss Saunders referred to as a cottage. It consisted of one room with a fire-place, a washstand that held a bucket, ladle, and a tin basin, a table with four chairs gathered around it, and a small cabinet. A loaf of bread and a small crock sat in the center of the table, and a lantern rested on the mantle. A curtain strung on a taught line separated the living area from a smaller area containing a bureau and a feather-tick-covered bed. Margarette set her bag down and let her gaze wander over the room. It was clean and tidy, and if she understood Miss Saunders correctly, it was to be their new home. Contemplating turning the small cabin into a home for her and her children filled her heart with joy. How she had longed for a home for her children.

Jens took a cautious step from behind her skirt. He looked up at his mother to ask, "We sleep here?"

Miss Saunders tweaked the coverlet on the bed and brushed at an invisible spot on the bureau. "I hope you will be happy here," she said formally.

"Thank you." Margarette didn't know what else to say. The tiny home was perfect. She hadn't expected to find a home and job so quickly. Surely the Lord was blessing her and letting her know she'd done right to bring her children here. The cabin was small, but there was privacy and far more room for the children to play than they'd ever had before. "Early tomorrow, I go big house," she promised.

"Good. Mr. Saunders prefers a large breakfast served promptly at six." Miss Saunders stepped toward the door, then paused, "Oh, I forgot to mention. There's a trundle under the bed. It will do for the boy." She exited, pulling the cabin's single door closed behind her. Margarette stared at the door, feeling confused. She didn't know the word *trundle* or what it might have to do with Jens.

Cautiously she approached the bed, still holding the baby who was squirming to be let down. Lowering herself to her knees, she lifted the coverlet so she could peer beneath the bed. Jens, copying her action, knelt beside her. Together they burst into laughter, and Jens clapped his hands as his mother drew the small bed from beneath the larger one.

"I sleep here!" Jens shouted, jumping on the bed, then feigning sleep.

"Jens," Margarette said while still kneeling. "We should thank Heavenly Father. We are safe now, and we have house."

The little boy hurried to her side, kneeling again.

* * *

Before leaving the small house the next morning, Margarette blew out the lantern and wrapped Annelise in her shawl. The sun was not yet up, and the air was chilly. Jens mumbled his wish to return to his bed since it was dark outside and he was still sleepy.

Nevertheless, he obediently clasped his mother's hand and walked beside her to the big house.

Miss Saunders was already in the kitchen when they arrived. Margarette instructed Jens to watch over his still-sleeping sister, who lay on her quilt in one corner of the large, comfortable kitchen, and immediately set to work learning Mr. Saunders's preferences and where the various supplies were kept. She made special note of each new word and phrase she learned in the process.

When Mr. Saunders descended the stairs, a steaming breakfast was waiting for him. He seemed to be in a jovial mood and invited Margarette and Jens to join him and his sister for breakfast. Reluctantly, Margarette set two more places and informed Jens he should watch his manners. Mr. Saunders read a brief passage from the Book of Mormon, then bowed his head to speak an equally brief prayer before heaping his plate. Margarette watched her employer surreptitiously, determined to anticipate his needs. She noted that he was younger than she had thought the previous day and not at all severe. His waistcoat strained at the seams, testifying of his devotion to hearty meals, and she vowed to prepare for him every tasty recipe she'd learned from her mother and even those her mother-in-law had insisted she prepare to suit Lars. She was surprised and grateful when the man complimented Jens on his excellent behavior and assisted the boy in cutting his meat.

Midway through the hearty meal, Annelise awoke, and Margarette scurried back to the kitchen to nurse her. When she finished, she found that her employer had already left the house for his office and Miss Saunders was engaged in clearing the dining room table. She hurried to assist her.

As the day progressed, Margarette learned not only her duties, but she learned that Miss Saunders was preparing to travel back east to live with her sister, who had four small children and was more in need of assistance than her brother. She learned too, that Mr. Saunders had become a Mormon against the wishes of his family and that his family disapproved of his insistence on staying in Nauvoo in spite of the loss of his wife in childbirth and the constant threat from mobs. Margarette didn't understand all that the other woman had to say, but she gleaned enough to know that her employer was a widower, that

Miss Saunders didn't approve of her brother's religion, and that Miss Saunders would be happy to leave his home in Margarette's care.

The following days were much the same, and Margarette felt she and her children were settling in quite nicely when Miss Saunders announced that they should visit the shops and make a few purchases. She wished to leave her brother well provisioned, and his new house-keeper needed to know at which businesses he had accounts.

She enjoyed the walk to the business district, and Jens had gained enough confidence to run back and forth between his mother and the various street crossings. In Denmark, he would never have been so brave as to let go of his mother's skirt, fearing dire threats from his grandfather. Even Annelise babbled and seemed happy to be out of doors in spite of a cold breeze coming off the river that made Margarette glad she'd bundled the children in their warmest clothing. As soon as she received her first salary, she would order thick coats for them. She'd learned during their voyage that Mary Bacon was an accomplished seamstress and that she planned to support her children with her needlework.

The shops were warm and cozy, and people greeted each other with small-town familiarity. A few nodded or tipped their hats to Miss Saunders, though she didn't return or acknowledge the greetings. Margarette noticed that to Miss Jane Saunders, visiting the shops was a grim responsibility instead of the adventure Margarette expected. She spoke only to the shopkeepers to whom she introduced Margarette as Mr. Saunders's new housekeeper, never mentioning her name.

Margarette tried to match her demeanor to that of the woman beside her, but she couldn't help smiling at the bright colors and enticing aromas she found in the shops or the broad wink the butcher directed toward her behind the staid lady's back. Several women complimented her children, and one offered Jens a peppermint stick. One made a point of mentioning that a service was to be held the following day on the temple grounds and that Brother Brigham was sure to deliver an address. This news delighted her, and she hoped that Mr. Saunders would allow her time off to attend the meeting. Seeing his sister's face, she thought it best to ask the gentleman herself.

Leaving the last shop with their string bags full, she heard a quiet voice greet her by name.

"Sister Jorgensen?"

Turning, she saw a familiar face. Before she could respond, Jens ran toward the young man calling, "Olaf, where is Matthew?"

Pleased to see Olaf, she held out her hand. The young Swedish man took it and in a mixture of Danish and Swedish with a little English thrown in, he expressed his pleasure at seeing her again, and then turned to answer Jens's question.

"Matthew and me work at brickyard. We share room in a house near work until Katrina and I wed. Today Matthew work on temple."

"Congratulations! It seems your betrothal has become official," she said in Danish.

"Ja, her uncle has agreed to my suit."

Margarette glanced quickly toward the large building that towered over the city. It was good to know that Matthew was helping to build it. She also found it comforting to learn he wasn't far away. She missed their daily talks and English lessons.

"We must be on our way." Miss Saunders spoke impatiently. The elegant tilt of her nose warned Margarette that her employer's sister did not approve of her stopping to chat with the Swedish workman. She hastily bid Olaf farewell and made ready to follow Miss Saunders.

"Miss." He touched her arm to stay her departure. "Someone has been asking for you. Someone from Denmark." There was a look of concern in his eyes as he reported the news in Danish.

"Soren?" She smiled hoping for news of her friends and that she was mistaken concerning the shadow she'd glimpsed in his eyes.

"This man did not sail on the *Carolina*."

5

The return journey seemed long and the bag she carried heavy. Miss Saunders didn't speak and seemed to be out of sorts. Margarette hoped that she wouldn't be dismissed because she had stopped to talk to Olaf. Annelise whimpered as though sensing her mother's worry, and Jens clung tightly to her skirt, nearly tripping her. Concern over whether she'd lost favor with Miss Saunders was only a small part of the worry that burdened her. *Had the person asking about her been sent by Lars?* She didn't believe her father-in-law would come after her himself. He was getting old, and he hated travel. Besides, there was no one to care for the farm in his absence should he come himself. Just as when he'd found Jory in Copenhagen after he'd run away and married Margarette, she expected Lars had hired someone to search for his grandchildren. Jens wouldn't go willingly with a stranger, and she knew he was afraid of his grandfather, but he was just a little boy and would be no match for a determined adult who was being paid to return him to Denmark. She found herself glancing over her shoulder and peering down side streets at frequent intervals.

She was glad to reach the Saunders's house with its plentiful trees and shrubs that hid it from the street and curious passersby. Jens seemed to relax too when they entered the kitchen, and he didn't protest when Margarette assigned him to watch his sister while she and Miss Saunders put away the supplies they had purchased and began preparing dinner. Annelise had started crawling just the past week and was more difficult to keep on the quilt where Margarette wished her to remain while she worked. Her stubborn insistence on practicing her newfound skill kept Jens busy chasing after her.

"I shall be leaving the first of the week," Miss Saunders announced. "You might as well begin preparing dinner by yourself tonight. I shall be in my room packing my trunk, should you need me." She walked stiffly from the room, leaving Margarette uncertain as to whether the lady was regretting her decision to leave her brother's home or anxious to be on her way.

It didn't take long to empty the two large bags and store their contents in the pantry that opened off of the kitchen. When the task was finished, Margarette turned her attention to preparing dinner. Her thoughts flew as she peeled vegetables and browned pork chops. She wondered if the inquiries being made about her might concern the bracelet instead of her children. The woman who placed it in Annelise's nappy might have told someone where she hid the piece of jewelry and sent him to retrieve it. But Margarette couldn't quite convince herself of that possibility. Some instinct warned her that Lars had guessed that she had emigrated to America to join others of her faith.

She was pretty certain that the woman who'd leaped into the Thames was the same woman she suspected of hiding the bracelet in Annelise's nappy. Every description she'd heard of the woman over the months they had been at sea perfectly matched the woman who had picked up her daughter that day. And though she had searched the crowds each time she was on deck before they sailed, she'd never caught a glimpse of her. If she were right, then the woman, if she were even alive, might show up in Nauvoo one day to demand the bracelet back. Knowing the ship's destination and that the ship carried a large number of Mormons was all she would need to know to lead her to look for Margarette in Nauvoo. If the woman had sent someone to find her, it wasn't reasonable to think she would hire someone from Denmark to conduct the search.

Her thoughts drifted to Matthew, and she wished she could talk to him and seek his advice. She missed him—and the Pedersens, too. She'd hoped to see them at the service tomorrow, but now she feared appearing in public. She didn't know what she would do if someone accosted her and demanded her children or if they were stolen away in a moment when her back was turned.

Jens was quieter than usual at dinner after they returned to their cabin. For the first time, she barred the door once they were inside.

She fed the baby and tucked both children in bed. Instead of putting on her nightgown and crawling into bed, she sat at the table and tried to think of what she should do. Nauvoo was the first place anyone, not just the woman looking for her bracelet, would search for a convert to the Mormon church, but there were other villages and towns with Mormon populations where she might not be so easy to trace. At the first opportunity, she would make inquiries concerning those towns.

She was tired, and her head began to droop. Chiding herself for staying up so late, she rose to her feet just as a light tap sounded on her door. She froze. Could the man seeking her have found her so soon? She almost ignored the tap but reasoned that Miss Saunders, who was leaving on Monday, may have thought of something more she needed to tell her.

"Who's there?" she called in a soft voice that came out more tremulous than she'd expected.

"Margarette? It's Matthew," came through the heavy panel. She flew to the door, fumbled with the bar, then flung it open. It was all she could do to refrain from throwing herself against Matthew's chest, seeing him standing on her stoop with his familiar grin. It felt like far more than two weeks had passed since they'd seen each other.

"Come in. How did you find me?" She reached for his arm to draw him inside. He ducked under the low portal, just as he had ducked the low ceiling in the *Carolina's* steerage. The familiar gesture brought an unexpected lump to her throat.

They stood, just looking at each other, then Margarette remembered her manners. "Please sit." She gestured to one of the wooden chairs. He sat, and she took the chair opposite him.

"Olaf told me he met you in front of the mercantile." Matthew started the conversation. "He inquired inside concerning your companion and was told she is Isaac Saunders's sister and that Brother Saunders had offered you a home and a position as his housekeeper. I made my way here, and—not wanting to disturb your employer— found a back way over the fence. Seeing a light in this cabin's window, I decided to take a chance that you might be the tenant."

She understood most of his speech. "I am glad you came." There was something dear about his crooked grin and the too long curls drooping toward his eyes. She found it difficult to look away from his familiar face.

"Olaf told me, too, about the man who has been enquiring after a Danish widow and her two small children." His eyes turned somber. "Do you think he is someone sent by your husband's family?"

"Who else could he be?"

"He may be connected to the jewels."

"No. I think woman jump from ship put little bag in Annelise's nappy. Man who died was chasing her to get jewels. He dead."

"You're probably right, but what are you going to do now?" He leaned toward her, pressing for an answer.

She shook her head. "I not know what to do. Soon someone will tell him where to find us."

"No, they won't."

"*You* found me."

"Because Olaf told me. And the only reason the woman at the mercantile gave him any information is because she knows he's a member of the Church. People here don't talk to outsiders much. They've been hurt too many times to trust someone who might be a spy for the Church's enemies."

"Today is first time I go out. I afraid go to meeting tomorrow. How will people know I member Church?"

"They'll know. Anyway, I have an idea that might help."

She clasped her hands together and listened as Matthew outlined his plan.

"Soren has not found a job, and Anna is still weak. Bishop Partridge found them a place to stay, but it is only temporary. Your house is small, but if they came here to live with you, they could help you with the children and watch for anyone suspicious. Then when you shop, Jens will not be exposed to curious eyes."

"Oh, yes." Matthew's suggestion sounded wonderful. "I have room for Anna and Soren. Anna needs to rest. She cannot rest when she worry. Tomorrow, I talk to Brother Saunders, ask . . . What is word? . . . I bring them here."

"Permission, ask for permission. Good. And tomorrow you must attend the church service. It will be held in the grove near the temple. You will be safe," he went on to assure here. "No one will dare bother you there. I'll find you, and you can tell me if Brother Saunders gives permission to bring the Pedersens here."

She nodded her head, and they continued to talk quietly a little longer about the children and their experiences since arriving in Nauvoo. At last, Matthew stood.

"May I see Jens before I go?" he asked. She led him to the curtain, then pulled it back far enough for him to see the tousled blond hair and sprawled body of her son lying on the trundle bed. She reached for the quilt that had fallen to the floor and pulled it over the sleeping child. Jens mumbled and burrowed beneath the warmth. Placing a finger against her lips, Margarette led Matthew to a large wooden box at the foot of her bed and pointed inside. Annelise slept in a nest of quilts inside the box.

"She crawl now," she whispered in response to Matthew's wide grin.

She walked him to the door and found saying good-bye difficult, though he promised they would meet again the following day. After barring the door, she prepared for bed, feeling more hopeful than she had before Matthew's arrival.

When morning came, she dressed the children in their warmest clothing and donned the better of her two dresses, a dark blue serge with a white, caped collar, knotted in front, before hurrying across the frost-covered lawn to the big house to prepare breakfast. She was surprised to find Miss Saunders there before her, looking cross.

"Mr. Saunders insists that a cold meal of bread and applesauce will do for his breakfast this morning and that he shall be content to wait for preparation of a simple repast for dinner so you may accompany him to the preaching." She clearly didn't approve of Margarette accompanying her brother. Or perhaps it was their destination of which she disapproved. Jane Saunders made no secret of her disapproval of anything to do with the Church.

Margarette was pleased that she needn't ask permission to attend the service, but she knew Miss Saunders was disappointed that her plans for elaborate meals on her last full day in her brother's home were set at naught.

Margarette arranged the table and sliced the bread that she had baked the previous day. It was her first experience baking the light bread the Americans seemed to prefer over the heavier dark bread she was accustomed to in her own land. It had turned out well, though she suspected it would not stay with a man as long as the heavy brown bread she had baked for Jory and Lars. She added butter and several preserves to the spread. Miss Saunders dished up bowls of applesauce and topped them with sweetened cream.

Brother Saunders read scriptures a mite longer than usual that morning, then urged them all to hurry with their breakfast. Jens needed little encouragement to eat quickly, and Margarette fed Annelise small bits of the sweet applesauce from the tip of her own spoon. When the meal was finished, Brother Saunders rose from the table.

"We shall take the carriage this morning, Sister Jorgensen. I shall bring it around in half an hour."

Margarette hurried to clear the table and do the dishes. She didn't wish to keep her employer waiting. In his enthusiasm to ride in a carriage and to see the temple up close, Jens tried to help her with the dishes, which proved more hindrance than help as his inattention to Annelise allowed her to crawl underfoot, but at last Margarette placed the last dish in the hutch. She gathered up her shawl and her daughter, and with Jens dancing around her she left the house. Her fears concerning the stranger were pushed aside as Isaac Saunders drove his matched team down the drive and halted in front of her. She would be safe from Lars's child snatcher beside her sturdy employer.

A brisk breeze lifted Annelise's silvery curls and ruffled Jens's thick gold hair as they waited for Brother Saunders to alight from the carriage to assist them into it, but they didn't have long to wait. He looked elegant in a long coat and top hat as he descended from the buggy to assist Jens, then Margarette, to the single seat. When they were all settled, he cracked a whip over the fine looking team, and they were on their way. Jens turned to smile, excitement dancing in his eyes, as he viewed the world from his elevated perch.

When they arrived at the grove, Margarette was startled by the size of the crowd of assembled Saints and was grateful for the arm Brother Saunders offered her. He carried the carriage blanket beneath his other arm. She balanced Annelise on one hip, holding her in place with her free arm. Jens took his usual place, clutching at Margarette's skirt, as they made their way on foot toward the massive building.

She noticed small groups of men and boys standing about, though she didn't see Soren or Olaf. Blankets were spread on the ground on which sat women, young girls, and families. Older boys raced about, dodging the blankets and weaving between clusters of adults.

Brother Saunders spread the blanket on the dry grass in a spot where the weak November sun evaded the nearby trees, then invited her to be seated. Instead of hurrying off to join one of the groups of men, he seated himself on one corner of the blanket. He encouraged Jens to sit close beside him, partially sheltering him from the chill breeze that served as a reminder that autumn had turned to winter.

"How did you come to join the Church?" he asked as though she were not his housekeeper but a friend. She explained about the missionaries who had taught her and her mother after her father's death and then politely asked about his own conversion.

"My wife met the missionaries while visiting her aunt. She was excited by their message and invited them to our home. At first, I was skeptical, but the more I studied, the more convinced I became of its truthfulness. My own family was appalled when we were baptized and berated me soundly. To gain peace, we removed ourselves to Nauvoo."

She wasn't certain of the meaning of all he said, but she understood enough to know his family, not just Jane, disapproved of his membership in the Church. "I too find family not like Church. My husband's family not allow me meet with other members or see missionaries. After husband die, I decide bring children to America, be near Church."

She found him surprisingly easy to converse with and patient with her stumbling English.

The meeting began with a lengthy prayer, followed by a sermon by Bishop Miller. A cloud covered the sun, and she shivered, finding it difficult to listen while worrying about her children catching a chill. She looked around once to see if Matthew or any of the people who had crossed the Atlantic with her were present. On the far side of the clearing, she discovered Matthew's English friends, and one of the little girls waved to her. Closer, her gaze happened on a severely dressed woman only a few years older than herself, who appeared to be frowning her disapproval of Margarette's sharing the carriage blanket with her employer.

Then Brigham Young rose to his feet and began to speak. Margarette forgot the cold and the disapproving woman. The lead Apostle spoke with knowledge and a power that impressed her and filled her with hope. He spoke of their enemies who were not content with the murders of Joseph and Hyrum, but who were continuing to harass the Saints, particularly those in the outlying farm areas. He spoke of the need for further organization, missionary work, and obedience to the principles the Prophet Joseph had taught them. Warmth crept into her heart, assuring her that Brother Brigham was a man of God and if she followed him she would be doing the Lord's will. The time passed quickly, and she was deep in thought when a third speaker arose.

"I think we should leave," Brother Saunders suggested as he leaned toward her. She became aware that Jens was restless and that Annelise was signaling she was ready to be fed. Around her were many blank spaces where families had been earlier. She realized that her face and hands felt like ice and that the baby's little fists were cold too.

Gathering up the children, she followed Brother Saunders to the buggy and was grateful for his meticulous care in bundling them beneath the carriage blanket for the ride back to his house. She looked around one last time for Matthew before the buggy began to move, but didn't see him.

There hadn't seemed to be an opportunity on the drive to the temple grounds to ask for permission to invite the Pedersens to stay with her. The ride back might be her only opportunity. It was only a short drive to the Saunders's house, so she couldn't delay.

"Brother Saunders," she began.

He took his eyes from the pair of horses and smiled encouragingly.

"You have been kind to me and my children. I apologize for asking favor." She carefully enunciated the words Matthew had taught her.

He raised a brow and smiled in a way that encouraged her to go on.

"There is elderly man and woman, travel with me on ship all the way from Copenhagen. They like loving parents to me. They have bad time finding place to live. Wife is weak and husband unable find work. I ask they stay with me . . . until Anna is strong and Soren find work?"

"The cottage is small." A faint frown appeared between Brother Saunders's eyes.

"They can have bed, and I sleep with Jens on trundle."

Isaac Saunders was silent for several minutes, then he asked, "Might this Soren be able to care for my horses and do odd jobs?"

"Oh, yes. He good fix many thing." She had no idea whether Soren knew anything about horses or not, but if he didn't, she would help him. There had been horses on Lars's farm, and she had fed and brushed them many times. She'd never ridden one of the large animals, but she'd learned how to harness them to the wagon and to muck out their stables.

"I suppose you could give it a try," he agreed, but Margarette could tell his agreement was without enthusiasm, except for the possibility of gaining someone to assist with maintaining his large estate. Regardless, she was overjoyed to gain his agreement.

"Thank you!" She clasped her hands together in her excitement. It would be good to have dear Anna and calm, steady Soren with her again.

* * *

After the large dinner Miss Saunders prepared, contrary to her brother's earlier instructions, her employer gave Margarette the remainder of the day off. She played quietly with the children in the cabin until they both fell asleep. Uncertain what to do with her first free time in a very long while, she longed for her mother's old Bible, but she'd been forced to sell it, along with her mother's ring and her winter cloak, to pay for their passage to America. As soon as she could accumulate enough coins, she would purchase a Book of Mormon, she decided. Perhaps Soren would help her learn to read it. Matthew had taught her enough to enable her to read simple words, but she longed to know more.

When Jens awoke from his nap, he pleaded to be allowed to play outdoors. In light of the stranger asking about them, she didn't dare let him go out alone, even to play in the enclosed garden, so she gathered Annelise in her shawl and agreed to a short stroll to the carriage house and back. She was surprised when Brother Saunders joined them. Jens was anxious to run and explore, but Margarette insisted he stay near. Her employer appeased him by lifting him to the top rail where he could pat the horses' noses from across the fence. Margarette was surprised by the look of pleasure on her employer's face as he assisted her small son. *Perhaps he is envisioning the way it might have been had his own child lived.*

"Brother Saunders," she began, but he interrupted her.

"Isaac will do when we are alone," he told her. Permission to address him by his first name made her a little uncomfortable. But perhaps formality was dispensed with much sooner in America than in Denmark.

"Thank you," she said, struggling to make the difficult "th" sound. "You kind to Jens."

"I have long wished for a son," he spoke quietly.

On the return walk to the cabin, she urged Jens to hurry. Darkness came early, though not as early as in her native land. She found herself growing cold as the shadows grew longer and the light began to fade. As they passed the large house, she noticed Jane and another woman standing beside a coach. She was glad Brother Saunders's sister had one friend to bid her farewell, even if she was the woman who had looked on Margarette in such a disapproving fashion earlier that morning. A sigh escaped Brother Saunders's lips. He too had seen the carriage. Looking like a small boy who had been ordered by his mother to be polite, he bid Margarette farewell near his back step and proceeded toward his sister and her friend. Taking Jens's hand, Margarette practically ran to the cabin.

Jens reached the door first and flung it open. He halted abruptly in the doorway. She stumbled into him and grasped at the doorframe to prevent herself from falling.

"Jens, hurry inside," she said. "I'm cold, and Annelise needs to be fed."

"Someone is here." Jens backed up a step.

She looked up to see a man's silhouette framed against the cabin's small window. The shadowy figure stepped toward her. Her breath caught in fear.

"Matthew!" Jens charged forward, recognizing their visitor a moment before she did.

Matthew caught the boy up in his arms and swung him around.

"I didn't see you at service this morning," Margarette said as Matthew collapsed on a chair with Jens on his knee.

"I saw you. You seemed rather busy." There was a strange note she did not like in his voice. It was like he was criticizing her for attending the service with Brother Saunders.

"Brother Saunders invite us to go to service with him. I not able to walk so far with the children. I grateful for his generosity." Generosity was a new word she'd learned from Jane. She hoped she used it correctly.

"What did you think of the service?" Matthew changed the subject slightly, excitement now shining in his eyes.

"It was good to see temple close and see many people believe gospel. I not understand first speaker say, but Brother Brigham talk to me. I understand." She smiled, remembering the warmth that had filled her as the leader had spoken.

"Some of the men I work with said that in August when the members of the Church met to discuss the matter of who should lead the Church, Sidney Rigdon claimed that God had assigned him to be the Church's guardian, but when Brother Brigham spoke, many people saw and heard the Prophet Joseph take shape where Brother Brigham stood. They took that as a sign that the Quorum of Twelve, with Brigham Young as the senior Apostle, should lead the Church."

"I wish I see," Margarette said. "Today I tingle all over when Brother Brigham speak. He man of God, and I think God want him lead Church."

"He's a man of practicality, too," Matthew added.

"What is meaning of *prac-ti-cality?*"

"Practicality means he thinks about how best to do things. I have heard much of his plans to organize us into groups by calling men to positions of leadership over ten or fifty families and to proceed quickly with the completion of the temple."

"Brother Saunders says Prophet make plans for Church go to Texas before he die and he assign Bishop Miller and Lyman Wight go there first begin preparations."

"I've heard that too, but I've also heard that he assigned others to discover all they can about upper California and the Oregon territory."

"I not like move again." She sighed.

"Speaking of moving, were you able to get permission for Soren and Anna to come here?"

"Yes!" She clapped her hands together. "How soon they come? It be good see them again."

"They are coming our house?" Jens slid to the floor and embraced his mother's knee. She was surprised the child had followed their conversation so well.

"Yes," she answered. "They not have house, so they come to us."

Jens danced about, clapping his small hands and laughing. Suddenly he sobered and returned to lean against her knee. He looked into her eyes, and she could see the happiness and hope shining in his.

"Matthew? Will he come stay also?" he asked.

6

"No, no." She felt heat creeping up the side of her face and was grateful for the dim glow of the lantern that hid her blushes.

"I will come to see you often." Matthew tweaked the boy's cheek. He seemed more amused than embarrassed by Jens's innocent question. "I will go now and let the Pedersens know they have a home. Expect them early tomorrow morning."

When he left, he disappeared in the direction of the trees behind the cabin. Margarette wondered why he didn't boldly use the front gate, which seemed more his style. *He's likely concerned for my reputation. With only two small children to chaperone, he doesn't wish me to become fodder for gossip.*

* * *

"Anna!" Margarette embraced the woman and insisted she lie down at once. She was shocked by how thin and worn her friend appeared. The hint of color that Anna had gained during their riverboat trip was gone. She noticed a gauntness in Soren as well.

The older woman sank wearily onto the side of the bed, and Jens rushed to her side. "Do you wish a glass of water, Grandmamma? I'm big now. I can get it for you." Margarette recognized the name Soren had taught the boy when he'd discovered that the Danish words for grandparents served only to frighten him.

"Indeed, you are a big boy," Anna said, touching Jens lightly. "I am so happy to see you and your sister and your dear mother again. I think I would very much like a small cup of water."

Jens rushed to retrieve a dipper of water while Matthew and Olaf carried the heavy trunk that had accompanied the older couple all the way from Denmark into the house. After bringing the water to Anna, Jens dashed about, getting in the men's way, but they didn't seem to mind.

"Where shall we put this?" Matthew asked. Margarette pointed to the spot where Annelise's box had sat earlier. She'd moved the crate and the trundle bed to the other side of the curtain that hung from the ceiling, to allow the Pedersens a small amount of privacy. The trundle could be pushed back under the larger bed during the daytime to make more space in the little house. The young men set the trunk where she indicated.

"We must go," Matthew said as he straightened. "We are on our way to deliver a load of bricks to the Almays. Brother Almay has decided it is time to turn their cabin into a fine brick home."

Margarette walked with them to the door and watched as the two men's long strides carried them down the path. Watching them walk away filled her with a strange melancholy. She drew her shawl around her shoulders. The morning was cold, and there was a heaviness to the thick clouds overhead that signaled an approaching storm and the beginning of winter.

"I help Matthew!" Jens rushed past her before she could close the door.

"No, Jens." She hurried after her son, only to see Matthew stop to scoop him up in his arms. Setting the child on his shoulders, he returned him to her.

"Jens, you must look after your mamma and little sister. The Pedersens need a big boy to help them become strong and well, too." He set the child back on his feet, adding, "You are needed here. Olaf will help me."

Jens showed his disappointment for only a moment, then straightened his shoulders in an attempt to look older. "Yes, I help everybody." He started back toward the cabin, then looked back at Matthew, "Come again soon, Matthew. We sad when you not come."

"I'll come often," Matthew promised, and Margarette found herself as pleased by his response as her son was.

Matthew and Margarette stood awkwardly looking at each other for several moments, then Matthew shifted slightly.

"I had best be on my way."

"Yes, I too have work," she agreed, but did not step away.

"All is quiet here. Does your employer sleep late?"

"Oh, no," Margarette laughed. "He awake early. Goes office before sun lights day. Today, he wake up early load sister's trunks on carriage. He take her to ferry begin journey to sister's home in Maryland."

"Ah, it is good that Soren and Anna will be here." Margarette wasn't sure what Matthew meant by that remark, but something about the way he said it brought a frown of annoyance to her face.

On her return to the small house, Soren insisted the children stay with him and Anna while she attended to the cleaning and dinner preparations at the big house.

It seemed strange to be alone in the Saunders's home, but she found that she accomplished her work much more quickly than when she had to keep reminding Jens to keep Annelise away from the stove and the stairs. It was also easier to scrub and dust her own way instead of worrying about pleasing Jane. As she knelt on the floor to scrub the brick hearth, she felt the hard lump that the little bag of jewels made beneath her knee. She wondered if she would ever know who had a right to claim the pretty gems.

Before her employer's return, she made her way to the cabin to nurse Annelise, whom she feared would be fussing. She was met by only a few feeble whimpers and a complete transformation of the cabin. A bright blue tablecloth covered the chipped table, and a lovely rug was spread in front of the fireplace. Curtains adorned the windows, and a set of pewter plates lined the mantle. Two small, framed pictures, one of the Danish countryside and one of the bustling port at Copenhagen, were tacked to an otherwise bare wall. An exquisite crocheted bedspread covered the bed, and a soft woven mat beside the bed would provide comfort for aged knees when their owners knelt there to pray. The Pedersens had turned the bare cabin into a home.

No, the love shared in the small house made it a home, but the objects the Pedersens had carried in their trunk certainly provided a warm and pleasing setting.

When Isaac returned for dinner late in the afternoon, he expressed dismay when he discovered that Margarette did not plan to join him for dinner.

"I do not enjoy eating alone," he told her.

"It would not be proper, now your sister is no longer here," she countered. She did not wish to invite gossip. Matthew's strange behavior just that morning had reminded her that she should be cautious in her behavior and give no one cause to question her character. Isaac didn't argue, but after dinner he appeared at the cabin door asking to be introduced to her guests. After a few moments, he invited Soren to walk with him.

Margarette found it impossible to keep her worry from surfacing. She didn't know what she would do if Isaac sent the Pedersens away. She loved them and couldn't bear to see them homeless, neither could she deprive her children of a roof over their heads with winter weather drawing nearer each day. The deep lines on Anna's face showed that she shared Margarette's concern.

When Soren returned, they heard his cheerful whistle first. His step was brisk when he stepped inside the cabin, and he was smiling. Margarette and Anna both heaved sighs of relief.

"Brother Saunders is a good man," Soren proclaimed. "He showed me the stable and a fine set of tools. He asked me to keep the fences and outbuildings in repair and to mend anything that our Margarette needs fixing in the big house. Each day, I will feed and care for his team."

"I help," Jens shouted.

"In exchange," the old man said, as he sat beside his wife and took her hand, "we are to share his table each evening."

Tears appeared in Anna's eyes, and Margarette said a silent prayer of thanks for leading her to the kind man who was providing not only a home for her and her loved ones, but was considerate enough to spare an old man's pride.

The following evening, they sat together at the large round table in Isaac Saunders's dining room. With charming thoroughness, Isaac put the Pedersens at ease, and Jens let it be known that he was happy to be seated between Isaac and Soren.

Margarette basked in a sense of well being for about a week, and then one evening as they ate dinner, Isaac brought up a disturbing subject.

"Two farms were attacked by mobbers last night. The families were turned out into the cold to watch their homes and barns burn and their stock driven off. One of the farmers received a whip lash across his face."

"What will happen to the families?" Margarette felt a familiar sickness. She couldn't bear thinking of entire families being turned out to suffer in the cold.

"Nab Johnson and the Coulters helped them round up what stock they could find and a few clothes that had been left untouched on a clothesline behind the house, then made room for them in their homes. Their homes are closer to Nauvoo, but not entirely safe from attack."

"Are any safe?" Margarette's concern caused her to ask.

Soren shook his head. "Just this morning, I heard from your neighbor, Edward Barnes, that he found a fellow attempting to break into the little house he uses for storage where his family lived before the brick kiln was established and he was able to build the fine house his family lives in now."

Margarette felt a stirring of unease. She'd heard no further reports of someone searching for her, but the peculiarity of someone breaking into a cabin so close by stirred her fears. She wondered if Matthew might have more news when he called. No definite arrangement had been made, but he frequently appeared at the cabin for a brief visit shortly before she banked the fire for the night. It had been two nights since his last visit, and she expected he would come this night if he were able.

"We must all be on our guard," Isaac concluded. "Now, a more pleasant matter. A famous singer from London, Miss Olivia Samuels, arrived on this afternoon's ferry from St. Louis. She was met by Lyman Hughes, who made her acquaintance while serving a mission in England. As it is but a few days before Christmas, Brother Brigham and the Apostles have prevailed upon her to provide a Christmas concert. It has been put about that Miss Samuels shall sing tomorrow night at the cultural hall. I have secured two tickets for her concert and would be honored if you, Sister Jorgensen, would consent to be my guest for the evening's entertainment."

Margarette lowered her head, not knowing what to say and wishing Isaac hadn't asked her to accompany him in front of the Pedersens and her children. She should decline. Appearing at the concert with Isaac Saunders was tantamount to announcing they were courting. She didn't think her employer thought that way about her, but he was merely being kind in making the suggestion. Still, she had a great love for music and might never be offered such a wonderful opportunity again.

"Dear Margarette, you must go," Anna urged. "You have had little pleasure in such a long time, and to hear one of Europe's most highly touted voices is not an opportunity to be missed."

"You needn't worry about the children," Soren added. "They will be safe in our care."

"Please say yes," Isaac pressed.

"I shall be honored to accept your kind invitation," she stammered and immediately wondered if she were making a mistake.

* * *

The children were asleep, and the Pedersens had pulled the curtain separating the one room into two when she heard Matthew's quiet tap on the door. She hurried to lift the bar and was dismayed to see exhaustion lining his face and his clothing dusty and disheveled.

"Come in." She touched his arm, drawing him inside the room. At once he stepped to the fire she was about to bank and stood before it rubbing his hands together. She reached for the teakettle that hung inside the yawning mouth of the fireplace and poured hot water over a spoonful of crushed peppermint leaves, then stirred in a few drops of honey. She handed the warm drink to him. He took it gratefully, seeming to derive as much pleasure from the warm cup as from the tea he slowly sipped.

"Brother Hicks says we shall have snow before morning," he said at last.

She had feared as much. Once she had delighted in the snowflakes she caught on her tongue and being pulled on a small sled by her father, but now she feared the discomfort and illnesses winter might bring. At least she and her children would be secure in their small home. And Mary Bacon had agreed to make warm winter coats for Jens and Annelise in exchange for the small amount Margarette was able to offer her.

She told Matthew of the news Isaac Saunders and Soren had shared at dinner and asked if he had heard more of the man searching for her. Matthew looked troubled.

"The men who attacked the outlying farms live in that area and are troublemakers who get worked up every time Thomas Sharp publishes his lies in his newspaper, the *Warsaw Signal.* However, no one seems to know who the man was that Brother Barnes scared away. He is described as being of medium height with dark hair and a fur hat pulled low, hiding his face. There have been other complaints of burglaries in houses set back from the road or hidden by trees. A few farms have reported the intruder too, but only small items such as a pocket watches, coins, warm clothing, and food have been reported stolen. The intruder doesn't limit his house breaking to Mormon homes, either. Consequently, his thefts are one more sin placed at our door."

"Do you think he is the same man who asked about me and the children?"

"The description is the same."

"Then I will not go tomorrow night." As much as she wanted to hear the singer from England, she would not risk her children's safety. Her mind began searching for a way to disappear. Her hand strayed to the now-familiar bag beneath her skirts.

"Go where?" Matthew appeared puzzled, and she remembered that he did not know Brother Saunders had invited her to attend a concert. Reluctance to tell him made her hesitate. She was being foolish; there was no reason Matthew should not know her plans. He was her friend and would be pleased at the opportunity offered her.

"A great singer from England, a woman who trained in Paris and Vienna, has arrived in Nauvoo. She is presenting a Christmas concert at the cultural hall. Brother Saunders has invited me to hear her tomorrow night, but it does not matter now. I shall stay home to watch over my children. They are my first concern."

Matthew was very still. He seemed to be suffering from some kind of pain. It was as she feared—it was not proper for her to attend the concert with Isaac Saunders. It would be presumed she was pursuing Isaac with his fine house and comfortable living. Isaac Saunders was one of the more wealthy men in Nauvoo, while she was a penniless widow and his employee. The gossips would say she didn't know her place.

"No, you should go. It is a great opportunity for you, and I will assist Soren in watching over Jens and Annelise."

Matthew's insistence that she attend the concert, followed by his hasty departure, left Margarette feeling unsettled until far into the night. If he felt it wrong for her to attend the concert, she wished he would have come right out and said so.

7

Snow fell before morning, but dawn brought bright sunlight, painting the City of Joseph in iridescent diamonds. By noon, the snow was gone, leaving a legacy of muddy streets. Margarette's thoughts went often to the previous night's conversation with Matthew, and in spite of his insistence that she attend the concert, she sensed that he wasn't happy that she would be going. She shared her doubts with Anna, who informed her that it was too late to withdraw her consent and that to refuse Brother Saunders at this point would be rude.

Following dinner, Soren brought the carriage around. Brother Saunders assisted Margarette to the second seat, then sat beside her. He tucked a robe over their laps to keep out the cold. Soren cracked a short driving whip over the horses' heads, and the matched pair moved forward with eager steps. Each step splashed bits of mud against the front of the carriage, making Margarette grateful for the robe that covered the skirt Anna had dug out of her trunk and insisted she wear to the concert.

Margarette had expressed concern to the Pedersens when Soren mentioned that he would be driving them to the concert, then returning later to take her and Brother Saunders back home. Even though this would save the horses from standing for two hours in the cold, it also increased her fear that someone might overpower Anna and take the children. Matthew's soft tap on the door minutes before she was to meet Isaac relieved her concern, and she'd bid Jens and Annelise good night before hurrying down the path to meet Isaac.

Though cold, it was a beautiful night, and Margarette enjoyed the short drive to the cultural hall. When they alighted from the carriage, it was to join a large throng of people slowly making their way inside the building. Most were laughing and stopping to speak with others who were clearly old friends. Isaac nodded and spoke greetings to a number of people. Occasionally, he introduced her to his acquaintances, but at length they made their way to seats with an excellent view of the platform that would serve as a stage.

Margarette looked around, drinking in the atmosphere of the brightly lit hall. Many of the women were attired in beautiful gowns, but others wore more serviceable dresses, and she wondered if anyone other than herself wore borrowed finery. She noticed a familiar set of shoulders several rows ahead of them. She craned her neck to see better.

"Is that Brother Brigham?" she whispered to Isaac.

"Indeed it is," he responded. Seeing her pleasure at recognizing Brother Brigham, he pointed out several other Church and city dignitaries and their wives in the audience. Then the crowd stilled as a gentleman in a long coat stepped onto the platform. He welcomed the concertgoers and then invited another well-dressed gentleman to pray.

Following the prayer, the man who seemed to be in charge made a dramatic gesture, bowing low and holding out a hand toward a tiny blonde woman who had been seated on the front row next to Lyman Hughes, whom Margarette remembered as one of the missionaries aboard the *Carolina*. The pale cream of the woman's silk and lace gown shimmered in the light of the lanterns placed around the small stage as she took the gentleman's hand and slowly mounted the steps. Jewels glittered in the pile of curls atop her dainty head, and her waist appeared impossibly small.

"Brothers and sisters," the announcer spoke. "Miss Samuels arrived recently in New York from London. Her arrival was celebrated by a quickly arranged baptism for her, her brother, her brother's fiancée and a small group of converts who left London rather quickly last fall before the ordinances could be performed there. From New York, she made her way here to keep a promise she made to Elder Hughes, the missionary who taught her the gospel. We are fortunate to have her sing for us tonight and to be able to claim her as one of our own. I give you now, our own lovely nightingale, Miss Olivia Samuels." The audience broke into thunderous applause, which ended abruptly when the singer raised her hands and began to sing.

Margarette felt the music as though it touched her very soul. It made her feel as she'd felt once long ago as a small child tucked between her parents in a sled that flew over snow-covered hills beneath a canopy of stars in far-off Denmark. One song after another brought laughter, then tears, then a joyous ache to her heart.

A short intermission came, and Margarette leaned back, still caught up in the wonder of Miss Samuels's voice. She had never experienced anything like it. Slowly she became aware of people around them visiting and greeting their neighbors. Two women stopped beside Isaac. Margarette recognized the woman who had glared at her when she'd attended the service held on the temple grounds. She was accompanied by another woman, who appeared to be an older version of the first woman and was most likely her mother.

"Brother Saunders, how good to see you again," the older woman exclaimed. "We have quite missed you and dear Jane."

"It is good to see you, Sister Waterton, Miss Hannah." He bowed slightly. "Business has been brisk, and I've been quite occupied."

"I see." Hannah Waterton gave Margarette a disparaging look.

Had Margarette known of the lady's tendresse for her employer, she would never have accepted his invitation for tonight, though she couldn't regret listening to Miss Samuels. She became aware that Isaac was introducing her to the ladies.

She stammered a response and held out a hand, which was ignored by the younger woman. While wondering what she could say to assure Miss Hannah that her relationship with Isaac Saunders was not what that lady seemed to assume, Miss Samuels returned to her place on stage, and a ripple of movement sent those standing back to their seats, including the Waterton ladies. Margarette continued to ponder the problem for only a moment, and then the music wrapped itself around her senses and she forgot all but the glorious sounds coming from Miss Samuels's throat.

At the completion of the concert, the songstress responded to two curtain calls before disappearing through a door at the side of the raised platform. Isaac placed the cloak Anna had also insisted on loaning her that night around her shoulders and offered his arm. Together they moved slowly through a crowd that seemed reluctant for the evening to end. On reaching the street, they found Soren waiting.

A fierce, cold wind carrying flecks of ice blew from the north. Isaac fussed over securing the carriage robe around her to protect her from it. Once he was satisfied that she was comfortably situated, he signaled for Soren to proceed. Giving the reins a shake, Soren urged the horses forward. The streets were frozen now, and no mud splattered as the team broke into a trot, their breath forming small clouds about their heads. The carriage had traveled only a few paces when Margarette saw something that caused her to draw in her breath in a quick gasp.

"What is it? Is something wrong?" Isaac asked.

"Those women . . ." She indicated two women standing with their arms clasped about each other. They were wearing identical gray cloaks. It was the cloaks that drew her attention. She'd seen one like them before. The woman on the *Carolina* who carried Annelise away, then returned her with the strange bracelet in her nappy, had been dressed just so.

"'Tis our songbird and Sister O'Connel. The O'Connels are newlyweds, recently arrived from England. It is rumored that the pair were in Miss Samuels's employ in London. I met them not long ago when he volunteered for the Nauvoo Legion." Isaac Saunders took great pride in his position as an officer in the Legion.

"Soren, please stop! I must see . . ." Soren pulled back on the reins, bringing the team to a halt. The horses stood, stamping their hooves impatiently and blowing white puffs of air into the frosty night. He turned to her, a question in his eyes.

"The woman on the ship, you remember? She wore a cloak like those two women are wearing." Understanding gleamed in his eyes, and he angled the carriage to give her a better view.

"What woman?" Isaac was clearly puzzled by their behavior.

As Soren urged the horses closer to the women, Margarette felt a stab of disappointment. Miss Samuels's cloak was lined with bright red silk, and black fur trimmed the cuffs and hem. Her former maid's cloak was unadorned, with a plain black lining. Neither cloak framed its wearer's face with Scottish plaid.

"I thought . . . A woman aboard the ship . . . wore a gray cloak. I think might be same woman."

"There must be hundreds of women with gray cloaks cut from similar patterns."

"I'm sure you are right."

"Was the woman aboard the ship important to you?"

"She gave me something I hope return." Margarette didn't elaborate.

Isaac signaled for Soren to go on. Slapping the reins across the horses' broad backs, Soren urged the team to a trot. Margarette turned her head, continuing to watch the two women.

The horses quickly carried them past the objects of her attention, and Margarette was satisfied that neither one was the woman she'd encountered that day in the London port. Miss Samuels and her former maid were both smaller than that woman had been, and their hair was much fairer. Isaac was right—there must be many women who chose the same fabric and design for their cloaks. She didn't know whether she was disappointed or relieved that neither woman was the woman she first thought one of them to be.

* * *

The prospect of visiting any of the merchants made Margarette uneasy since learning that someone had been asking for her, but a few days after the concert, she found it necessary to make one of her rare trips to the mercantile. After purchasing the needed items, she stopped at the butcher's shop. While examining a large fowl that she planned to roast for Isaac's New Year's dinner, she overheard the butcher discussing an odd incident with a stout gentleman with whom he appeared to be on friendly terms.

She didn't mean to eavesdrop on the conversation, but in her eagerness to improve her English, she'd trained her ear to listen for new words. Conversation at Isaac's dinner table and Matthew's continued efforts had gone a long way toward building her confidence in her ability to speak and to understand, and the snatches of conversation she encountered in the various shops were greeted as a welcome challenge to her new skill.

"Of course, it was assumed he was a Mormon," the butcher said in a loud jovial voice.

"It's always the case. Robbers and hooligans suppose that because the newspapers describe us as a lawless people, they will be welcome in our midst and sheltered from the law. Consequently, they arrive in large numbers to steal and counterfeit. Then when they attack Mormons, our neighbors applaud, but when the non-Mormons are the victims of these lawless predators, the attacks are assumed to be at the behest of the Mormons," the portly gentleman who stood at the counter expressed his observation.

"Do you think he's the same crafty fellow Bishop Morely came nigh to capturing a fortnight ago among his chickens?"

"It's hard to say. But he fits that fellow's description, and several others have seen him. Maud at the mercantile swears he's the same fellow who was enquiring a month ago about someone to translate Danish. She sent for Sven Bjornsen, who, though he's from Norway, speaks all of the Scandinavian tongues. He said the man was looking for a woman and two small children."

Margarette thought her heart would stop beating. She inched her way closer to the pair. Listening was more than a game now.

"Did he find the woman?"

"No. Brother Bjornsen said the fellow had shifty eyes, and he suspected it was a trick, so he sent the fellow on a fool's errand to a distant township." The two men enjoyed a chuckle.

"Doesn't seem he found anyone who could speak his lingo there, either." The butcher shook his head in mock sadness.

"Those fellows from over Warsaw way caught him sleeping in a haystack. They figured that since the fellow spoke some foreign tongue, he was one of ours. They roughed him up good, I hear. When he limped to Brother Yates's farm and his missus recognized the coat he was wearing as one stolen off her daughter's clothesline, Brother Yates chased him halfway to town, where he sneaked aboard the last riverboat headed back to New Orleans."

"Guess we won't see that bounder again 'til spring." They guffawed merrily, then noticing Margarette standing near, the butcher asked, "What can I help you with today?"

She quickly placed her order, then began the walk back home. All the way, she found herself thinking about the conversation she'd over-heard. Could it be that she was finally free? She wished she knew more about the man who was rumored to be searching for her. When she reached the cabin, she told Soren about the conversation, and he promised to find Sven Bjornsen and see if he could learn more.

* * *

Christmas passed quietly, and now the new year arrived with little fanfare. Margarette saw little of Matthew, who dropped by frequently to visit the children and to check on the Pedersens while she was involved with cleaning and cooking at the main house. It almost seemed that he was avoiding her, and she wondered if she had somehow offended him. She found that she missed him and the lessons he'd taught, which had been mixed with an exchange of varied topics and ideas.

One sharp, clear January day, Isaac returned to his home early. There had been a recent snowfall that painted the town white, and the team's harnesses jangled in the frosty air as he drove up the lane to the stable. Margarette peered from behind a curtain, noting the fine picture the man and his horse made against the snowy backdrop.

Soren met Isaac at the stable. From the kitchen window of the main house, Margarette could see them speaking together before Soren led the team inside the shelter and Isaac turned toward the house with long, brisk steps. He seldom entered the house by the front door anymore, so she met him at the kitchen door to take his hat and coat.

"I have just begun dinner preparations," she began to apologize.

"It's not dinner that concerns me," Isaac told her as he paced about the kitchen. "I'm afraid it is bad news. Word has just reached the Twelve that the Nauvoo charter has been revoked."

"Revoked? What does that mean? Must we leave Nauvoo?"

"Not at once, but soon. For now, it means that we shall not be able to defend ourselves against our enemies. The Nauvoo Legion is to be disbanded and our city offices have no standing. Lyman Wight is leaving for Texas as soon as he can pack up his wagons. He requested that I accompany him."

"How long shall you be gone?" she asked with some alarm. If Isaac closed up his house, she would be without employment.

"I told him I couldn't go at this time, but would perhaps join him later. It is impossible for me to be ready to leave by the end of the week. I have a great deal of business to transact and the house to sell before I can leave Nauvoo."

This reassured Margarette somewhat, but eventually he would leave. When that happened, she wondered what she would do. She, her children, and the Pedersens were settled quite comfortably in the cabin, and food was plentiful. It was unsettling to contemplate the loss of the home and the position that was providing her with her first comfort and security since her father's long-ago drowning.

That evening, when she finished tidying the kitchen and hurried down the path to the cabin, her thoughts were on Isaac's news. She was anxious to share the information with Soren and Anna. Perhaps together they could make plans.

Most days, the older couple kept the children at the cabin while she tended to the big house, an arrangement that, in addition to allowing her to complete her work more quickly, saved the children from daily exposure to the cold winter air. She made several trips back to the cabin each day. At first she went to check on Anna and to nurse Annelise, but now that the little girl had learned to hold a cup and to toddle about the cabin on her own and Anna was well again, she went merely to spend a little of each day playing with the children and assuring herself they were safe.

She pushed open the door and stopped short. Matthew was seated at the table with Jens on one knee. Her heart began to behave strangely, and when he smiled, her own smile erupted like the sun after rain.

Truth be told, she was hungry for just a glimpse of the man she'd come to think of as her dear friend, and she was glad to be able to assure herself that he was well. Fevers and aches still plagued the river town when the weather turned cold, and there seemed to be a great deal of illness going about. Hearing of so much illness, she worried about Matthew, who spent the better part of each day outdoors delivering loads of brick or working on the temple.

"Have you heard news?" she asked as she turned to hang her cloak on a hook behind the door. Without waiting for an answer, she hurried on. "Brother Saunders says the Nauvoo charter has been revoked, and we are without a way to protect ourselves from the criminals who enter our city."

"Yes, I learned of the action earlier today and came to warn all of you of the need for greater care when you go out. The Twelve are taking steps to ensure our safety," Matthew said. "They tried to ward off this action, but when their efforts failed, they asked the Legion to continue to keep order within the city in an unofficial capacity."

"But if the Legion is disbanded, what can they do?" Anna asked.

"They can't take any official steps, but their presence alone may serve to discourage vandals, especially if they patrol the city in groups," Matthew pointed out. "All of the boys and men will be asked to contribute time to keeping our population safe."

"But without judges or policemen, the lawless element will have free reign in our city," Anna expressed her concern.

"This is but one more trial of our faith," Soren said. "If we hold to the gospel and trust in God, we shall be safe whether we live or die."

Margarette believed Soren's words with all her heart, but she couldn't help wondering why, in a country with a constitution that promised freedom to worship, following God's Prophet had to be so hard.

When Matthew stood, declaring that it was time for him to seek his own quarters, he asked if Margarette might accompany him a little way. Surprised and pleased, she reached for her shawl, but Anna pressed her fur-lined cloak toward her.

"It's much too cold for just a light wrap," she insisted.

"Thank you," Margarette murmured as she stepped through the door, closing it tightly behind her to prevent heat from escaping the cabin. She pulled Anna's cloak close against her throat and followed Matthew, who led the way along the narrow path. Near a large tree, he stopped and turned to face her.

"Soren told me about the conversation you overheard a few days ago," he said. "Olaf and I went to see Sven Bjornsen."

"Did you learn anything more?" Margarette asked. She put out a hand to touch his sleeve.

"You'll freeze." He placed his gloved hand over her bare one. "I shouldn't have asked you to come outdoors."

"It doesn't matter. What did you learn?"

"Only that the man who was beaten was angry because no one would speak to him and that he'd been pursued by Mormons and anti-Mormons alike. He said he took his papers to a captain of the Nauvoo Legion, showing his authority to remove two children from their mother and return them to their grandfather who is their legal guardian, but the captain said the papers were worthless here. Sven said that the man claimed his purse had been stolen in St. Louis when he stopped to ask questions concerning the Mormons. Without money and no cooperation from the law, he'd turned to petty thievery to acquire warm clothing and food. He was fearful that when he returned to Denmark, his employer would have him arrested."

"Then it was Lars who sent him here." Margarette shivered. "You are certain he has gone?"

Mistaking her shudder for a reaction to the cold night, Matthew placed an arm around her and drew her close. "He's gone. You needn't worry. Elder Hughes was one of the missionaries who taught me the gospel in England, and we have visited several times since my arrival here. I learned that a few days after Miss Samuels's concert, the two were wed in Brigham Young's parlor before rushing to board the last paddleboat headed toward New Orleans before the ice closed off the river. They plan to meet her brother and his wife, who have been taking a slow honeymoon journey down the eastern coast while trying out a new steam-powered vessel. I was in the crowd that accompanied Elder Hughes and his bride to the boat, and I myself saw the man whom Sven described as he leaped aboard the sternwheeler at the last possible minute."

"But what if he only remains aboard until he reaches St. Louis or some other town closer than New Orleans?

"There won't be another boat until spring." He drew her face against his shoulder. "He has no money to buy a horse and no way to transport the children if he does manage to find them, until he gains some funds. Besides, I heard that the captain who spoke with him left orders to run him out of town if he shows up here again. I think you can feel assured of your children's safety for a few months at the very least."

"Thank you." She drew her head back and looked up into his eyes. Something she saw there held her captive.

He too seemed to be caught up in some kind of spell. He leaned forward across the short space that separated them. His lips barely brushed hers, then he pulled back abruptly, releasing his hold on her so unexpectedly that she almost lost her balance.

"I'm sorry," he apologized. "I had no right . . ." He turned away, hesitated a second or two, then plunged into the trees. He was out of sight before she could gather her wits about her.

"Wait!" she called, but the only response was the crackle of ice-laden branches stirring in the cold wind that suddenly sprang up.

8 ☜

"It's a beautiful evening, the first such of the season. Would you care to take a drive up to the temple mount to check on the progress being made on the temple?" Isaac sat on the stool Margarette used for reaching the higher cupboards, watching her finish washing and drying dinner dishes. She couldn't recall when he started joining her in the kitchen on evenings after the Pedersens returned to the cabin, taking her children with them following dinner, but it was now a well-entrenched habit. He was a well-educated man with many interests, and she found their discussions enlightening. She suspected he was as lonely as she was, without a spouse with whom to discuss the day's events. Her thoughts went to Matthew, but she promptly attempted to bring them back to the proffered invitation and the April evening scented with blossoms from the many orchards found in Nauvoo.

Thinking about Matthew still had the power to bring a flush to her cheeks and a quick remembrance of the kiss he'd given her that cold, January night. It wasn't the kiss that brought a hint of color to her cheeks—she blamed that on the hot dishwater her hands were in—but his apology. She hadn't really minded the kiss, but there was something embarrassing about Matthew's apology for the stolen kiss, followed by his hasty retreat. Added to that was the care he took now to only visit the cabin when she was absent. She feared the impulsive kiss had somehow made him regret their friendship. Since January, she'd only caught a few brief glimpses of him.

"All right," she consented with a smile directed toward Isaac. She usually avoided Isaac's invitations, ever mindful of Miss Hannah Waterton's expectations in her employer's direction, but the buds were swollen on the trees, and a few hardy flowers were showing their faces. The winter had been long, and the cabin had grown small. She was in no hurry to return there tonight since she'd caught a glimpse of Matthew cutting through the woodlot minutes earlier. She missed him, but she wouldn't burden him with a friendship he no longer wished to continue.

When the last dish was in its place, she gathered up her shawl and strolled beside Isaac to the stable where he hitched just one horse to a light buggy. After checking the straps and buckles, he assisted her to the high seat, then climbed up beside her. Giving the reins a shake, he set the horse at a lively trot. The seat was narrow, and she found that each jolt of the wheels bumped her up against Isaac, which didn't particularly disturb her, though it felt strange to sit in such close proximity to a man after the passing of nearly two solitary years since Jory's death.

When they reached the temple grounds, she was awed by the spectacular structure and amazed by how much it had grown during the winter. Even though dusk had arrived, dozens of workers still swarmed over the unfinished building. Isaac brought the buggy to a halt, and together they watched the activity for several minutes.

"Would you like to explore on foot?" he asked at length.

"Oh yes." She was anxious to see as much of the temple as possible. It was a lovely building, and one she felt a deep yearning toward.

Isaac jumped down, secured the horse, then held out his arms to her. Instead of taking her hands, he encircled her waist, lifting her easily to the ground. His hands stayed at her waist several seconds longer than necessary, leaving her a bit flustered.

Seeming not to notice her discomfort, he tucked her hand into the crook of his arm and led the way across the open space before the temple. She gazed in wonder at the intricate carvings on the stones. Upon reaching the steps, Isaac continued up them until they could peek through an open door into a large room. They didn't enter, but made their way carefully around the temple to the other side.

Isaac led the way to a small grove some distance from the building itself, where he suggested they rest a moment on a smooth log, positioned like a bench, from which they had an excellent view of the temple and the city below it. Behind them, the trees exhibited their new, pale green wardrobes, creating an almost secluded arbor around them. After a few minutes of quiet contemplation, Isaac rose to his feet and began to pace a few steps one direction, then a few steps back to the log.

Margarette watched him, sensing he was deeply troubled about something. She also was surprised to note he looked much younger than he had the first time she'd seen him. The paunch was gone, and his cheekbones stood out where before there had been fullness. An overall look of softness had disappeared, and she wondered if it was her fault. Was she not feeding him as well as his sister had? She remembered the rich sauces and desserts Jane had insisted he eat and his requests for simpler meals. Perhaps Jane was the one at fault, making him appear more stout and older than his years by pushing richer dishes on him than he wished. Margarette became aware that her employer was really a handsome man.

He ceased his pacing to stand with one foot braced on the log, looking down at her. "I received a letter today from Lyman Wight," he said.

"Is he well?" she asked politely.

"He is in excellent health and has suggested I join him."

Margarette's heart began to pound. Had Isaac brought her to view the temple to soften the blow of announcing he'd soon have no need for her services?

"If I can find a buyer for my home, I would like to leave by the end of next month," he went on to say.

"Has it been decided, then, that the Church will remove to Texas?"

"It was decided before the martyrdom." Isaac sounded impatient, as though he'd argued this point before.

"I understood the Twelve had assigned others to a variety of locations where we might go."

"There is no need to look any farther. Brother Wight has already begun laying the foundations for a settlement."

She didn't respond to this statement. She'd heard it said that Joseph Smith had expected the Church to be established in the tops of the mountains, and from what she knew of Texas, it didn't sound like the place that the Prophet had prophesied would be a place of refuge for the Saints. Besides, Brother Brigham had made no announcement concerning removing to Texas, and she was quite convinced that wherever the Saints eventually settled, the Lord would make that destination known to Brother Brigham. It didn't seem likely, either, that resettlement was imminent, judging from the amount of building she'd noticed taking place. Many of the first settlers were building fine brick homes, and newcomers were not content to stay in the older houses for long. Nauvoo was growing and expanding at a rapid rate.

"But the temple hasn't been completed. Surely, we shan't be asked to leave before it is finished."

"Brother Wight has selected a location with a small hill where we can begin anew without being rushed or harassed. He assures me it is a fine location for a temple."

"So much sacrifice has gone into this one."

"I'll be leaving the end of May. Will you go with me?"

Margarette hadn't seen Isaac move, but he now knelt on one knee before her.

"I can't . . . It wouldn't be proper . . ." She didn't wish to insult him or to lose her job, but surely he knew that accompanying him to Texas would set tongues to wagging.

"I said that badly."

She noticed a sheen of perspiration on his brow.

"What I meant to say is, will you do me the honor of becoming my wife?"

Margarette could only stare in shock. She hadn't expected his proposal, yet a voice inside her head derided her for being a fool. He'd shown her more attention than that of employer for housekeeper right from the beginning. He was no more than ten years her senior. They were both young, healthy, and lonely due to the loss of their mates to death.

"The children," she gasped. "And there's Miss Waterton."

"Your children seem to like me well enough." He smiled. "I shall be pleased to treat them as my own and hear them call me Papa. Jens would make any man proud to call him son. As for Miss

Waterton, I fail to see that she has any say in the matter. She is Jane's friend, not mine."

"I do not know what to say," Margarette said in shock. She wasn't naive enough to miss seeing the immediate advantages to marrying Isaac. Her children would have a father and be safe from Lars. Isaac was a successful businessman and would surely build a fine home in Texas, and theirs would be the best of accommodations on the journey. He was kind and generous, attractive too. If she refused, she would be without a home. Not only she and her children would suffer if she refused Isaac's offer, but the Pedersens would also. She feared turning him down might be an act of irresponsibility.

"You needn't answer at once." Isaac smiled and took her hand. "By now, I know you well enough to know you will wish to make my offer a matter of prayer. I esteem you highly and am convinced we shall do very well together."

She opened her mouth, though she didn't know what would come out of it. Her English had improved vastly over the winter, due to Isaac's patience and Soren and Anna's insistence that they speak English when they were together. Before she could get a word out, a giggle erupted from a short distance away. Startled, Isaac rose to his feet and looked around, frowning into the trees.

"Come out here at once," he ordered in the voice that Margarette suspected made his employees and Legion recruits tremble. The giggle changed to a sob, and after a moment, a little girl stepped into the clearing. Her apron covered her face, and her small shoulders shook. Long, brown, unkempt hair from a loosened braid fell across her shoulders.

"Were you spying on us?" Isaac demanded.

The child's hiccupping sobs turned to wails.

"Leave my sister alone!" A second little girl charged from behind a large tree. Her fists were doubled, and she looked prepared to do battle on her sister's behalf. The second child was smaller than the first, and her hair was a paler hue. She had a deep scowl on her face as she moved belligerently toward Isaac.

"Alice! Nancy!" Recognizing the children from their transatlantic journey, Margarette leaped to her feet and dashed toward the little girls.

"You know these children?" Isaac peered toward Margarette, then toward the sobbing child. While he was thus occupied, Alice rushed forward and landed a kick to his shins.

"What!" With one hand, he grasped Alice's shoulder, preventing her from repeating the action. She continued to punch and scratch instead.

"Alice, stop that," Margarette said over her shoulder to the little scrapper. Kneeling, she swept seven-year-old Nancy Bacon into her arms. "Don't cry. Brother Saunders didn't mean to frighten you." She attempted to soothe the more sensitive child.

"Me? What did I do?" Isaac grasped both of Alice's hands in one of his in an attempt to quell her attack and prevent another blow to his throbbing ankle. Without warning, she burst into tears too. Isaac released her as though she were a hot coal he'd mistakenly plucked from the fire. Just as she appeared about to renew her attack, Margarette spoke to her in a commanding tone.

"Alice, come here at once." The five-year-old shuffled toward her, her eyes downcast. When she stood in front of Margarette and her sister, Margarette reached a hand toward her, drawing her closer. With an arm around each of the little girls, she asked, "Now, suppose you tell me what this is all about? And where is your mother?"

"He yelled at Nancy." Alice scowled toward Isaac.

"We were playing a game," Nancy whispered. "We were hiding from Mum and Darren."

"A game!" Isaac snorted. "Their folks probably think they're lost."

"Not lost!" Alice's bottom lip protruded in a defiant gesture.

"Girls, this is Brother Saunders. He's a very nice man and my friend. He didn't mean to scare you." Margarette tried to make peace between the children and Isaac. She motioned him closer. When he was a few feet away, he crouched so he could look them in the eye.

"Pleased to meet you," he said, holding out his hand.

Nancy timidly shook the offered hand, but Alice looked him over critically before reluctantly extending her own small hand.

"Does your mother know you're hiding on this hill?" Margarette asked.

Nancy hung her head, her guilt apparent.

"Nope, it wouldn't be hiding if we told our hiding place." Alice spoke in a matter-of-fact voice.

Margarette thought she saw Isaac hide the smallest hint of a smile.

"It's too dark to play hide-and-seek anymore today," Isaac pointed out. "How would you like a ride in my buggy back to your house?"

"May Sister Jorgensen come too, even if she doesn't want to get married to you?" Nancy asked, her solemn round eyes casting nervous glances back toward the trees.

Margarette felt her cheeks flame at the child's innocent question.

"Can I hold the reins and yell giddyap at your horse?" Alice wanted to know.

"We'll all go," he rolled his eyes, evading the question.

Margarette took both girls' hands, leading them toward the buggy.

When they reached the buggy, Isaac handed Margarette up to the high seat, then picked up each of the girls and passed them up to her. Without enough space on the narrow seat for the four of them, Margarette attempted to hold both girls, but as soon as Isaac settled himself beside her, Alice scooted onto his knee and reached for the reins.

"Now look, young lady . . ."

"Giddyap, horse," the small tyrant yelled, and Isaac found himself scrambling to keep his seat, hold onto Alice, and gain control of the horse's reins.

"Where do you live?" he finally managed to ask.

"Go this way until we get to the river, then back this way," Alice swung her arm, indicating a jaunt to the south.

"It's that house," Nancy spoke up, contradicting her sister's instructions as she pointed to a sod and wood structure they were passing no more than five minutes from the temple site. Isaac reined in the horse, bringing the buggy to a halt. Not trusting Alice in the driver's seat, he carried her with him as he leaped down to tie the horse to a post. Once the horse was secure, he reached back for Nancy without releasing Alice.

"What are you doing with my sisters?" A youth charged from the front door of the humble home swinging a fire poker.

"You should watch them better," Isaac growled.

"Darren, it's all right." Margarette scrambled down from the buggy seat unassisted and hurried toward the boy. "Brother Saunders gave your sisters a ride home after we discovered them in the woods beyond the temple."

"I drove Brother Saunders's horse," Alice announced as she slid to the ground. Isaac set Nancy on her feet, and she too ran toward her brother.

"Brother Saunders is Sister Jorgensen's friend, and he's ever so nice except when he yells. He likes her and wants her to go away with him."

Margarette felt a blush climb her cheeks again at the child's candid remarks. "Nancy." Margarette knelt beside the little girl and captured her hands in her own. "Listening to other people's private conversations is not kind, and telling others things you weren't supposed to hear is rude."

"I'm sorry." Nancy began to cry again. "I didn't mean to listen to Brother Saunders."

"We were hiding." Alice seemed to think that was sufficient excuse for their behavior.

"Mum is going to send you to bed without any dinner," Darren threatened. "She warned you about running off."

"Didn't run off," the five-year-old insisted. "We was playing a game."

"Where is your mother?" Margarette asked the boy.

"She's out looking for these two." His irritation with his younger siblings was evident. "I wanted to look too, but she said I had to stay here in case they came back."

"Nancy! Alice!" A swish of skirts brought Mary Bacon dashing toward her daughters. In an instant, she was on her knees, pulling them to her. Damp streaks ran down her cheeks. Finally, she straightened and turned to face Margarette and Isaac while keeping a firm grip on each of the girls. "How can I thank you for finding my girls?" she asked.

"Wasn't lost," Alice muttered.

"They were playing near the temple," Margarette said. "Brother Saunders was kind enough to offer them a ride home as it had begun to grow dark."

"I don't believe we've met," Mary lifted her eyes to Isaac's and held out her hand.

"Mary and her children traveled to America on the same ship as my family." Margarette turned to provide Isaac with an introduction. He was standing still, staring at Mary as though he were viewing a vision. They both appeared oblivious to her and to the children. "Mary, this is Isaac Saunders. Brother Saunders, this is the widow Mary Bacon," she continued in a lame voice.

"Pleased to meet you." Isaac released Mary's hand. Mary's words were lost in the commotion of Darren attempting to usher his sisters inside the house through a door that hung by only one hinge.

"I'd better get them settled." Mary turned toward her children. "Thank you again." Her words drifted over her shoulder to Isaac and Margarette as she disappeared through the sagging door.

"I'll be by tomorrow to fix that door," Isaac called after her.

Without saying another word, Isaac took Margarette's arm. Once more, he settled her on the buggy seat, then took his own place beside her. Several times, Margarette glanced at his face in the moonlight. His features appeared stiff and unyielding, leaving her wondering what would happen next. Might he make a complaint against Mary? Would he pursue his matrimonial suit now that they were alone again? And how should she answer?

Accepting Isaac's offer, she knew, would be the wisest course of action, and she was being immature to consider turning him down, yet she felt a strange reluctance to commit herself once more to a husband, even one as kind as Isaac. She felt certain that marriages based on kindness and respect were more likely to succeed than those based on romantic fantasies, as hers to Jory had been. She wasn't a giddy girl now, and she had observed that few couples shared the ongoing excitement that she'd sensed between her parents and that she thought she'd found with Jory. Loving each other so many years and still treasuring each other like the Pedersens did was rare indeed.

Then there was Isaac's determination to follow Lyman Wight to Texas to consider. This disturbed her a great deal. Without a pronouncement from Brother Brigham that this was the correct course, how could she go? She and her children had suffered a great deal to be with the Church, and if the main body of the Church chose not to settle in Texas and she went with Isaac, then all would have been in vain.

Isaac drove without speaking for several blocks, then startled her with a sudden burst of laughter. "Your friend surely has her hands full with that little one."

"Indeed, she does." Margarette looked at him sideways, surprised by his laughter. His chuckle became contagious. "She is forever dragging her older sister into trouble. Mary tries to control Alice's wilder impulses, and Darren is a responsible youth who takes his role as the man of the family in all seriousness, but Alice does try their patience. It's regrettable she doesn't have a papa to rein in her wilder enthusiasms."

Soren heard the clop of the horse's hooves as they turned up the drive and hastened to relieve Isaac of the task of caring for the animal. While Soren saw to the animal's needs, Isaac escorted Margarette across the back lawn to the path leading to the cabin. Her mind mulled the question he'd proposed, and she wondered if he would demand an answer before bidding her good night. She wondered if Isaac might be the answer to her many prayers asking God to help her care for and protect her children. Would she be placing them in jeopardy if she refused his suit? Was she foolish to even consider rejecting Isaac's magnanimous offer? She lifted her skirt clear of a puddle and felt the familiar lump pinned to her petticoat. Matthew and Soren had urged patience concerning the jewels. Was patience the answer to her current dilemma? She would wait until she received God's confirming warmth in her heart before giving her answer, just as she had determined to do with the bracelet.

"Sister Waterton has chided me for failing in my social duties of late," Isaac interrupted her thoughts in an unexpected way. "Jens informs me he is about to celebrate his fourth birthday, and it seems to me that a birthday might be an occasion to invite a few children and their mothers to my home for tea Friday next."

* * *

Isaac didn't press her for an answer, but he did pursue his plans for the children's party he had proposed. A few days before the party, Margarette made one of her infrequent trips to the mercantile.

"Margarette." She turned to see Matthew standing just outside the shop where she'd gone to purchase supplies. He held his cap in his hands, worrying the brim and appearing ill at ease.

"Matthew!" Gladness filled her heart, and she stepped closer. She'd seen little of him for months and couldn't believe her good fortune at happening on him while shopping.

"Do you have time to walk with me for a few minutes?" His voice was low, and his eyes didn't meet hers.

"Of course." She smiled as she took his arm.

At first, Matthew's steps were slow, and he seemed weighed down by some serious matter. He led the way down the walk and entered a shady path that led to the river. Sunlight sparkled on the water, and the sound of birds in the trees lent an air of tranquility to the April morning, though Matthew seemed unaware of his peaceful surroundings.

"What is it?" Margarette feared he was about to tell her that Lars's spy had returned to continue his search for her.

"I shall be leaving Nauvoo in two weeks' time," he announced, and his steps grew faster.

"Matthew! Are you going to Texas too?" She stopped so abruptly that Matthew stumbled. She couldn't believe Matthew would choose to be part of the party leaving to join Lyman Wight. Isaac hadn't mentioned the names of those who would be in his party, but she hadn't supposed that Matthew would be among those going.

After a moment, Matthew turned to face her. His cheeks were pale, and he appeared almost ill. "I've been called to serve a mission."

"A mission?" She didn't know why she hadn't considered that possibility. Over the past few months, many of the men in the community had been asked to leave their homes to preach the gospel in distant places.

"Will you be returning to England?" She felt suddenly bereft. Though she hadn't seen much of Matthew recently, she'd taken comfort in knowing he was nearby and that he checked on the Pedersens at frequent intervals.

"No, four of us will be journeying to Alabama, Mississippi, and Georgia."

"I shall miss you, and Jens will be heartbroken when you no longer come to the cabin." She blinked to clear the moisture that threatened to spill over her lashes.

"Shall you truly miss me?" He appeared pensive for a moment, then broke into a grin that Margarette thought didn't quite reach his eyes and made her wonder if he was not pleased with the call he'd been given.

"You shall be so busy with your own new life, you won't have time to miss me." He took her arm again. He seemed to be memorizing her face with his eyes. "I'd best be getting you back to your shopping and hurry back to my own labors. It would never do to be fired before I can quit."

He walked so quickly it was all Margarette could do to keep up. He seemed overly anxious to part from her. And when he left her standing before the mercantile with no more than a wave, something heavy settled in her breast.

9

Margarette hummed a tune she'd heard at a recent meeting as she put the finishing touches on a tray of teacakes. Her toe brushed something soft, and she looked down to see Annelise reaching for a cake that was just beyond her chubby fingers. Stooping down, she picked up the baby to return her to the quilt spread in one corner of the big kitchen. She handed her daughter two wooden spoons and a rag doll Anna had made for her.

"No, no," Annelise tossed down the items and rose on wobbly legs. Giving her mother an impish grin, she staggered across the room with outstretched arms, intent on reaching the dessert-laden table. Margarette sighed. Anna had taken Jens to the cabin to dress him in his best clothes for the party, leaving her to contend with her strong-willed daughter while finishing preparations for the tea party. Now that Annelise was walking and no longer nursing, she was into everything, and right now she was intent on eating teacakes.

Swooping down on the child, she swung her into her arms, then relenting, broke off a crumb to stuff into the toddler's rosebud mouth. While the baby was still savoring her treat, Margarette returned her to the quilt, and this time when she set Annelise down, she reached under her skirt for the familiar little bag. She shook out the contents for the fascinated baby. She'd discovered by accident several weeks ago while changing her clothes that Annelise loved playing with the shiny bauble. Annelise lunged for the bracelet, turning it over in her small hands several times and pointing to one gem after another prattling an unintelligible tale. With Annelise occupied, Margarette set out small plates and a row of glasses.

As she worked, she mulled over the reasons she'd thought of for Isaac's sudden decision to throw a children's party with Jens as the guest of honor. She supposed it had something to do with his proposal, wanting her to be seen playing his hostess. And he was a good man, who doubtless wished to make a favorable impression on the boy he hoped would soon call him Papa. Whatever his reasoning, it seemed like he was pressuring her to accept his suit, though he hadn't addressed the subject once since that night on the temple hill. In fact, she hadn't seen much of him, other than at meals for a week and a half. He'd suddenly become very busy after work. She had much to be grateful to Isaac for and had no right to resent even subtle pressure, she told herself. Isaac would make a steady and kind husband and father.

There was no reason she could think of for the strange reluctance that made her hesitate to link her life with Isaac's. After all, the children were her first concern, and she no longer held childish notions concerning falling in love with a romantic hero.

The clap of the knocker on the front door brought her musing to an end. She looked around the dining room to be certain everything was in place, then hurried back to the kitchen. From the entryway, she could hear Isaac greeting his guests and ushering them into the drawing room. Amid greetings from several women and the high-pitched voices of children, she recognized the overly bright trill of Hannah Waterton. She wasn't certain why Isaac had invited the single woman to the party, but Margarette knew so few people, she'd been happy to leave the guest list entirely to Isaac.

Hearing approaching steps, she removed the bracelet from Annelise's grasp and slipped it back into its hiding place. The doors from the dining room and the kitchen opened at the same time just as she dropped her skirt back into place and reached for her daughter. Isaac escorted Miss Hannah into the kitchen from the dining room as Anna ushered Jens, with his slicked-back hair and best shirt, through the kitchen side door.

"Most of our guests have arrived, Sister Jorgensen," Isaac announced. "Miss Waterton has offered to assist Sister Pedersen in serving tea to the ladies while you and I take the children outside." Margarette didn't miss the startled expression on Hannah Waterton's face that turned to dismay, or the amused one on Anna's.

Alice and Nancy Bacon came running the moment Isaac, holding Jens's hand, stepped outside. Margarette was happy to see the girls and pleased that Isaac had thought to invite them to the party. She guessed he'd done so when he'd gone to their home to repair their door. Jens smiled his welcome to Alice, who promptly claimed Isaac's free hand and began tugging him toward a red cart pulled by a pony. Almost a dozen children had gathered on the lawn, and Isaac and Soren took turns leading the pony as it pulled the cart in wide circles beneath the trees. Margarette, with Annelise perched on one hip, helped the older children begin a croquet match. After all of the children had a turn riding in the cart, Isaac led them to the wide porch where Anna and Mary were setting out lemonade and teacakes.

Amid a great deal of laughter and noisy enthusiasm, the children chose their cakes and carried glasses of lemonade to various tables placed in shady spots beneath the trees. Alice insisted that Jens sit beside her on the step, and Nancy joined them.

"I should check that there's still plenty of refreshments for the ladies," Margarette said to Isaac, but he was absorbed in conversation with Mary and didn't seem to hear her. She hurried inside anyway. After all, the smooth running of Isaac's household was her responsibility. Inside the kitchen, she found Anna replenishing lemonade pitchers and hurried to help her. She set Annelise on her quilt and handed her the spoons.

"I can do this," Anna protested. "You should stay with the children."

"They're all right. Both Brother Saunders and Mary Bacon are with them." She reached for lemons, sliced them in half, then pressed a half to the juicer and gave it a quick twist.

"Unless I miss my guess, Miss Hannah is with them now too. I saw her dart out the door just after you came inside," Anna pointed out. "Or perhaps I should say Miss Hannah is with Brother Saunders. That woman chases him mercilessly. She borrowed her nephew and invited herself today because she couldn't bear to pass up an opportunity to come here."

"Why, Anna, how do you know that? It's my understanding the Watertons are old friends of Brother Saunders and his sister."

Anna chuckled. "The moment Miss Hannah planted herself by the hall window to watch the children play outside, the whispers in the parlor began." She took the tray from Margarette, "Now you get back out there and rescue poor Brother Saunders."

Margarette wasn't sure whether she wanted to rescue him, or if he needed rescuing, but she supposed it was her responsibility to check on the children and make certain more lemonade wasn't required. She snatched up Annelise, who had wandered from the quilt to empty a low shelf of baking pans. She shoved the tins back in their place and, with her daughter once more perched on her hip, hurried to the back door.

Stepping outside, she let her eyes drift over the scene, looking first for Jens. She found him standing beside Nancy at the far side of the lawn. He was holding a heavy croquet mallet while she seemed to be instructing him in its use. The sound of breaking glass brought her head around in time to see Alice teetering on the edge of the sawhorse and plank table that held the refreshments. Her glass lay in splinters on the porch and Alice was about to fall among the broken fragments.

"Alice!" Margarette lunged toward the child, catching her by an arm as the temporary table tipped, sending its contents plunging to the floor.

"Oh no!" she heard Isaac yell, followed by Mary's scream. Margarette whirled around with Annelise held to her hip with one arm and Alice clinging to her other side in time to see Isaac stagger backward off the porch step to land on his behind in the grass. Clutched in his arms was the lemonade pitcher, the contents of which was slowly running down his face and dampening his hair. Smeared across his coat were a dozen or so teacakes.

"Isaac, oh, dear Isaac," Miss Hannah rushed to his side, then drew back, holding her gloved fingertips to her face. Mary stood as though frozen in place.

Annelise began to wail, and Margarette could feel little Alice trembling against her side. A picture arose in her mind of the thrashing Jens would have received from his father or grandfather had he precipitated such an accident. She pulled Alice closer in a protective gesture.

A sudden burst of laughter rang out. Shocked, she stared at Isaac. Had he hit his head? Mary must have feared the same thing, because she shook off the shock that held her and dashed toward the step leading to the lawn. Alice pulled away from Margarette, launching herself toward the man who sat in the grass laughing. Colliding with her mother on the top step, Alice sent Mary propelling, her arms like a windmill, trying to regain her balance. As Alice struggled to right herself, she bumped her mother, sending Mary sprawling onto Isaac's lap. Alice flung herself toward them, her sticky fingers enveloping them both in hugs, along with shouts of apology, tears, and laughter. Isaac appeared in no hurry to free himself of either Mary's billowing skirts or Alice's sticky kisses, Margarette noticed. Isaac and Mary's reaction to each other on meeting and their preoccupation when spoken to earlier suddenly came to mind. Isaac had volunteered to repair the widow's broken door; had he found other needed repairs that had kept him busy the evenings he'd been absent from his home?

Margarette cradled Annelise in her arms, shushing her cries, while watching the odd spectacle before her. She concluded that Isaac wouldn't ask her again to go to Texas with him. From the corner of her eye, she saw Miss Hannah's shoulders slump. The spinster's voice was sharp as she called to her a little boy with a rip in the knee of his pants, whom she scolded all the way down the driveway as she made her way to the front gate. Margarette felt an odd sort of pity for her former rival; she wasn't sure what she felt for herself beyond a relief-tinged numbness.

Anna took charge of sorting out children and mothers and sending them on their way while Margarette set about cleaning up the shattered glass and Soren removed the saw horses and planks. Isaac insisted it was his duty to see Mary and her daughters safely home before returning to change his attire. When Margarette began piling plates and glasses on a tray, Anna took Annelise from her, called to Jens, and turned toward the cabin.

Margarette had swept up the last crumb from the parlor and was drying the last of the glasses when Isaac returned and rushed upstairs. A few moments later, he descended the stairs in a fresh shirt and jacket. He assumed his usual place on a high stool where he often watched her finish up the day's household chores. When she finished, he asked, "Will you walk with me?"

She nodded her head, gathered up her shawl, and led the way across the porch. Isaac offered his arm, and she took it. They walked in silence for a time. When they reached the pasture where his horses grazed, Isaac stopped. Turning toward Margarette, he took both of her hands in his.

"I've sold the house," he said. "The new owner will arrive in two weeks' time to make the final arrangements."

Margarette couldn't stop the sharp stab of pain that accompanied his words.

"A fortnight ago I made a proposal to you, and I am now in need of your answer as I will be leaving for Texas at the end of the month."

She noted with a touch of sadness the lack of emotion in his voice. "I think your heart would choose another."

"It is to you I have spoken."

"I'll not hold you to that proposal. You and I have both had occasion to discover the fleeting nature of happiness, and I would not hold you to a promise made before you became aware of one who can bring you lasting joy. Go to her."

"It is true that Mary and her children have awakened feelings inside me that I thought to never experience again. I have made myself useful to her on several occasions since we first met, but I have not spoken to her or in any way hinted that there can ever be anything but friendship between us."

"You'll need to move quickly if you are to persuade her to accompany you to Texas."

"But what shall become of you and your little ones? I do care about you, you know."

Margarette was touched by the anguish and true concern she detected in his voice. His arms came around her, and she leaned her head against his coat.

"I do not know, but I trust the Lord will watch over us as He has done before." She spoke softly into his shirtfront and prayed she had the faith to match her words.

Taking hold of her arms, he leaned back, watching her face. "I shall make it a condition of the sale that you and your children—the Pedersens, too—shall have the continued use of the cabin as long as you are in need of it."

Tears filled her eyes. Isaac truly was a good man. She experienced a twinge of regret that she hadn't been able to accept his offer. Perhaps she might have married him for the peace and security he would have given her children if she hadn't noticed the growing affection between him and Mary. Peace, the first real peace she'd felt since the night of his proposal, crept into her heart and seemed to whisper, *Mary will love him as he ought to be loved, and you will not be left without comfort.* She clung to that hope.

With nothing more to be said, Isaac escorted Margarette to the path leading to the cabin. When he would have continued to her door, she laid a hand on his sleeve to halt his steps. "I would like to walk alone for a few minutes."

He nodded his head and bid her good night.

She took her time walking the short distance to the cabin, her mind filled with questions. She was grateful her family would not be without a roof over their heads, but what could she do to bring in an income? Was there a possibility the new owner would require a housekeeper?

"Dreaming?" A voice broke into her thoughts, bringing her to a halt.

"Matthew?" His voice sounded strange.

"I saw you near the pasture. I assume I am to wish you happiness."

"Happiness?" His words made little sense. "I fear there will be more uncertainty than happiness in my future. Brother Saunders has sold the house and will be on his way in little more than a fortnight's time. I do not know if the new owner will have need of a house-keeper." Her words ended with a catch in her voice.

Suddenly Matthew was beside her. His arms circled her shoulders, and he drew her to him. To her, it was a feeling of being home after a long journey. Silent tears ran down her cheeks.

"I don't understand." Matthew's voice was hoarse. "I thought you were to marry and accompany him to Texas."

"I don't wish to go to Texas. Here in my heart," she touched the spot where her heart beat a ragged tempo, "I doubt it is God's will that we follow Lyman Wight to Texas."

"I have been attending meetings two or three nights each week in preparation for my mission. There is much talk among the elders that Brigham Young and the Apostles are leaning toward northern

California as our place of refuge." He was silent for several minutes, and she could see him chewing on his bottom lip as though deeply troubled. "It is widely expected that Brother Saunders will wed you before he leaves. How can he abandon you because you do not share his vision of Texas as the gathering place?"

Margarette straightened to her full height and said with some heat, "He is not abandoning me. I released him from his promise, though I had not yet accepted nor refused him. I do not love him as a wife should love her husband, and he has met someone else who brings joy into his life. He has promised me continued tenancy of the cabin as long as I need it, and I will continue to pray for his happiness and continued faith in the Lord."

"I see I owe him an apology. It is myself I should berate."

"But you have done nothing wrong—save abandon me when I thought we were friends." She ended on a wistful note.

"It was harder than you'll ever know," he murmured.

The flutter she felt once before, when Matthew kissed her, tickled the space inside her chest. "Oh, Matthew, I expected hardship when I ran away from my father-in-law's farm, but loneliness has been the hardest burden to bear. Discovering you had grown weary of our friendship, I was hurt and lonely and in need of a friend. I enjoyed Isaac's friendship, but it lacked something, and I could not commit to becoming his wife. Besides, I'm not looking to marry again. Protecting Jens from his grandfather and providing my family with financial security were the only reasons I considered accepting Isaac."

Matthew placed an arm around her and stroked her hair. Several times he swallowed, and Margarette could tell he was struggling to keep his emotions in check. "Margarette, dear, sweet girl," he whispered. "I did not grow weary of our friendship. I only thought to free you to accept Brother Saunders's suit should you be inclined to do so. I came here tonight to bid a dear friend farewell as I found I could not leave without seeing you one last time. I leave tomorrow."

"So soon?" Tears sprang to her eyes. He was leaving just when she thought they might be friends again.

"Shortly after the sun rises. I don't know how long we shall tarry in the South to preach the gospel, but as soon as we are summoned home, I shall come straight to you." He brushed at her tears with his fingertips.

"I shall be waiting," she promised, "for I have missed my dearest friend.

"Don't let Jens and Annelise forget me." He tried to lighten the somber moment. His fingers slid down her cheeks to cup her chin. He pressed a kiss to her trembling lips, then stepped back, leaving her oddly shaken.

"Good-bye for now," he said. "Will you write to me?"

"I don't write very well," she responded. "But I will try."

"That is all I ask for now." He started to walk away, then turned back as though he'd forgotten something. "Margarette, should you need to leave Nauvoo before I return, I will make every effort to get here in time to help you. If you must go without me, I promise I will find you."

10

A wave of sadness swept over Margarette as she stood in the driveway watching the last of Isaac's wagons turn onto the street that led down to the wharf. She would miss him. She would miss Mary, too, though she was happy for her and pleased that her friend had agreed to a hasty wedding and to accompanying Isaac to Texas. She wondered if she would see either of them again. Isaac and Mary's departure, following so closely on the heels of Matthew's leave-taking, left her feeling more alone and vulnerable now than she had been at any other time since the day Matthew had introduced himself to her aboard the *Carolina*.

Once the wagons were out of sight, she stepped back inside the empty house. Getting a bucket and scrub brush, she went to work, cleaning and polishing to make the house ready for its new owner. Isaac had warned her that the new owner was not a member of the Church and that there was no promise that she would be hired to work for him. Tenancy of the cabin was the only guarantee he had been able to secure for her.

She scrubbed the kitchen floor and shook out the curtains in every room. If the new owner found a sparkling clean house, surely he would be more inclined to ask her to continue caring for it. It was a beautiful late spring day, making her pessimism concerning the future hard to maintain.

"Ma'am, are you Mrs. Jorgensen?" She hadn't heard the arrival of the owner of the voice.

"Yes, sir." She looked up from her task to smile a greeting at the man who stood in the doorway. He was smartly dressed and had an impatient frown on his face. "You must be Mr. Rundell." She felt at a disadvantage to be caught sitting on the floor and hurriedly scrambled to her feet.

"Indeed, I am." He pulled the door wider and stepped inside the parlor where Margarette had just finished dusting the baseboards. He looked around, casting a critical eye toward the window, where she had pulled the curtains aside to allow sunshine to wash the room. Isaac had insisted on the curtains being opened wide after his sister left the house, and she'd gotten used to the light, airy feeling of sunshine streaming through the windows.

"Would you like me to show you around?" she asked.

"I believe I can find my way." With his hands clasped behind his back, he wandered to the next room. When he began to climb the stairs, Margarette gathered her cleaning supplies and retreated to the kitchen, where she seated herself on the stool Isaac had frequently claimed and wondered if she should begin dinner preparations. She could hear Mr. Rundell moving about in the upstairs rooms, opening and closing drawers and doors. Half an hour later, he found her in the kitchen, still waiting.

"I believe the house will do quite admirably," he announced. "My furnishings will arrive promptly at eight tomorrow morning. Please be available to assist Mrs. Rundell as to placement. We will discuss further employment after Mrs. Rundell has had an opportunity to meet you and judge your qualifications." He bid her good day and departed, presumably for the hotel. Margarette watched him walk toward the street with a sinking heart. Kraft Rundell was nothing at all like Isaac Saunders. His personality was cold and aloof, and if his wife was anything like him, Margarette's work was about to become unpleasant—if she even continued to be employed.

* * *

Claire Rundell was a complete surprise when she arrived the next morning. From behind the kitchen curtain where she watched, Margarette's eyes opened wide when instead of the dour matron that Margarette had steeled herself to meet, she saw Mr. Rundell assist a dainty young woman attired in crinolines, lace, and bows to alight from his buggy. She leaned heavily on her husband's arm as they made their way to the front door. She appeared to be as fragile as an exquisite china doll.

The Rundell buggy was followed by two heavy wagons loaded with household goods and driven by two black men. Peering from the back of one of the wagons were several more black faces. Margarette stared in astonishment as the men jumped down from their wagon seats and stood with their shabby hats in their hands, waiting for instructions. A large woman bustled around from the back of the second wagon, followed by two young girls who appeared to be in their teens. One carried a toddler, not much bigger than Annelise, on her hip. The women stopped beside the men and appeared to be waiting.

Margarette stepped into the dining room and from there to the small parlor to greet the Rundells. On seeing her, Mr. Rundell said, "I shall conduct Mrs. Rundell on a tour of the house. You may acquaint the women with the kitchen." She stared after him in astonishment. He hadn't introduced her to his wife or offered a greeting. She could only assume the women she was to acquaint with the kitchen were the black women he'd left standing on the lawn. As she moved back toward the kitchen, deeming it an unspoken order to use that entrance, she heard Mrs. Rundell complain to her husband.

"Kraft, dear, it is so small. How shall we manage until you can arrange to enlarge the house?"

The Rundells didn't seem to have any children, and the house, with its four large bedrooms, enormous master suite, two parlors, a dining room, kitchen, and pantry, seemed spacious to Margarette. There was even a cold cellar and a smoke house. She shrugged her shoulders and hurried outside to invite the waiting women inside.

Margarette felt a little nervous introducing herself to the people gathered on the lawn, though she made an attempt not to stare. She'd never seen black skin and hair that curled like lambs' wool before arriving in New Orleans, though she had heard of a black race of people, native to Africa, who had been brought to America to labor as slaves in wealthy households, a practice she found reprehensible. The black waiters and porters aboard the paddlewheel boat that brought the *Carolina*'s Mormon passengers to Nauvoo had been the gentlest, most polite people she'd ever met. It hadn't occurred to her that they might be slaves.

After introducing herself, the older black woman said, "Call me Julia." She pointed to the older man and said, "That's my man. He be Lester. Caleb, Rosie, and Trixie be our young'ns, and Timothy be Rosie's."

"Mr. Rundell said I should show you the kitchen," Margarette said.

Julia nodded her head and signaled for the two girls to follow her. They picked up heavy crates that the men had lifted from one of the wagons and followed as Margarette led the way. Inside the kitchen, the black women began shifting items from the crates to shelves and cupboards. As soon as one of the large crates was emptied, Rosie placed Timothy inside it and offered him a knotted rag to play with. After a few moments, Julia began preparations for a meal, leaving Margarette feeling superfluous. The woman and her daughters didn't speak much or show either enthusiasm or disappointment concerning the large kitchen Margarette had found pleasant and inviting.

Feeling unneeded and out of place in the kitchen that had been the center of her days for seven months, she slipped into the parlor when she heard Mr. Rundell's voice. He was standing near the open front door while his wife stood on the bottom step of the staircase that led up to the bedrooms. He gave the two black men orders to begin unloading the wagons. There followed a flurry of orders and counter orders that kept the two servants rushing up stairs and back down again. Furniture was placed in first one spot, then moved to another. Claire Rundell frequently turned to her husband and to Margarette, asking their opinions concerning placement, but seldom followed their advice. Instead, she would sweetly tell Kraft to have the item placed in an entirely different place. After almost an hour, Margarette caught sight of Julia slipping along the upper hall toward the master bedroom and concluded that the woman had discovered the back stairs Margarette hadn't thought to point out to her.

At length, Mrs. Rundell declared she was exhausted and must lie down to restore her strength.

"Take her upstairs," Mr. Rundell instructed. After a moment's hesitation, Margarette realized he was speaking to her. The young wife leaned heavily against Margarette as they moved up the stairs.

She hadn't done any lifting or unpacking, yet her steps seemed weighted with fatigue. Margarette wasn't sure how she was going to release Claire's grip and find sheets to put on the huge bed Lester and Caleb had hauled up the stairs earlier.

When they reached the master suite, she was surprised to find it in perfect order, a deep feather bolster on the bed, curtains at the long windows, rich rugs dotting the floor, and the comforter on the bed turned down. A luncheon tray waited on a small table.

Julia greeted her mistress with clucking sounds and the swift removal of her dress and petticoats before loosening her stays and ushering her into bed. In moments, Mrs. Rundell was propped in bed with pillows behind her back and the tray across her lap.

"You done too much, Miz Claire." Julia spoke in soothing tones as if she were speaking to a fractious child.

"There's just so much I must see to," Claire said with a sigh before biting into a thick slice of ham.

"Well, I'll go downstairs now," Margarette excused herself.

"Julia take care of Miz Claire just fine," the colored woman said, and Margarette left the room with a heavy heart. She wasn't needed in the kitchen or anywhere else it seemed. It was becoming clear the Rundells didn't need a housekeeper. Julia was obviously accustomed to managing the Rundell household.

The next few hours passed more smoothly. Margarette made a quick trip to the cabin to check on her children and to ask the Pedersens to keep Jens from running to the main house to play after his nap as he usually did, then she hurried back to the big house. She would miss the freedom Isaac had allowed her and her children. When she arrived at the house, Kraft Rundell was just finishing his lunch in solitary splendor in the dining room.

"What would you like me to do this afternoon?" she asked him.

"Take care of organizing the house."

"But won't your wife want to supervise?"

"Just get as much done as you can before she wakes up. The servants will mind you. They're accustomed to taking orders from an overseer. Let Lester and the girls know they can set up their tent in the woods after the house is in order. Caleb knows to fetch me in time for dinner, and Julia will take care of getting Mrs. Rundell dressed." He reached for his hat. "I have orders that need to be handled at the office. As soon as I return, you may return to your own quarters for the evening."

Putting the house in order proceeded without fuss as the men placed furniture where she thought it should go and the two young women scurried about, adding the finishing touches of pillows, scarves, and bric-a-brac while Julia worked in the kitchen and entertained little Timothy.

"Do you think Mrs. Rundell will want that chair in the large parlor or in the smaller one?" Margarette asked Rosie while directing the men in the placement of the last of the furniture. Jane Saunders had confided to Margarette that Isaac's first wife had used the smaller parlor as her own sitting room, taking advantage of the morning sun to sew or read.

A look of panic crossed the young girl's face, and she backed away from Margarette. "Rosie do what Rosie told," the girl mumbled.

Margarette felt a stab of annoyance. These people knew Mrs. Rundell far better than she did; surely they should know her tastes better than she could be expected to know them. It was irritating, too, the way they always spoke of themselves in the third person and never spoke to her unless she asked a question. They were polite, but not friendly. Her spirits plummeted. Even if Mrs. Rundell decided to keep her on as housekeeper, working with people who kept her at a distance would be difficult.

"Caleb go now," Caleb reported to her as the large clock in the hall chimed the hour.

"Oh, yes, Mr. Rundell will be expecting you." She watched the long-legged young man hurry toward the kitchen. Moments later, she saw him cross the lawn, heading for the stable where Soren leaned against the board fence, the buggy and team waiting.

"We're almost through here." She smiled at the two girls who were dusting and polishing before adding embroidered tablecloths and crocheted doilies to tables and bureaus. They made no response but kept on working. Margarette joined them, and when at last she could see nothing more to clean or straighten, she announced that they were finished unless Mrs. Rundell wished anything rearranged when she came downstairs.

Lester and the two girls stood, watching her expectantly. She remembered Mr. Rundell mentioning something about a tent. "You've done an excellent job," she told them. "Mr. Rundell said when we finished arranging the house, you should set up your tent in the woods."

"Tent?" It was almost a screech. Margarette looked toward the stairs where Claire now stood, once again elegantly attired. Her long, auburn curls were drawn atop her head in a formal coiffure, a glimmering necklace encircled her throat, and her skirts were wider than they'd been that morning.

"Are there no slave quarters in this dismal place?" she asked in an imperial manner.

"Slave quarters?" Margarette gasped with a hurried look toward Lester, then back at Claire Rundell. Her suspicions were confirmed. That Julia and her family were slaves explained much that had puzzled her about them. If she didn't need her job so badly, she would have left at once. The thought of working for people who were slave owners sickened her.

"Claire, I told you before we left Atlanta that we wouldn't be moving to a plantation and that keeping slaves isn't a common practice in this part of Illinois."

Margarette hadn't heard Mr. Rundell arrive. He stood at the foot of the stairs looking up at his wife, a weary expression on his face. Before he could say more, a high-pitched wail came from the kitchen. Rosie cast a frightened look toward her mistress, then bolted toward the kitchen to quiet her son.

"And that's another thing," Claire pointed an accusing finger at her husband. "You said I could only keep the most essential household slaves, and then you let Rosie bring that baby. Bessie would have been of much more use to me, and Timothy would have fetched a good price."

The memory of Margarette's problems with her in-laws brought a bristling to her heart and a great deal of sympathy for the young black mother. *How could she even think of separating such a young child from his mother?*

"Claire, we have no need for a large staff, and Mr. Saunders assured me that Mrs. Jorgensen is an excellent cook and housekeeper,"

Kraft tried to placate his wife. He turned to the two black men and in a soft voice suggested they unpack the tent and remove it to a spot deep in the grove of trees that ran across the back of the property.

"I don't want to see an unsightly tent when I look out my sitting room window." The childish whine in Claire's voice appalled Margarette as much as did her words. "You said there was a cabin . . ."

"Mrs. Jorgensen's family has the use of the cabin until the Mormons move on." He sounded more coaxing than firm.

"You allowed Mormons on our property?" Claire's voice rose to a shriek. "Make them leave!"

"I can't do that." Kraft attempted to reason with his wife. "They built this city, and I purchased Saunders's business and home with a good faith clause that allows Mrs. Jorgensen and her family to stay until they are ready to leave."

"Why don't the Mormons just go? Civilized people don't want them here." Claire's voice was cold and uncaring, and Margarette wondered which of them was truly more civilized. "If you can't make them leave, then the darkies and the Mormons will just have to share the slave quarters."

"The cabin is one room, and there are already five of us living in it!" Margarette said, then more firmly added, "Mr. Saunders gave me a signed paper, giving me exclusive use of the cabin until I have no further need of it."

"You! You're a Mormon!" Claire shook a trembling finger at Margarette. "Get out of my house."

Margarette looked to Mr. Rundell. Looking sad and embarrassed, he signaled that she should leave.

The tears didn't begin to fall until she reached the cabin. Anna looked up as she stepped through the door, then rushed to fold her in her arms. "Oh, my dear," she said, patting Margarette's back. "We'll manage somehow. The Lord didn't bring us all this way to abandon us now."

"She was just so horrid," Margarette said in choking gasps. "They brought slaves and that nasty, spoiled woman was angry with her husband because he didn't sell Timothy."

Jens buried his face in her knees. He looked up at her with a worried expression on his face. "Is Timothy the little horse I saw in the corral? I was hoping I might get to ride him."

"No, darling." She swept her son up in her arms, hugging him fiercely. "I know nothing about the horses Mr. Rundell brought. He brought some people with him—people with dark skin—who have to do everything he and Mrs. Rundell tell them to do. Mr. Rundell owns them just like he owns the horses."

"Just like I had to do everything Bedstefar said?" He hung his head and looked sad.

Margarette hugged him tighter. She had hoped his unhappy time in his grandparents' house had faded from his memory.

She nodded her head, unsure of how to explain the difference to her young son. She wasn't certain there really was a lot of difference.

"But who is Timothy?" Jens persisted. "Is he a little boy like me?"

"Yes, he's a little boy, but littler than you. He's about as big as Annelise."

Margarette's eyes met Soren's, and she saw anger there. "I met the young man. Caleb, he said his name was. He was worried because I harnessed the horses, which he said was his job. He kept his head down, never looking me in the eye. I had a suspicion he was a slave. Slavery isn't illegal here, but it's one of the reasons people in this area and over in Missouri are against us. They're afraid we'll tip the political scale by making some of these frontier states 'free' states."

"Every state should be a free state, and every person should be free," Margarette stated emphatically.

"I agree with you, girl," the old man said, "But there are those who don't believe black people are people or have feelings like we do. To them, black people are highly profitable beasts of burden."

"Come, eat your dinner, dear," Anna coaxed.

Margarette sighed, remembering the many evenings they had joined Isaac at his table. Without a job, how would she feed her family? Soren was old and finding work he could manage would be difficult, and she had no skills beyond housekeeping and cooking. They would be all right for a few weeks—both Isaac and Matthew had left them whatever food supplies they couldn't take with them before they departed, and she had saved a small amount from her wages. Soren and Anna still had some of the meager savings they had brought with them from Denmark as well. Beyond that, she could only trust in the Lord.

"Come, Jens. Sit by Mamma." She led her son to the table. Annelise, with one of Anna's sashes anchoring her to her chair, banged her spoon against her plate.

"I think that is our signal to begin," Soren chuckled before bowing his head.

* * *

Jens pushed a small wooden wagon Soren had made for him across the floor, imitating the clopping sound of horses' hooves. Soren settled near the fireplace with his big Danish Bible, and Anna sat close to him, a basket of mending by her side. Annelise whimpered and pleaded to be held. Margarette picked her up and began pacing the short distance between the fireplace and the table with the little girl in her arms.

"What is the matter, sweet one?" she whispered in a soothing voice as she moved with smooth, rhythmic strides. "Are you getting a new tooth?"

When her arms grew tired, Margarette tried to distract her daughter with a drink of cool water. When that failed, she tried a drop of clove oil on her gums. Annelise would not be comforted, but tugged and pulled at Margarette's dress.

At last, Margarette reached for the little bag she kept hidden beneath her skirt. Annelise clapped and reached for the bright band of jewels. In minutes, the baby was contentedly sitting on the rag rug in front of the fireplace, playing with the bracelet. Margarette watched her for a few minutes, then turned to gather up her knitting. She had promised to complete four pairs of stockings for the brethren who were laboring to finish the temple.

A knock sounded at the door, and Margarette's heart leaped before she remembered that Matthew was far away and would not be knocking on their door anytime soon. Setting aside her knitting, she rose to her feet. When she reached the door, she was surprised to find Kraft Rundell standing there, looking ill at ease. She invited him in and introduced him to Soren and Anna, who eyed him with suspicion.

"I came to apologize," he said, "and pay your wages for these past two days. Mrs. Rundell's words were harsh, but she was raised on a large cotton and sugar plantation in Georgia and has never known anything but the Southern way of living. Everything here is strange and frightening to her. Our first child is due to arrive early in November, and in her delicate condition, I think it best not to upset her, therefore I won't be able to continue your employment. I will stand by the agreement concerning this cottage, however."

Margarette didn't know what to say. She could remind Kraft Rundell that she too was far from everything she'd previously known in her life. She could point out that she hadn't had the luxury of being spoiled while carrying either of her children, and she certainly hadn't been rude, nor expected slaves to wait on her. And she had a legal right to remain in the cabin. She remembered the words Soren had read aloud to them all one recent evening. "Pray for them who despitefully use you." The Rundells didn't have the gospel to guide them, but since she did, it was her responsibility to forgive them and pray that they would receive the truth. She decided it was best not to say what was on her mind.

While she was trying to think of something positive to say, Mr. Rundell took a step toward the table, where he placed a coin. "I was hoping Claire would take to you so she would have a white woman to help her when her time comes."

Margarette felt her spine stiffen. There was nothing she could do for Claire that a colored woman couldn't do just as well, and since Claire didn't consider slaves or Mormons her social equals, Margarette was glad she wouldn't have to see her every day.

"What is that baby playing with?" There was an odd note in Kraft's voice. She saw him stoop, then remove the jeweled bracelet from Annelise's grasp. The baby began to scream, and Margarette rushed to pick her up. After months of protecting the bracelet from being seen by anyone, she'd forgotten about it tonight when Kraft's knock had come to her door. She stifled an urge to jerk the pretty bauble from his hands and give it back to Annelise.

She watched him turn the bracelet over several times in his hands and hold it up to the lantern to see it better. "Unbelievable," he muttered, oblivious to Annelise's cries and attempts to snatch it back.

"Where did you get this?" He turned to Margarette, excitement in his voice. She saw Soren move closer, his shoulders hunched, signifying he meant to intervene if their visitor attempted to take the bracelet.

"It came from the old country." She didn't believe there was any reason to share the full story.

"A strange heirloom. The setting is worthless, but the gems are the most magnificent I've ever seen." He looked up as though attempting to assure her of his qualifications for judging the jewels. "I've had a great deal of experience in buying and selling gemstones. These appear to be nearly perfect, and if you'll allow me to examine them more closely to assure that I'm not mistaken as to their value, and if my estimation proves valid, I'll make you a fair offer."

"I've no desire to sell the bracelet."

"You can't mean to continue living in squalor when you have a valuable asset such as this in your possession." The shock on his face was unmistakable.

"Annelise likes it." Margarette held out her hand to reclaim the bracelet.

"Only a fool would allow an infant to chew on gems worth a king's ransom." He thrust the bracelet toward her and slammed his way out the door.

11

Building in Nauvoo continued at a frenzied pace all summer, and immigrants arrived in large numbers. The lumber mill and brick works did a booming business. Neither Soren nor Margarette were able to find regular employment, though Soren spent a few hours most days helping at the temple site and occasionally hired out for a day doing rough carpentry work. But by July, most of their supplies were running low, and Margarette was forced to carefully weigh each meal she prepared. Each night, the three adults knelt to ask God to show them how to provide for the children. They always included a plea for Matthew's success in spreading the gospel and for his protection.

They occasionally saw members of the slave family and knew that they had pitched a tent in the grove of trees that bordered the pasture. If spoken to, they responded politely, but their nervous behavior suggested they had been warned to have nothing to do with the occupants of the cabin. Jens pleaded to be allowed to watch Mr. Rundell's fine horses run in the pasture and to play with the little boy he'd heard about, but Margarette felt it best to avoid contact that might bring trouble to her family or censure for the slave family.

Olaf and Katrina called on them one Sunday evening to report that they were now married. Olaf carried a bucket of milk, which he presented to Anna. He'd recently found employment with a farmer outside of town, he told them. Being a farmer at heart, he'd gladly given up his job several months ago at the brick works to accept the farmhand position that included a small cottage as part of his wages.

"My employer makes a practice of donating Sunday morning's milking to the widows and the poor in Nauvoo," he told Anna and

Margarette. "Each Sunday I drive into town with the milk. If there is a service, I attend it, but before I leave the farm, Brother Davis and I fill the back of the farm wagon with buckets and jugs of milk to deliver to those in need. Matthew asked me to look in on you while he is away, Margarette and Anna, and today Katrina decided to accompany me, so it seemed a good time. From now on, you can count on me bringing you milk each week."

"Thank you," Margarette told Olaf, and she instructed him to thank the kind farmer for whom he worked. She then hugged Katrina. "The children need the milk," she said with a lump in her throat. She congratulated them on their marriage and wished them happiness. The warmth that filled her heart assured her that Heavenly Father was aware of their plight and had answered her prayers.

A few days later, a knock on the door one afternoon while Soren was away working on the temple brought a surprise. Margarette opened the door, and there stood Hannah Waterton and her mother. Startled, Margarette stammered a greeting.

"Hello," Hannah said. "May we come in?"

Margarette opened the door wider, and the two women brushed past her. They greeted Anna politely and took the wooden chairs she offered them. When all four women were seated and Annelise was snuggled on Margarette's lap, Hannah began. "The women of the Nauvoo Relief Society have set a goal to increase our contribution to the construction of the temple by preparing the needed furnishings for the inside of the temple. We came by to ask if you have the skills needed to hem curtains or make lace cloths."

"I can make lace," Anna said. Margarette wondered where they would find the funds to purchase the thread Anna would need for such a task.

"Some of the sisters are increasing their gardens to enable them to provide meals for those toiling at the temple site as well," the elder Sister Waterton said.

"We don't have a garden," Margarette told them. "As long as Brother Saunders was here, we were allowed to take what we needed from his large garden, but the Rundells have many mouths to feed and have not offered to share the fruits of their garden, even though Soren planted and cared for it until their arrival." Margarette felt a lump in her throat. She wanted to help, but she had no skills beyond being able to cook and clean. Sister Waterton and Anna began discussing patterns and designs for the temple cloths. Anna brought out a shawl she said she intended to unravel so that she could reuse the lovely white thread for an altar cloth.

"Sister Jorgensen," Hannah spoke quietly. "I have been less than welcoming of you and feel I must tell you I sincerely repent of my unkindness. It was foolish of me to entertain expectations where there were none and to hold you responsible for my disappointment."

Again, Margarette was at a loss for words. Hannah's frank honesty took her by surprise. "You were not unkind," she managed to stammer. "Mr. Saunders was considerate of me and I regretted many times that his kindness was often mistaken by others for interest." She'd probably said more than she should have. She didn't wish to embarrass either of them, but the confession seemed to leap from her lips.

Conversation between the two became easier, and they found they shared many of the woes that befell single women in a society where couples are the expectation. Margarette was thrilled to discover that Hannah, as she insisted on being called, had a bright, quick mind and many interests. She didn't seem annoyed or put off when Margarette stumbled over or forgot an English word.

"Like most women, I would like a home and children of my own, but I don't know how to catch the interest of the kind of man I admire. I grew almost to adulthood in a Quaker community, and though I was given an education beyond that which most women receive, I never learned to make polite conversation or flirt with gentlemen." Hannah's blunt manner was beginning to be less shocking to Margarette. "My manner scares away those I would befriend, both male and female."

"You're welcome to visit me anytime. I would be glad for us to become better acquainted." Margarette discovered that she meant the offer, and when it brought a smile to Hannah's austere countenance, she made another discovery—Hannah was almost pretty when she smiled.

"We must be on our way." Sister Waterton rose to her feet, and her daughter followed her action by standing too.

Margarette walked with them to the door and stepped out onto the stoop just as an anguished scream rent the air.

"A child has been injured!" Hannah began running in the direction from which the scream had come. Margarette thrust Annelise toward Anna, then began to run too, followed by her son.

"Come back here, Jens," Anna called.

Margarette didn't stop to order him back to the cabin, even though she knew they might be rushing toward danger. An urgent voice inside her head seemed to be propelling her forward, telling her not to waste time arguing with the boy. They stopped when they reached the fence circling the pasture behind the stable. There, Caleb leaned, sobbing against a post, a long horsewhip in his hands. Tied to the post was little Timothy, his bare back revealing a long red welt. Tears ran down his frightened, confused little face, and he silently writhed, trying to escape the pain.

"What are you doing?" Hannah's voice was its own kind of whiplash, though she didn't speak loudly. She turned her back on the grieving man to hurry to the ragged little boy and began working to untie the cord that held him to the post.

"Caleb." Margarette touched his shoulder. "Why would you do such a thing?" The small time she had spent with the young man had shown her no hint that he was capable of such cruelty.

"Miz Claire, she say whip dat boy five lashes cuz he not stop crying, but Caleb cain't do it." He buried his face in the crook of his arm, and his big shoulders shook.

"Miz Claire is your mistress?" Hannah whirled to face him with the child in her arms. There was a fierce light in her eyes.

"Yes ma'am. She sell him down river, I don't do what she say."

"Can she see us here?"

"She can't see this spot from the house," Margarette answered for him.

"Jens." Hannah beckoned Margarette's son closer. "This baby needs your help. When Mr. Caleb hits that post with his big whip, you scream like he's hitting you. Can you do that?"

"Yes, ma'am," Jens answered bravely, though he looked to his mother for confirmation that he should obey the lady.

"Do it, Jens. As soon as the whip cracks."

"Now!" Hannah hissed at Caleb. The black man straightened, drew back his arm, and delivered a stinging blow to the fencepost. Jens screamed, then offered a shaky grin.

"Not so much force this time," Hannah ordered. "If she's listening, she knows you don't want to do this. Jens, instead of screaming this time, call, 'Mamma' just like your little sister does when she's sad."

Both Caleb and Jens complied with her orders with tears in their eyes.

On the fourth strike, Hannah prompted Jens, "Don't scream this time." The only sound that followed the slash of the whip was Timothy's hiccupping sobs. After the fifth blow, there was only silence.

"I know her kind," Hannah whispered. "She'll be watching to see if you struck yourself so she can punish you if you spared the boy. Here, Margarette, take the boy to your cabin. His mother can come for him after dark." Margarette reached for the baby, but before she could turn away with him, she saw Hannah draw a long pin from her hat and draw it along her arm, creating a dark red line that puckered and bled. She smeared the blood on Caleb's hands and shirt. She then picked up the whip and let her blood stain its tip, the droplets forming small beads on the dusty ground around the pole as well.

"Come Hannah, we must leave at once." Sister Waterton calmly buttoned her daughter's sleeve, took the pin from her now trembling fingers, and with an arm around Hannah's shoulders, led her toward the gate at the far end of the pasture.

Margarette raced toward the cabin with the injured toddler in her arms, listening with each step for Jens's soft patter following her. Anna met them at the door. She didn't ask questions but led them inside where Margarette practically collapsed on a chair.

"You're safe now, baby." Jens crowded close to the injured little boy, patting his grimy knee. "My mamma will take care of you."

"Mamma!" Annelise toddled to her mother and tugged on her dress, indicating she wanted to be held. The sight of her mother holding another baby didn't seem to please her.

"Here," Margarette rose to her feet. "Anna, you must hold him while I see to his back." Timothy's little fists clung to her when she attempted to transfer him to the other woman.

"It's all right, Timothy." She attempted to soothe him. "She won't hurt you. Jens, sit on the trundle bed with Annelise, please, and keep her out of the way while I fix Timothy's sore back. She'll be content if you give her this to play with." She unpinned the small black bag and handed it to him.

She tested the teakettle and found it still warm. Pouring a small amount of water in a bowl, she proceeded to wipe away the grime that mingled with tears on Timothy's face and hands. She carefully cleaned the lash mark across his back and applied a soothing film of butter to the wound. Once he was clean and she had ministered to his injury the best she could, she went in search of a suit of clothing Jens had outgrown. It was too large for Timothy, but an improvement over the rags he'd been wearing.

When Timothy wiggled, indicating that he wished to be put down, Anna set him on the rag rug near Jens and Annelise. Annelise slid from the trundle bed and carefully walked around the little stranger, then she picked up the damp cloth her mother had set down and approached Timothy with evident determination.

"Dirty." She attempted to scrub Timothy.

"No, no, darling." Margarette took away the cloth and picked up her daughter. Jens remembered the black waiters on the boat that carried them from New Orleans to Nauvoo and had satisfied his curiosity then by asking questions, but how could she explain to Annelise the difference between her pale pink skin and little Timothy's deep ebony hue?

"Look, little one," Anna brought her sewing basket to the table. She held up a length of blue yarn. "Pretty," she said.

Annelise nodded her head and repeated the word. "Pwitty."

Next Anna showed her a bit of yellow yarn and again said, "Pretty."

Annelise reached for it. "Pwitty."

Seeing where Anna was headed with her yarn, Margarette retrieved the bracelet from where Annelise had dropped it on the trundle bed. She pointed to each gem and declared each pretty, then she pointed to her baby's hand and said, "Pretty." Next she touched Timothy's hand. "Pretty."

"Pwitty," Annelise echoed. Suddenly she clapped her hands and slid to the floor. With her chubby little legs churning, she rushed to

Timothy, bent over, and kissed the top of his woolly head. "Pwitty," she announced.

* * *

It was late, and all three children were asleep when a timid knock came to the door. Soren peeked through the window, then removed the bar to admit Rosie and Caleb. Rosie's eyes were red and swollen. Caleb shuffled his feet and looked downcast.

"Rosie baby?" Rosie queried.

Margarette put her finger to her lips and led the worried young mother to the trundle bed where Timothy lay curled between Jens and Annelise. She reached for him, drawing him to her breast while tears ran unchecked down her cheeks. He opened his eyes, patted his mother's cheek and promptly fell back asleep.

"How he be?" Caleb asked, guilt and worry making his face look pinched and drawn, reminding Margarette that even though Caleb was the size of a grown man, he was still a young boy.

"He'll be all right if his wound doesn't become infected," Margarette said.

"Caleb ain't never gonna hit nobody with a whip ever again, even if Miz Claire order him whipped or sell the whole fambly."

"What Rosie gwine do wif dis baby?" Rosie asked while clutching Timothy close.

"Tomorrow, bring him here," Margarette told her. "He can play with my children and be safe while his back heals. There's a path through the trees that leads from this cabin to a little clearing behind your tent. If you follow it back to your tent now, and again to bring him here in the morning, Mrs. Rundell won't see a thing."

In the days to come, Timothy's arrival before dawn each morning and the soft rap on the door late in the evening signifying that someone from his family had come for him became the framework of Margarette's days. Soren warned her that she might find herself in big trouble if the Rundells found out she was interfering with one of their slaves, but he spent a good share of his day playing with the little boy, and he made the child a toy wagon much like the one he'd made for Jens. Once, he admitted that he'd discussed the matter with Bishop

Morley, who had commiserated over the unfairness of the situation but had urged him to be as cautious as possible while continuing to protect the child.

Annelise's jealousy of Timothy changed to an air of possessiveness. She never called him Timothy; to her he was Pwitty. Each morning, she awoke searching for Pwitty, and she insisted the little boy sit next to her while they ate their breakfast, and they sat side-by-side on the rug in front of the fireplace playing with blocks, Annelise's rag doll, and the wagons, until their heads began to nod and it was nap time. Pwitty replaced the bracelet as her favored source of entertainment.

Timothy seemed to thrive on the care and attention he received from the Pedersens and Margarette's family, especially Annelise. Whatever mischief she got into, he was right beside her. Hannah became a frequent visitor to the cabin, and she never failed to bring a small gift, such as a succulent strawberry, for the child she'd rescued. Whatever the gift, he divided it to share with Annelise.

"Pwitty gib Lisa," he always said as he handed a share to her.

He was soon running about the house, trying to keep up with Jens, and his vocabulary grew daily. Though he was wary of Caleb for a few days, he soon seemed to be healed both emotionally and physically, once more delighting in his uncle's horsey rides, which he insisted Uncle Caleb give Annelise and Jens too. Only at night when Rosie came for him did he show any sign that all was not well in his world. He would cling to his mother and whimper as though the day's separation had been unbearable.

Shortly after Timothy had become a part of her daily household, Margarette opened the front door one morning to find a small bunch of turnips on the front step. Another morning, there was a bucket of green peas. Sometimes there were potatoes or beans. She wondered how Caleb was acquiring the simple gifts, for she assumed he was trying to assist her since she was caring for his young nephew, until he showed up at her door unusually early one morning with a skinned rabbit he had caught in the woods.

"Thank you," she said. "And thanks, too, for the vegetables you've been bringing."

He looked puzzled. "This be the first time Caleb bring Miss Margarette somethin'. Caleb not take vegetables. He only catch rabbit today and bring him for Miss Margarette to make stew so boys grow big, strong."

She accepted the rabbit gratefully, and it made a fine stew, added to the mysterious vegetables that appeared regularly on her doorstep. Each night, as she tucked the children into bed, she felt a wave of gratitude for the Lord's blessings—the generous gifts of milk, vegetables, and an occasional rabbit to keep them healthy.

One hot, sticky night, she heard a knock on her door. It was later than usual for someone from Timothy's family to come for him. The Pedersens had gone to bed, and the children were asleep too. She opened the door, her fingers to her lips, prepared to caution Caleb or Rosie to speak softly.

Instead of Caleb, Kraft Rundell stood on her doorstep.

"May I come in?" he asked. For a moment her mind seemed to freeze. She couldn't let this man see his littlest slave asleep on the trundle bed with her children inside the cabin.

"Everyone is asleep, and the house is quite stuffy," she improvised, stepping outside and drawing the door shut behind her, but she was too late.

"That's our little Timothy," he said. "Why is he here?"

Nothing but the truth came to mind. But if she told the truth, would she and her family be punished? And what would happen to the innocent child?

"I'm waiting for an explanation."

Her back stiffened, and she found herself unable to hold in the angry words. "Mrs. Rundell ordered him whipped because he cried. I brought him here to tend to his lash marks, and it seemed the best solution to keep him here during the day to free his mother to do her work without distraction and save your wife from having to hear the sounds a baby naturally makes."

"Whipped?" he appeared stunned but quickly recovered. "My wife is not well, and perhaps it is best to keep a noisy child from bothering her. The boy is a valuable piece of property I would not want damaged, so I will see that you are compensated for your supervision of him. I intend to give him to my son as soon as he is born."

Margarette bit her lip to keep from saying anything that might make the pompous man before her change his mind about leaving

Timothy in her care. She had entertained the belief that Kraft was not so inhumane as his wife and that he had allowed Rosie to keep her baby because he didn't want to separate a baby from its mother. The idea of giving dear little Timothy to the Rundells' child as if he were a toy or a new coat stirred almost uncontrollable anger deep inside her.

"I should have been informed of the arrangement, but it is no matter and shall likely work out for the best. I'll have a word with Rosie tomorrow and let her know I will not tolerate secrets being kept from me in the future."

Margarette wondered if he had any idea how callous and ridiculous he sounded. Slavery was an evil practice and no mother, certainly not Rosie, should be censured for protecting her child. She wasn't certain whether keeping her thoughts to herself was wise judgment meant to spare her loved ones reprisal or if it was cowardly hypocrisy, but she said nothing that might antagonize him.

"This matter quite distracted me from my purpose in coming here. I am prepared to make you a generous offer for your bracelet. I can give you enough to build a fine home, provide for all of your family's needs, and send your son to University."

"It isn't . . ."

"No, don't give me your answer now. Think about it for a few days." Kraft reached into his pocket and produced a letter. "Oh, I almost forgot. This post arrived several days ago, addressed to you." He handed her a thin envelope, then turned away, moving with ease along the path that led to his house.

12

Margarette turned the much-handled envelope over in her hands and saw with pleasure that the letter was from Matthew. She hurried inside the cabin and seated herself at the table, pulling the lantern closer that she might see better. Before she could open it, another soft tap sounded at the door. Slipping the letter into her pocket, she hurried to answer it.

"Rosie saw Massah Rundell come to Miss Margarette's door, so Rosie hid in da bushes," Rosie whispered with a fearful glance over her shoulder.

"I think it will be all right," Margarette tried to reassure the girl. "He knows about Timothy, and he said it was all right for you to bring him here each day. He said he would talk to you about keeping secrets from him, but he didn't sound angry."

"Massah Rundell is not a bad master like some," the girl said with quiet sincerity. "He never order whippings. He not like Miz Claire and her papa. Her papa sell Rosie to bad master. Massah Rundell buy Rosie back from master who put baby in her belly."

Margarette's heart ached for the young girl. "Rosie, how old are you?" she asked.

"Rosie be 'most fifteen," Rosie answered as she walked toward the trundle bed. She stood for a moment looking down at the three sleeping children.

Margarette wondered what Rosie's thoughts were as she gazed down at her dark child nestled between Margarette's children with their fair skin and near-white hair. She hoped the young mother saw only three sleeping children, equally beautiful in their innocence.

After Rosie left carrying her son, Margarette seated herself at the table again and carefully slit open the envelope Mr. Rundell had brought her. *Dearest Margarette,* she read.

We have been beset by many trials since our arrival here—a few dogs, too. We have not been blessed to find many souls who are eager to hear the Word, but by much suspicion and hatred. The faithful few who have been baptized are preparing to remove themselves to Nauvoo, or should the Church move westward, they will endeavor to meet up with the Saints along the way. The people here live in much squalor and are quite remote from one another. Each shack, whether it houses a single bachelor or a family of twenty, has an abundance of vicious, underfed dogs. The people and their dogs are suspicious of strangers and have threatened to do us bodily harm. Most nights we sleep in haystacks or in the woods. We have much to be grateful for in that the Lord has blessed us to escape our enemies and has provided us with sufficient food that we do not grow faint.

Elder Blake received a missive from Brother Brigham this day stating that it is his expectation that the residents of the City of Joseph will leave that fair place come spring, and he urges the Saints from the Southern states to join in the exodus. Some are making plans to journey to Nauvoo forthwith. Elder Blake and I have speculated that we will be allowed to journey with them to be reunited with our families. I miss you and the children and desire our speedy reunion, but I'm pleased to be serving the Lord, for it is in His Gospel that our hope for eternity is grounded.

I must hurry with this missive as the hour grows late and I wish for the messenger who brought Brother Brigham's letter to carry it with him when he departs at first light. Until we meet again, I pray for heaven's watchful eye over you.

Yours in the Lord,
Matthew

Margarette wiped away a tear and brought the letter close, clasping it against her breast. She missed Matthew more than she could say. After a moment, she reread the letter and pictured him sitting at a table, straining to see by lantern light just as she was doing. It made him feel nearer. At last, she folded the paper, tucked it back into her pocket, blew out the lantern, and joined her children on the trundle bed. She fell asleep with Matthew's dear face before her.

Sunday, Olaf and Katrina brought word that those charged with the murder of the Prophet Joseph Smith had been acquitted by a biased jury. They also informed her that the anti-Mormon raiders were becoming more active and that a family but two farms away from the one where they lived had been raided two days earlier. Stock had been driven off or wantonly killed, the family evicted, and the house and barn set on fire. After that, each week brought more stories of families forced from their homes in the dead of night, husbands beaten or tarred, women assaulted, and all of their possessions destroyed or stolen.

By the end of summer, rumors were rife that the Mormons would soon depart, and the anti-Mormons were growing more aggressive each day. They were being so bold as to sneak into town to wreak havoc and destroy property. Nearly two hundred farms were burned. The Twelve sent word for all those on outlying farms to move into Nauvoo for protection. As the farm families arrived in town, they began doubling up with town families who were willing to take them in. Katrina's aunt and uncle made room for them, and Olaf's employer sought space for his cattle in town as there was a great need for the milk they provided for the city families.

After visiting Margarette one Sunday and seeing the large pasture where Kraft's team and a pony grazed, Olaf approached him seeking permission to graze four cows in his pasture. They struck a bargain allowing the cows to use the pasture and half of the stable in exchange for Olaf arriving twice a day to milk the animals and turn over half of the milk to Julia for the Rundell family's household use. Olaf, with his employer's permission, left a jug of the milk with Margarette each day as well.

Shortly after being blessed with a steady supply of milk for the children, Soren convinced Anna to join him, even though the long walk would be difficult for her, to attend the October conference being held in the uncompleted temple. Margarette decided to take the children, including Timothy, and attend too. Jens walked beside Soren, who assisted his wife over the steeper spots, while Margarette held a toddler in each arm.

The meeting was a dedication of sorts, since the decision had been made to dedicate the individual rooms as they were completed, and they met in a large downstairs room for the ceremony. They were out of breath, and the two smaller children were fussy by the time they arrived and found seats. Still, it seemed wonderful to Margarette to attend a service held inside the structure, unlike the many she had attended before on the outside. Brother Brigham made a formal announcement that the members of the Church would leave in the spring for the Rocky Mountains in far-off northern California. The announcement filled Margarette's mind with trepidation. She could barely manage to feed her family; how would she find the means to travel over two thousand miles to establish a new home? The solemn prayer offered by Brigham Young a few minutes later renewed her determination and hope for her children's future.

On the long walk back to the cabin in the late summer heat, the words from the prayer, "Lord, we dedicate this house and ourselves to Thee," echoed in her mind, renewing her resolve to find a way to stay with the body of the Church and to see her children receive the blessings of the temple. Hearing Brother Brigham speak of a timetable for their exodus from Nauvoo had increased her concern for her ability to transport her family west, but worshiping with her fellow Saints seemed to renew her faith that the Lord would not let her and her family be left behind. Still, as she walked, her practical side warred with her faith, and she struggled to bring her mind to the practical considerations such a journey would entail.

Margarette was grateful for the milk and the frequent anonymous gifts of garden produce that appeared mysteriously on her stoop, but with summer at an end and instructions from the Church leaders to prepare to leave the city in the spring, she became obsessively worried about feeding her family and preparing for the trek. Her children couldn't live on charitable gifts of vegetables and milk alone. The few occasions when Soren was able to work, she and Anna already hoarded the coins to purchase flour.

She discussed the matter with Soren and Anna, and the three set aside a day to fast and ask the Lord to help them.

One crisp fall day shortly after their fast, Soren opened the front door to find a large basket of potatoes and two big squash. It was to be the last of the garden produce they would receive from their anonymous benefactor. Margarette and Anna were overjoyed by the gift, which if used wisely would carry them well into the winter. That same day, Kraft Rundell gave Margarette a five dollar gold piece for Timothy's support and renewed his offer to buy the jeweled bracelet.

"It is worth many thousands of dollars," Mr. Rundell persisted. "Surely you can see the folly of allowing it to be a child's plaything."

Margarette was sorely tempted to sell the bracelet. She no longer allowed Annelise to play with it, but she wasn't certain she had a right to dispose of it. What if she sold the jewels and then the rightful owner came to claim them? And hadn't she decided a long time ago not to sell the bracelet unless prompted by the Lord to do so?

"I'm sorry, but no. I cannot sell the bracelet," she told him.

"I learned today that the Mormons will be leaving Nauvoo next spring and that your leaders have advised that each Mormon family acquire a wagon, oxen to pull it, and sufficient supplies for a long journey. I came here to offer you all that you will need for your journey plus enough to build a fine new home when you reach wherever you decide to settle." He smiled, expecting that she could not refuse this offer.

Saying no was becoming harder, but she managed to say it.

"My offer continues to stand." He seemed certain she would eventually accept his offer.

After he left, the two women discussed what would be the best use for the gold coin. Their needs were many, but they resolved not to spend it. Instead, it would be the beginning of a fund for the purchase of the supplies they would need when it came time to move west.

As they discussed the matter, Hannah arrived for her weekly visit. Anna and Margarette asked about her plans for the spring exodus.

"I'm not certain I shall be going," Hannah said, to Margarette's astonishment.

"But why not? It will not be safe to remain here, and your father is one of the fortunate ones who can afford a wagon and supplies."

"It's not that my faith has faltered nor that I'm not convinced of the gospel's truthfulness, but of late, I have felt that perhaps there is a reason I haven't been blessed with a husband and children. I'm quite convinced it is the Lord's will that I return to Pennsylvania and live among the Quakers again," Hannah confided with downcast eyes. "I may even travel."

"Oh, Hannah," Margarette threw her arms around the woman who had become her friend. "Don't give up. Someday you'll have a home and family of your own. Who knows what opportunities may arise after we have found a place where we will be safe from the hatred and jealousies found around us here? I have heard that there are more men than women on the frontier, so don't give up hope that you'll find a husband."

"I don't think my future lies west, but I shall miss you, dear friend." Hannah dabbed at her eyes with her handkerchief.

"You will find it much harder to remain faithful to the gospel when you have no one around you who shares your beliefs." Margarette spoke from her own experience in Denmark after her mother's death.

"I know, but I shall endeavor to remain true to God. I shall read my Book of Mormon each day and pray. It's just that I feel so strongly that this is something I must do."

After Hannah left, Margarette felt troubled as she thought about the other woman's words and how strong her conviction was that God had a particular work for her to do. She sought out Anna.

"Anna, am I wrong to refuse to sell the bracelet? While still aboard the *Carolina,* I felt impressed that I should not part with the bracelet until I felt certain it was God's will that I do so. Could it be that the jewels are the answer to our prayers and I am too blind to recognize God's answer?" she asked, thinking about Kraft Rundell's latest offer.

"I don't know," Anna said. "Knowing of your concerns about the jewels and about finding the means to leave Nauvoo when the Church moves to the place prepared for us in the mountains, I have looked at the matter from many directions. You did not take the bracelet from anyone and are not guilty of theft or coveting that which is not your own. Whether the woman who hid the jewels had a right to them or if the jewels belonged to the man who died that night aboard the *Carolina,* we will never know. He is dead and presumably the woman is also. Perhaps she had nothing to do with secreting the bracelet in Annelise's nappy, and the jewels appeared there because the Lord knew you would need them. I can only advise you to continue to ask God whether you should use the jewels to secure your family's future or to continue to hold them in trust."

"You are right, Anna." She hugged the older woman. "It is not a decision for me to make. Only the Lord knows what use, if any, should be made of the gems."

* * *

Margarette sat up in bed. Something had awakened her, but though she strained her ears to hear, the night was silent. She listened for several minutes and was about to lie back down when she heard a whisper of sound coming from behind the curtain that separated the cabin into two rooms at night.

Little light made its way through the cabin's two small windows, but the little there was revealed a figure creeping from behind the curtain.

"Soren?" she whispered.

"Shh." He moved closer to the door, and she saw him test the plank that barred the door. She slipped out of bed, pulled on her shawl that doubled as a robe, and joined him. Together, they stood like statues listening for they knew not what.

The sound of pounding hooves was the first sound that broke the peace, followed by a frightful uproar of shrieking women, shouting men, and the clanging of metal objects. Soren and Margarette peered through one of the small windows. At first they saw nothing, and then a bright light appeared through trees, now denuded of their foliage.

"What is—" she started to say, and then she knew the answer before Soren shouted, "Fire! The tent is on fire."

He jerked at the bar, and then flinging open the door, he began running down the path. Margarette would have followed, but a small, sleepy voice behind her called out for her. Turning swiftly, she lifted Jens back onto the trundle bed.

"You must stay here and help Anna watch your sister. Timothy's home is on fire, and I must go help them."

"No, Mamma," he began to cry. "If you go, the bad man will get me."

Margarette stopped. Neither she nor Jens had mentioned for many months the man who had been searching for her and the children, so why was Jens suddenly afraid?

"What is it, Jens?" She hurriedly knelt beside the low bed. "Why do you think that man has returned?"

"I was naughty," he admitted sheepishly, but with round scared eyes. "I didn't stay by the cabin like you said when I went out to play this afternoon. I ran down the path to the pasture to see the horses and Olaf's cows. I saw the man running through the trees."

"But why did you think he had come to get you? He might have been a thief, attempting to steal Mr. Rundell's horses."

The door flew open and Soren stumbled into the room. Gunfire sounded some distance away.

"Quick, bar the door." Anna stumbled from behind the curtain, her long gray braid that was usually wound tightly atop her head hung over her shoulder, reaching past her waist.

"Thank goodness you're all safe," the old man struggled to get the words out. "I was almost to the tent when I saw horses with riders milling about. They were carrying torches and shouting, 'Get out, Mormons.' The tent was burning, and those poor black women were running into the bushes. One of the raiders clipped Lester across the back of his head with a rifle, and two of them had Caleb cornered against the stable when Mr. Rundell came running across the grass with a shotgun. He fired once, and they took off on their horses yelling, 'We ain't through with you Mormons. We'll be back.' I was afraid some of them might have come this way and set a torch to the cabin."

"Those poor people. I'd better go see if I can help." Margarette started for the door. Remembering her son's fear, she added, "I think the man you saw was one of the men who set fire to Timothy's tent. He's a bad troublemaker, but he didn't come looking for you."

"It might not be safe to go," Anna protested.

"I think the raiders have gone," Margarette responded. "The women will need comforting, and Mr. Rundell might blame Lester and Caleb."

"I'll go with you," Soren offered.

"No, you stay here and keep a watch out for any mobbers who might sneak back this way. It might be best if you don't light a lantern," she added.

Pulling her shawl tight around her shoulders as she ran, she approached the place where Rosie and her family had pitched their tent. Nothing was left but a smoldering pile of rubble. Seeing Julia standing near the smoldering mess, she grasped her arm.

"Rosie? Little Timothy?" she gasped, winded from her run.

"Dey hidin' in the woods," Julia said. "Dey plenty scared."

"Julia," Kraft shouted. "Get up to the house and assure your mistress she's safe. The fools who mistook us for Mormons are gone. Stay with her until I return."

Julia began a rapid trot toward the big house.

"Mistah Rundell," Lester's voice came out of the darkness. "Lester got de hawses. Dat Caleb, he find de cows. One of dem been kilt." He emerged out of the darkness, gripping two horses' halters, one with each hand, while the big animals minced and attempted to rear. "Where Lester put dem?" he asked, and Margarette realized the stable had also been burned to the ground.

"Tether them to a post," Mr. Rundell shouted back. "Then go help Caleb."

Margarette walked slowly around the perimeter of the trees, calling softly, "Rosie, Trixie, come out now. They've gone." It was several minutes before Rosie crept from the bushes with Timothy in her arms. Trixie followed with round, scared eyes peering nervously around the clearing. Seeing Margarette, they rushed to her side. *They're only children themselves,* Margarette thought, putting a comforting arm around each of the girls.

After a few minutes, Trixie asked, "Where we gwine sleep?"

"Timothy be cold," Rosie added.

Margarette removed her shawl and handed it to Rosie to wrap around her baby, then she said, "Stay right here. I'll be back in a moment."

She walked toward Kraft, who stood beside the fence, stroking the noses of his matched team as he watched Lester and Caleb drive three cows and a pony toward him.

"Mr. Rundell," she began, "the girls and little Timothy are cold. Have you thought about where they should sleep for what is left of this night?"

"Sleep?" he sounded puzzled. His eyes went to where the tent had stood, then to the house. "Claire won't hear of them spending a night in her house."

"May I make a suggestion?" She attempted to conceal her exasperation. With four empty bedrooms in the Rundell house, it seemed absurd to even be carrying on a discussion of where the burned-out family should sleep.

"Go ahead," he sighed, and she suspected his thoughts were not terribly far from her own.

"You might think about keeping Julia in the house to watch over Mrs. Rundell. She could even sleep on a rug outside her door or in her mistress's dressing room to protect her. It might make your wife feel more secure. When you and your men finish repairing the fence, perhaps you'll want Lester and Caleb to take turns standing guard and sleeping in the kitchen. I can prepare pallets on the floor at the cabin for the girls and Timothy."

He gave her a long look and nodded as though terribly exhausted.

As tired as she was, sleep didn't come easily for the remainder of the night. From the restless tossing on the pallets, she knew Rosie and Trixie were not sleeping well either, and when they prepared to leave for the big house before dawn, Timothy cried and clung to his mother, begging her not to go.

The following afternoon, she learned that Mr. Rundell had been unable to acquire another tent as both canvas and oiled linen were in great demand for the wagons the Mormons were having built. He came to her door to ask if the girls could stay with her another night. She agreed, but he remained on her step. He seemed eager to express his views of the current situation in the city.

"Something has to be done about the thieving outlaws who are destroying homes and running off livestock," he complained.

"The Nauvoo Legion used to patrol the streets and keep out those bent on trouble and destruction, but since the state took away our charter, the legion has no legal authority," she reminded him.

"There are some who still wish to band together for the city's protection, and I'm not the only non-Mormon who has signed up to assist in defending our property. The Mormon leaders have promised to leave in the spring. It is only the riffraff who are causing trouble and refusing to stop their harassment. They want to take over the city without paying for the property, expecting it will fall into their hands without any expenditure on their parts. They mean to drive everyone—Mormon and non-Mormon alike—out of the city and steal our property."

"I'm glad you've signed up to help in our defense."

"I don't have any sympathy with Joe Smith's religion, but I see a great future for Nauvoo. If left in peace, it is likely to become the state's capital, and my fortune will grow with it, but if it becomes inhabited by squatters and thieves instead of the respectable people who, given time, will purchase the fine homes and businesses here, my investment will be lost. I expect it will be necessary to post a guard all winter to prevent the burning of the city. Tomorrow I will take my horses to the stable where my company's animals are boarded and hire a guard to watch them."

Before he left, he again renewed his offer to purchase the jeweled bracelet, and again Margarette declined, though she was becoming more convinced each day that she was being a fool.

Two weeks passed, and November arrived with little change in the conditions or sleeping arrangements. Margarette expected to hear any day that the Rundell heir had been born. She seldom saw Claire, but she heard about her progress from the girls who shared the cabin at night. It seemed that Claire became more cross each day as her body grew more unwieldy and rumors of trouble spread throughout the city. She made impossible demands on her servants, and the day came that Rosie and Trixie stumbled into the cabin in tears.

"She say she gwine sell us cause they ain't nuff work for all o' us an' Massah Rundell's business ain't doing so good. Miz Rundell say Julia can take care o' the house and da babe, she don't need Rosie and Trixie no more. She say she sell Lester, too, cuz he gettin' old and don't do nuff work. She keep Timothy cuz he gwine b'long to her son an' she gonna hire Irish girl for nanny," Trixie blurted out.

Rosie was too devastated to even speak. She clasped Timothy in her arms and sobbed until the boy was crying too.

"I don't think Mr. Rundell will let her do that," Margarette tried to offer a measure of hope.

"He so het up 'bout his baby gwine be borned, he let Miz Claire do anything she want," Trixie argued.

The following night, pebbles were tossed against their door. Though the sound was slight, Margarette was instantly awake. She saw the girls scramble to their feet and tiptoe toward the door fully dressed, as though the slight sound was a signal for which they had been listening.

"Wait," she called out, causing them to jump.

They stood framed in the moonlight that spilled through the window, and it was clear that they were scared and uncertain which way they should turn. Margarette knew at once what they planned to do. She also knew that running away was dangerous. The mobs that harassed the Mormons wouldn't hesitate to capture and punish runaway slaves.

"Do you have a plan?" she asked, before opening the door to see Caleb, Julia, and Lester waiting on the stoop. "Come in," she motioned for them to enter. After casting a nervous glance over her shoulder, Julia led the way.

"You telling on us?" she asked, her tone belligerent.

"Please, Miz Margarette, we cain't take no mo'. We a fambly, and we ain't gwine be split up and nebber see each other again. Rosie ain't givin' up her baby, and I ain't neber gwine whip nobody again."

"I'll not try to stop you," she attempted to reassure the family. "My concern is that you don't get caught and returned in chains."

"Everything is arranged, and I'll look after them." Hannah Waterton stepped into the room.

Margarette stared in astonishment, but before she could speak, Soren and Anna pushed aside the curtain separating their sleeping space from the remainder of the room.

"I've had my suspicions you were the one coming here at night," Soren said to Hannah. "I never said anything and I won't, but if I can figure it out, others will too, and you won't be safe around here anymore. Most of the folks in Nauvoo don't hold with slavery, but some do, and the troublemakers trying to drive us out of our homes would love to catch a Mormon helping black folks escape their masters."

"I don't plan to come back," Hannah said.

"Do you have enough money to buy food and make a new start?" Margarette asked. A strong impulse was growing in her heart.

"We have enough to reach the underground if we're careful—and we intend to be careful."

"But if you are delayed or have trouble?" Margarette turned partly away, fumbling for the pin beneath her skirt. She pulled out the small bag and dumped the bracelet on the wooden table. Using a butter knife, she pried apart the clasps holding a large golden stone. Picking it up, she placed it in Julia's hand. Warmth filled her chest, telling her what she did was right.

"If this is as valuable as Mr. Rundell says it is, it will get you all the way to Canada and help start your new life."

Julia's eyes grew large and round. "No, Miz Margarette. We cain't take no jewel."

"If we get caught wif that rock, Massah know for sure you hepped us," Lester added.

"All right," she plucked it from Julia's hand and presented it to Hannah. "There's no reason a woman such as yourself shouldn't own a valuable gem. You know what to do with it. Now go with God's blessing."

"Just a minute." Anna rushed forward. "Jewels are hard to spend, and it might be best not to sell that one until you reach the end of your journey. Take this." Margarette watched Anna hand Hannah the five dollar gold piece they'd set aside to obtain supplies for their expected trip west.

When they were gone, Margarette seated herself at the table, where she gathered up the bracelet and the small knife. Methodically, she freed the four remaining jewels from their settings. Kraft would ask about the bracelet again, maybe even demand to see it. It wouldn't do for him to see that one stone was missing. She would hide the other jewels in various places, and tomorrow she would drop the faux silver bracelet minus its jewels into the river.

13

"Mrs. Jorgensen, wake up. I need your help!" Shouting and hammering awakened Margarette before dawn. She opened her eyes, then promptly closed them. It was Kraft Rundell! Had he discovered the slaves were missing already?

She climbed out of bed and pulled on her cloak for modesty's sake and went to the door. The moment she released the bar that held it closed, Mr. Rundell burst into the cabin. His hair was wild, and he'd forgotten his coat, though a cold November wind blew.

"The baby is coming, and I can't find Julia. You'll have to help Clair."

"Do you want me to go for the midwife?"

"No, there isn't time. Hurry."

"All right, you go ahead, so she won't be alone. I'll dress as quickly as I can and then go to her."

"You must hurry. She's in a great deal of pain."

"I'll only be a moment, and I'll send Soren for a midwife." She nudged Mr. Rundell toward the door. The moment it closed behind him, she threw off her cloak and pulled her dress over her head.

"You decent?" Soren called in a whisper through the curtain.

"Yes, I'm putting on my shoes." Soren was beside her at once.

"I'll go for Sister Johnson. Anna is awake and knows we're leaving. I told her to fasten the bar behind us."

Margarette reached once more for her cloak.

* * *

"Claire, you're a grown woman, not a little girl." Margarette's patience had grown thin after two hours of Claire's complaints, threats, and screams. On arriving at the house, she'd discovered Claire was not as close to delivery as she'd believed herself to be, but she was extremely petulant and demanding.

Soren brought word from the midwife shortly after Margarette was ushered into Claire's bedroom that the midwife would come as soon as possible, but that she was occupied with another delivery that she could not leave.

"No one else can make this easier for you," Margarette tried to reason with the nearly hysterical young woman. "You can scream and cry and threaten if you want to, but it will only make the pain harder to bear. Neither Julia nor your papa are coming, no matter how much you yell or sulk."

"I don't want to have a baby."

"Whether you want to have a baby or not, this baby is coming. There's no changing your mind now."

"But it hurts," Claire whimpered, and then she pounded her fists against the bed in a screaming frenzy.

Margarette dreaded what the girl's behavior would be like once her labor really became advanced. "Yes, it hurts, but your complaining is making it hurt more. The more you relax, the easier your pains will be and the sooner your baby will come."

"I want Julia, not you. You're too bossy."

"You get me or no one, and I'm not a slave you can order about," Margarette snapped back, then regretted losing her temper. She knew very well that giving birth the first time was not easy, and she suspected that Claire, like herself four and a half years ago, had received little prior information concerning what to expect. Margarette, too, had gone without a midwife, but in her case, she'd been attended by her mother-in-law who had been rough and critical, slapping her when she screamed from pain and fear. Memories of that frightening time softened her voice and gentled her irritation with the spoiled young woman's childish behavior.

"Hush." She seated herself beside Claire and stroked her hair. "I know you're frightened and uncertain. Childbirth is never easy, but you really can make it less painful by relaxing and breathing slowly. When the pain starts, don't fight it. Relax and let it flow over you. Count if you like, so you'll know if the contractions are lasting longer and you're getting closer to delivery."

Daylight came, and the morning wore away while Margarette coaxed and bullied Claire into accepting what she must do. Sometimes they walked slowly across the room and back again, and sometimes Claire huddled on her bed and cried. Margarette talked, patiently explaining the different stages of labor and alerting Claire to what would be expected of her. She talked about the baby and the joy found in caring for an infant. Sometimes Claire docilely followed Margarette's instructions and other times she screamed and threw anything within reach.

It was early in the afternoon and Claire's breathing was beginning to change when the bedroom door opened and Sister Johnson stepped into the room, taking charge at once. A large woman wearing a snowy white apron, she rolled up her sleeves and plunged her hands up to her elbows in a basin of water Margarette had instructed Mr. Rundell to heat. Margarette had heard it said that the only purpose behind having new fathers boil water was to keep them out of the midwife's hair, but her confidence in the midwife soared as the woman took the time to ensure her hands were clean. Though Mrs. Johnson's manner was abrupt and a little too hearty, Margarette could see that her hands were gentle as she checked Claire, who thrashed about, continuously groaning.

"It will all be over in no time," Mrs. Johnson cheerfully announced as she tied strips of cloth to the bedposts for Claire to grasp when the time came to push. Fitting the young woman's hands into the loops, she said, "In a few minutes, you'll feel an urge to bear down. When I say push, you best push with every bit of strength you possess."

"Will it hurt?" Claire whimpered.

"Land sakes, child. Of course it's going to hurt, but it'll feel so good to be able to do something about getting your babe birthed and the hurting over with, I expect you won't care." She chuckled as though she'd said something funny.

The midwife turned to Margarette with a small pouch of herbs and instructed her to steep them in hot water and bring the tea back to the birthing room for the new mother. "Soon's this young'un gets here and the mamma counts fingers and toes, she's going to want some soothing herbal tea. Set a flannel blanket close to the fire, too, to wrap the wee one in."

Margarette dashed into the hall, nearly colliding with Mr. Rundell. "It won't be long now." She offered a quick word of reassurance to him as she sped toward the kitchen. When she returned, she found the baby almost free and Claire pushing with all her might.

The baby emerged, screaming without any encouragement from the midwife, who chuckled and announced, "You have a healthy baby boy with as fine a set of lungs as his mamma!"

Margarette took him from Sister Johnson, gently cleaned him with warm water, then wrapped him in the heated blanket before carrying him to Claire's side.

"You did well." She smiled at the exhausted young woman and tucked the baby in the crook of her arm.

Claire smiled back weakly before turning her head to study her son. She appeared almost shocked at the sight of the wiggling, red-faced infant in her arms. Lifting her eyes to meet Margarette's, she grinned triumphantly. "I did it. I did it all by myself."

"I think your husband will be very happy to see you and his son." Margarette turned away to fetch Kraft Rundell.

She took advantage of the midwife's plans to stay the night to hurry home to her own family. As she stepped through the door, Annelise ran to her with tears streaming down her face. "Pwitty gone," she sobbed.

"Oh, Sweetie," she held her daughter close. "Pwitty is with his mamma. I'm sure he misses you and is sad. But he's happy too because he can be with his mamma every day now."

* * *

Margarette had her job back by default, but it provided barely enough to feed her household, and the coins she and Anna were able to put aside were few. Claire threw a tantrum when she learned that her servants had run away, but her husband said little within Margarette's hearing. He hired two young men to patrol his property at night and posted a notice at the mercantile that he was in need of a wet nurse and a nanny. A fourteen-year-old orphan from England applied for the nanny position, but there were no responses to the plea for a wet nurse.

Claire was irate when faced with the necessity of nursing her own child. "I'm not a field hand. Ladies of my station don't do anything so undignified," she argued, but between her hungry child's cries and her own discomfort, she was finally persuaded to let the baby nurse, though she never stopped complaining about the indignity of it.

Claire's expectations and Margarette's realities were constantly at odds with Claire assuming Margarette would manage her household and always be available without regard for Margarette's own family. Mr. Rundell tried to hire more servants, but the Mormons were leery of working for one who didn't share their faith. Besides, every man, woman, and child was already working long hours to prepare for the evacuation of Nauvoo and to complete the temple. Between Claire's demands and the escalating tension between the city's residents and the violent gangs anxious to drive out the Mormons and confiscate their property, the next two months were filled with turmoil.

On the day in December that Brigham Young and Heber C. Kimball began giving endowments to faithful Latter-day Saints, Soren and Anna among them, Margarette received another letter from Matthew. It was only a few lines, but her heart leaped with joy as she read:

> *The Mississippi Saints are prepared to depart as scheduled, and Elder Blake and I have been given permission to return to Nauvoo once we have successfully conducted our flock to St. Louis where they will cross the Mississippi and proceed under the leadership of John Brown.*

The Nauvoo Saints' departure was set for April, as was the formal dedication of the temple, but conditions became so intolerable that by January the Brethren began preparing several companies to depart at a moment's notice in spite of a colder-than-usual winter. This knowledge increased Margarette's sense of panic. There was likely no way she could be prepared by April and certainly not any sooner. She wished she could discuss the problem with Matthew. If they pooled their resources, they could perhaps find a way to stay with the Saints on their migration. She chided herself for her wishful thinking. She was aware that even if Matthew reached Nauvoo before she was forced to evacuate, their financial situation would not improve, as he was as poor as she.

The first wagons left Nauvoo early in February amidst weather so bitter cold that some wagons were able to cross the river on ice, though most employed the ferry. Each day saw the city become a little more empty, and at night, fires were often seen, signaling the destruction of a home or business. Marauders dressed in black invaded the city, making venturing out increasingly dangerous.

The few immigrants who arrived from other areas were generally at the end of their funds and too poor to go farther. Instead of bringing assistance to those under siege in Nauvoo, they added to the drain on resources. Food supplies became scarce, businesses closed or dwindled, and even if Margarette had the money to purchase a wagon and outfit it, none were available. The fresh milk her family had enjoyed for many months ended too, as Katrina and Olaf left Nauvoo with Katrina's uncle, and Olaf's employer sold his remaining cows to various families with young children who hoped the cows would provide nourishment for them on the long trip ahead of them.

Claire complained bitterly concerning her lack of servants and the plainness of the meals Margarette served. She watched the doors apprehensively at night and cowered in her bed each time she heard shouting in the streets or saw the flicker of torches in the distance. Her acid tongue vilified the Mormons and blamed them for the slump in her husband's business. When the young nanny served notice that she had been invited by a Mormon couple whose family included an expectant mother and five small children to travel west with their wagon company in exchange for her help with the children, Claire demanded to be allowed to return to her papa's plantation in Alabama.

"I will not live in this uncivilized place any longer," she stormed. "Your business is almost bankrupt, and I do not intend to be poor."

"Just a little longer," her husband pleaded. "The Mormons will soon be gone, and there will be peace here. Business will improve, and we'll be able to replace our servants."

"I'm leaving on the first riverboat to arrive after the ice melts," Claire threatened. "Papa warned me that I would regret coming to this awful place." She relented slightly to add, "But you may come get me and our son when those awful people have gone."

Margarette pressed her lips together in anger. Claire never concerned herself with Margarette's feelings when she spoke out against the Mormons, and every time she didn't get her way about something, she blamed the Mormons.

"Papa will be happy to help us find dependable servants to replace Julia and her ungrateful family."

Margarette didn't miss Kraft Rundell's grimace at the mention of Claire's papa.

Claire and Kraft argued for several days, but with the first whiff of spring, Claire ordered Margarette to pack her trunks, and on the last day of April, the deep boom of a boat whistle was heard over the steady drip of rain. A short time later, Kraft brought the buggy around, and Margarette found herself sitting in the back seat between mounds of luggage, holding young Stephen, who had been named for Claire's papa, for the ride to the dock. Claire and Kraft didn't speak much during the short trip or while the steward led them, with Margarette carrying the baby, to the best cabin the boat had to offer. When it came time for Kraft to bid his wife and son farewell, his eyes filled with tears.

"If only you'd be patient until the end of summer," he said. "There's not more than three thousand Mormons left, and they'll soon be gone."

"Three thousand is still too many," Claire sniffed. "And those rude, uncouth frontier men running amok here every night can't tell the difference between Mormons and civilized Christians."

"I'll come for you soon," Kraft promised when the deep whistle of the boat sang out a warning of its imminent departure.

Margarette shifted the baby to his mother's arms and turned toward the gangplank. Kraft joined her on the dock's thick, wooden planks a few minutes later. They stood together in the rain, watching the big paddle wheel turn and the riverboat drift out into the current of the river. The tempo of the rain increased, sending a torrent of water slashing toward the river. Kraft pulled a flask from his pocket and drank deeply.

A few minutes later, he escorted Margarette to the buggy and helped her climb inside. Once he was seated beside her, he picked up the reins, but didn't signal for the horses to move out. Instead, he sat staring out over the water as rain dripped from the buggy's canopy.

"It's time we come to an agreement over those gems." His voice was cold. "I no longer need a housekeeper, and the longer you delay your departure, the greater the danger you and your family face here. My business is in ruins, and I cannot make an offer as generous as I did earlier, but I have access to a wagon, six oxen, and enough supplies to see your household to the Pacific Ocean if you desire to go that far."

"Excuse me," a large, fair-haired man with a scarred face interrupted. He stood a few feet from the buggy with a battered portmanteau at his feet and rain dripping from his hat brim. "I just arrived in town, and I am in search of a woman and two small children who arrived here approximately eighteen months ago from Europe."

"That describes half the town," Kraft said, setting the horses in motion with an impatient flick of the reins. Margarette sat as if frozen while the buggy's high wheels churned through fresh mud. The man's accent was clearly Scandinavian. This man was no bumbling idiot such as Lars had sent before, and Mr. Rundell was correct when he said the brief description the man had given described half the women in Nauvoo, but she knew that she was the woman the man was seeking. She ducked her head, letting her bonnet brim hide her face. They rode in silence for several blocks.

"Months ago, I removed the jewels from their settings and hid them in various places lest vandals discover the bracelet and carry them all away." She resumed their earlier conversation as though there had been no interruption. "The setting, as you said, is worthless, so I dropped it in the river. I'll accept your offer in exchange for two of the jewels."

"I want them all."

"Would you deprive my children of the entirety of their heritage?"

"Three, then, the ruby, the diamond, and the emerald." His jaw was set, making it clear, he didn't wish to bargain further.

"Not the emerald. That stone is the dearest to Annelise."

"All right, you keep the emerald, and I'll take the sapphire."

"How soon can you arrange for the wagon?"

"I'll have it brought around to the stable at first light tomorrow morning. You can add whatever goods you wish from the cabin and be at the ferry before noon."

14

Margarette ran from the buggy to the cabin, her mind filled with turmoil. She longed for the quiet assurance that she'd felt when she'd given the topaz to Hannah to tell her she was doing right to give three more of the jewels to Kraft Rundell. Her mind flew back to the day of her baptism when the tall missionary had told her she must always study out questions in her own mind just as she had the decision to be baptized, then ask Heavenly Father if she were making the proper choice. She'd studied this problem over and over in her mind, and the news that a stranger was asking about her certainly propelled her toward believing the acceptance of Mr. Rundell's offer was the right thing to do. Still, she'd feel better if she were filled with burning warmth instead of icy fear.

There was so much to do, and setting out in a wagon with two elderly people and two small children to find those who had already left the city seemed a daunting prospect. She knew nothing of camping in the wilderness. Would they face hostile Indians or ferocious wild animals? She shuddered.

"Soren! Anna!" she called as she stepped through the door. "We're leaving . . ." A tall shadowy shape rose from a chair and advanced toward her.

"Margarette! Dear Margarette." As arms reached for her, she stumbled forward, blinded by her tears.

"Matthew, oh, Matthew, you have come."

With Matthew's arms holding her fast, she was oblivious to all else in the cabin until she heard Jens's giggle. Drawing back, Matthew caught her hands in his, and they stood looking at each other for several minutes until she became aware of the smiling faces surrounding them.

"How long have you been here?" she asked.

"Elder Blake and I arrived this morning on the riverboat. Wilford Woodruff was on the same boat as he was just returning from his mission to England. We were met by Orson Hyde, and he and Elder Woodruff hurried to the temple to formally dedicate it, and I came straight here."

"Goodness, I just came from the wharf." Margarette hurried to tell them of all that had transpired. "So you see, we must pack and be ready to leave tomorrow morning."

"It is much less than he offered before," Anna noted.

"Yes, but both his situation and ours are far more desperate now. With the more comfortably situated Nauvoo residents already gone and rabid mobs preventing the usual commerce, Mr. Rundell's business has been hurt greatly."

"Are you sure Mr. Rundell will keep his word to deliver the wagon and oxen?" Matthew asked.

"Yes. I've not known him to ever go back on his word. Though he and I disagree on many matters, he is not a cruel or undependable man."

"He's only a fool where his wife is concerned," Anna muttered, not quite under her breath. "We must begin packing our things at once," she added in a louder voice.

"Is Matthew coming with us?" Jens shouted with hope in his voice.

"Yes, I mean . . ." He stopped, his ears growing red. "I think your mother and I need to take a walk."

* * *

She'd almost forgotten what it was like to be so happy. With their fingers interlaced, they walked slowly through the trees toward the back of the small grove. She had so much she wanted to tell Matthew, and there were so many things she wanted to hear about his mission, but they seemed to silently agree there was no time for that now. Moving slowly, they merely reveled in being together again. She had missed the easy companionship that she'd learned to rely on during their voyage to America. He paused before they had gone far, mindful of her concern regarding the stranger looking for her and her children.

Turning to face her, he took both of her hands in his and slowly lifted them to his lips. "I have missed you more than words can tell," he said. "I'm glad I arrived before your departure from the city. I have no money and no employment. I have no goods to contribute, only a strong back and a determination to see you and your children safely to Zion. I had expected to have more time upon my return to prepare to follow the Brethren, but if you are to depart tomorrow, I feel I must act quickly. It is my fondest wish to be beside you on your journey west, and I will not allow you to be subjected to coarse gossip. Therefore, if you will allow me to accompany you, I think we should be wed before our departure. Will you accept me as your husband?"

"Yes, Matthew." She didn't hesitate, though she hadn't desired to marry again. If they had more time, her conscience wouldn't allow her to capitalize on their friendship by tying Matthew to her and her children in this way. "I greatly feared departing without your strong assistance, and I too, see the necessity of avoiding gossip or censure."

Still holding her hands, he drew her closer as though he would kiss her, and then changing his mind, he said, "If I hurry, I might be able to find Elder Woodruff still at the temple. He said he too leaves tomorrow, following a public dedication of the temple, to join the remainder of the Twelve in Iowa. With your permission, I shall obtain a license and ask him to perform the ceremony before he leaves."

* * *

Margarette found it took less time than she had anticipated to pack her few belongings and those of her children. She'd brought little with them from Denmark and had acquired only a few items of clothing since their arrival. It took longer to pack Anna and Soren's trunk, as most of the household items they had been using in the cabin belonged to them. When they finished, the cabin looked bare and unfamiliar.

During a pause in their labors, Margarette explained to the children and the Pedersens that she and Matthew had decided to marry. The children greeted her news with enthusiasm, and the Pedersens behaved as if they had expected the announcement.

Only Margarette's best dress and their quilts were left to pack by the time Matthew returned. He'd changed his clothing and, along with his best suit, he wore a wide grin. Seeing his smile lifted her spirits.

"Elder Woodruff said to meet him at the temple in half an hour," he said, placing an arm around Margarette's waist and whirling her about.

"Now? We're going to be married today?" she gasped, backing up a step when he released her. She hadn't expected that preparations could be made for sooner than the following day before their departure.

"That's right."

"Then may I call you Papa?" Jens raced across the room and leaped into Matthew's arms.

"Papa! Papa!" Annelise twirled and danced around the room and ended up hugging Matthew's leg.

"I'd be proud to have you call me Papa," Matthew assured the boy before setting him back on his feet.

"Well, by all means, you must hurry," Soren ushered them toward the door. "We'll watch the children, and the Lord will help us keep them safe while you are in His holy house."

Margarette slipped behind the curtain to change into her best dress before kissing the children and leaving the cabin to walk stiffly beside Matthew. Little waves of panic left her speechless. Marriage to Jory had proven to be a disappointing experience. Of course, Matthew wasn't Jory, and unlike her first husband, he was kind and gentle. He shared her faith, too. There were worse things than marrying your friend, she assured herself. Besides, there was no other way to ensure her children's safety and her good name.

When they reached the temple, they were met by a small group of men and women in white temple robes who had just completed a private dedication of the temple. Elder Woodruff invited them inside and spoke triumphantly.

"Notwithstanding the many false prophesies of Sidney Rigdon and others that the roof should not go on nor the house be finished and the threats of the mob that we should not dedicate it, yet we have done both."

When the time came to kneel across from each other at the altar and recite their vows, Margarette was thrilled to recognize the lace cloth Anna had made by unraveling her best shawl, then painstakingly tatting it into an altar cloth. Soon the cloth was forgotten, and Margarette's attention focused on the man who was about to become her husband and on the wondrous blessings and promises given them. The enormity of the step they were taking caused her to tremble, and then a quiet peace filled her heart, melting the last of the ice that lingered from the morning's encounter with Lars's spy.

At the conclusion of the brief ceremony, Elder Woodruff reminded them that when the Saints reached their destination far to the west, beyond the mountains, a new temple would be built and that they must go there with their children and Brother Brigham's recommendation to be united eternally.

Leaving the temple a short time later, they discovered that night had fallen. Margarette wondered if the glow she felt within her would be enough to light their way home. She let Matthew take her hand, and they moved with slow steps at first, still caught up in the wondrous experience of being within the House of the Lord. Once they left the temple grove behind, they began to move more quickly, lest they attract attention from any of the undesirable element who prowled Nauvoo's streets at night stirring up trouble.

A block from the Rundell property, they heard the pounding hoofbeats of approaching horses coming up behind them. Matthew acted quickly to pull Margarette behind a hedge, where they crouched, their shoulders touching, as they waited for the riders to pass. Instead of passing, they drew rein a short distance away.

"I tell you, I saw someone walking this way," a voice said.

"Probably heard us coming and took off running," a second voice said.

"You think it might've been that Mormon who lives in the big house up ahead?"

"I heard he ain't a Mormon."

"Don't matter if he is or he ain't. He's sidin' with the Mormons. 'Sides, Captain Thomas already spoke for that house soon's we git the Mormon vermin cleaned out of this here place."

"I'm thinkin' of movin' Miss Katy and her girls inta that big church they built up there on the hill," another voice bellowed. Loud guffaws followed. Hearing the men speak such of the beautiful edifice where she'd just experienced the most wondrous moments of her life hurt like a sudden jab to the center of Margarette's chest.

She felt Matthew squeeze her hand in shared empathy. She returned the gentle pressure and continued to listen. She'd counted at least three separate voices. The men sitting astride their horses in the middle of the road may have been drinking, but they didn't sound intoxicated—at least not yet. She figured the big house and property they were discussing were Mr. Rundell's. With her two small children and the elderly Pedersens alone back in the cabin, the words she heard filled her with dread. It was all she could do to remain still and refrain from running back to the cabin as quickly as possible to assure herself they were safe.

As if sensing her desire to rush to her children's defense, Matthew's grip tightened.

"Are we gonna burn that fella out tonight?" It was the first voice again, and it nearly brought a gasp from Margarette.

"Thomas ain't ready to make his move yet, and he don't want the house burned. He said we should be patient until a few more of 'em leave."

"I was just thinkin' of helpin' a few of 'em decide to leave." Chuckles followed.

"Well, we ain't gettin' nothin' done sittin' here," the voice sounded impatient. "Let's get goin' and see if anyone else has got somethin' planned."

Neither Margarette nor Matthew moved for several minutes after the last hoofbeat faded away. Then they followed the hedge, staying in the shadows until they reached Mr. Rundell's pasture.

Once they gained the darkness of the small wood grove, Margarette and Matthew moved faster. When they came to the cabin and saw it resting peaceably in its hidden glen, they stopped. Matthew drew Margarette close, simply holding her until their breathing steadied. After a moment, she sensed that he had something he wanted to say but wasn't certain how to proceed.

"Shall we go in?" she whispered.

"All the way back from Mississippi, I planned how it would be when I saw you again. I was going to see if I could get my old job back at the brick works and save every penny to buy a wagon and team to take us to the Rocky Mountains. When it became clear our plans would have to be rushed, I thought I would bid you good night at your door tonight. I figured we would begin our marriage when we were safely away from here and you'd had a chance to get used to the idea, but after hearing those foul men, not half an hour past, plot against the innocent people of this city, I cannot leave you to fend for yourself one more night."

"No, Matthew, I do not wish for you to leave me even until morning," she burrowed closer against the chilled night air. "You are without lodging and have no other place to go. Our wedding night can wait, but I will feel safer if you stay in the cabin tonight."

He picked up her hand. "My mother wore a thin gold band on her hand that had belonged to her mother. I want you to wear that ring until I can buy you a finer one." He slipped the plain ring on her ring finger. "I took it with me tonight because I thought it would be needed when we spoke our vows." He placed a kiss over the ring after settling it in place. "I have something else for you, too." He grinned the mischievous smile she'd grown to love during their long voyage.

"I met a strange old man in Mississippi who claimed to be an Indian, though his skin was as white as my own. He wore a small leather bag suspended from a thong about his neck. He said it was a medicine bag and that his people believed in placing tiny mementos of important occasions in their lives inside the bags to remind them of who they are and to keep evil away. In his medicine bag was a blue-green turquoise stone. He said the ancient Inca and Aztec Indians carried beautiful emeralds in their medicine bags that were mined in South America and that they considered the gems to be sacred. He made this bag for me, but I want you to have it. It will be a safer way for you to carry your remaining gems than pinning them to your underskirt."

"After I give three to Mr. Rundell in the morning, there will only be the emerald left to put in the bag." She told him about Timothy and his family and Hannah. When she finished, he placed the leather thong about her neck, then kissed her long and tenderly. The kiss was unexpected, but not unpleasant, and Matthew had hinted several times that he expected their marriage to be a real marriage, so she didn't pull away. When she felt an ache for more growing inside her, she broke away in confusion. She hadn't expected to experience feelings she thought had ended when Jory had turned on her in violent frustration.

To cover her confusion, she took Matthew's hand and led him inside the cabin. They were met with warmth and laughter. Anna presented a feast prepared from the last of their food that could not be stored and taken with them.

"Are you my papa now?" Jens asked Matthew.

"Yes," Matthew assured him.

"Can we still be friends?"

Matthew set Jens on his knee. "Papas and sons are the very best kind of friends. When we get to the mountains, we'll go fishing together, and you can help me build a cabin for all of us to live in. When you want to talk, we'll find an old tree stump to sit on, and we'll just talk 'til everything is all figured out."

Matthew knelt with Margarette and the children while Soren and Anna sat nearby for prayers. Annelise insisted Matthew kiss her good night, and he was pleased to oblige.

"Am I ma'weed too?" she asked with her arms around Matthew's neck.

"You're my little girl, my princess angel, so I guess you can say we're all married together." He kissed her nose and tucked her beneath the quilt he said he remembered from their voyage a year and a half earlier.

When the children were asleep, Matthew told Soren about the conversation he and Margarette had overheard.

"That doesn't surprise me," Soren said. "I've feared for some time that Mr. Rundell will not be safe even after we are gone. We must warn him before we go."

Soren and Anna tried to insist that the newlyweds take their bed while they slept on the pallets Rosie and Trixie had used.

"No," Margarette shook her head. "This may be your last night to sleep in a real bed for a long time. We are young and more able to sleep on the floor."

* * *

Margarette found that sleep did not come easily. Matthew had placed the straw pallets side-by-side, but in the narrow room, her back brushed the trundle bed where the children slept, and Matthew was in danger of bumping his head on the fireplace stones on the other. The familiar sound of the children breathing, mingled with Soren's soft snore, should have lulled her quickly to sleep after a day so long and full, but she was too conscious of the man who lay beside her, her hand clasped in his, her head resting on his shoulder. She sensed he was not asleep either.

* * *

She didn't have time for a moment's embarrassment on finding herself wrapped in Matthew's arms when she awoke. A wild whoop from Jens was all the notice she received as he launched himself from the trundle bed to land on top of them.

"Matthew stayed all night," he shouted, throwing his arms around both their necks.

"Yes, he did." She laughed at her son's exuberance. "Now everyone needs to hurry. Anna set out a cold breakfast for us last night, and as soon as we finish eating, we need to start loading our wagon."

Margarette collected the jewels from their various hiding places. The emerald she placed in the medicine bag; the others she returned to the little bag that had previously held the bracelet. This she dropped in her apron pocket.

After a few bites of bread, Margarette and Matthew left to meet Kraft Rundell. Margarette breathed a sigh of gratitude when she saw the large wagon with a billowing linseed oil–treated linen top and six sturdy oxen waiting beside the pasture fence. Mr. Rundell stood near the front of the wagon.

"It appears your Mr. Rundell has converted a freight wagon into a prairie schooner," Matthew whispered.

"Is that bad?" Margarette whispered back.

"I think it will be fine since freight wagons are built to haul heavy loads long distances."

"Good morning, Mr. Rundell," Margarette spoke.

"Who is this?" Kraft pointed to Matthew with suspicion in his voice.

"This is Matthew Holmes," she answered. "He has been gone for more than a year on Church business and just returned yesterday. We were married last night."

"And our deal?" He brushed off word of their marriage, concerned only that he get the promised jewels.

"Mr. Rundell, we've known each other for almost a year. In that time, I feel we've both had ample opportunity to learn that we both keep our word. Here are the jewels." She held out the small cloth bag. Into his outstretched hand, she poured the three large stones. The rising sun struck them, sending a kaleidoscope of colors flashing in its light. He smiled in satisfaction before closing his fist around the gems.

Seeing the brilliant glow of the jewels, Margarette felt a moment's regret, but a glance at the sturdy wagon and animals waiting to carry her loved ones to safety brought a burning warmth to her chest. The jewels were just stones, but her children, and Matthew, Soren, and Anna were her life. The gems were of no moment compared to the opportunity to follow Brother Brigham to a refuge where they would be free to practice their religion without fear. At last, the assurance came that the jewels should pass to Kraft Rundell. She touched the leather pouch hidden beneath her bodice. Keeping the emerald was right too.

"Mrs. Jorgensen," Kraft's voice softened. "I have no reason to be angry with you or to blame you for my business failures and my wife's decision to take my son and return to her father's plantation. I have treated you with less than gentlemanly courtesy when I should have expressed gratitude for your kindnesses. I was wrong to insist on three of your gems in exchange for a wagon and oxen. Your first offer of two of the jewels is more than fair payment." He reached for her hand, startling her by pressing a hard lump into her palm.

"Mr. Rundell," Matthew spoke up. "Last night we overheard some rowdies making plans to take over your house and property. They accused you of being a Mormon sympathizer on the grounds the Mormons haven't driven you out."

"They'll leave me alone once everyone knows Mrs. Jorgensen and her family are gone." His arrogance was back.

"I wouldn't count on it, sir," Matthew said. "Hatred mingled with greed doesn't usually listen to reason."

15

"That's the last of our belongings." Matthew handed his worn portmanteau up to Margarette, who stowed it in one of the wooden boxes near the back of the wagon. Since they owned no furniture, the wagon was roomier than she had expected. The wagon seat itself was just a large box filled with salt pork, dried beef, sugar, tea, coffee, and salt. It could be lifted off and used as a table. Behind the seat were barrels of flour, cornmeal, dried beans, and dried fruit. A feather tick sat atop the barrels, forming a comfortable bed. A large box near the back of the wagon held an assortment of tools, fishing gear, ammunition, ground cloths, a small tent, tin plates and cutlery, along with a few spices. The Pedersens' large chest fit near the back of the wagon beside two boxes with fitted lids, one of which held an odd assortment of seeds, boots, blankets, and clothing. Margarette's family's clothing and personal items went into the other. Water barrels were loaded on the sides of the wagon, along with a box that held lanterns, kerosene, a tin basin, several heavy pieces of iron cookware, and a washtub.

"There was a list of the supplies Mr. Young said each family of five needed posted at the mercantile." Kraft eyed the fully stocked wagon with satisfaction. "Everything on that list is accounted for except the cattle. I couldn't find a cow, but I got these." He pointed to a crate of chickens at his feet, which he helped Matthew attach to two hooks beneath the wagon. Flaps could be lowered around the mesh wire sides to keep the chickens dry when it rained. And from the looks of the sky, it appeared the flaps would soon be needed.

Matthew helped Anna to the wagon seat and handed up the children. Jens sat beside Anna, but Annelise preferred to bounce on the feather tick.

"Are you familiar with oxen?" Kraft asked Matthew.

"No, sir. I don't see any reins, and I've been wondering how to . . ."

"I'm familiar with oxen," Soren put in.

"I am too. Lars and Jory had oxen," Margarette said. "We'll teach you."

"I think we're all set then," Matthew said.

"Except for one thing." Kraft reached for a rifle he'd left leaning against a post. He handed it to Matthew. "The list included a rifle, so I got one for Mr. Pedersen, but since you're younger and more likely to be able to defend the bunch of you, I'll hand it over to you, though I've been told I could be fined for placing a gun in a Mormon's hands."

"Thank you, Mr. Rundell," Margarette said, "for outfitting us properly and for the return of the sapphire." Kraft had placed the jewel beside the emerald in the medicine bag during one of her trips back to the cabin to retrieve the items she and the Pedersens were taking with them.

He looked uncomfortable, then admitted, "The remaining jewels are worth far more than a wagon and supplies, but it's all I can give you for them now. I lost a great deal during the past months, but with the jewels to finance a new start, my business will soon flourish again, and my wife and son will return to me."

"I hope it will be as you envision," Margarette said in a quiet voice. "But remember what Matthew told you."

* * *

Margarette felt conspicuous and even a little guilty as she walked beside the lead ox. Most of those who peeked from behind curtains or nodded to her as the wagon lumbered by were still in Nauvoo because they were too poor to leave. She couldn't help wondering what would become of them. She wished she could gather them all up and take them to safety with her. Brigham Young had left a committee behind to arrange for the sale of property with the objective of paying off debts and outfitting the poor for the trek west, but gradually those left behind were coming to the realization that no one was going to buy what they could soon simply take.

As they approached the river, she felt a sharp sting on her back, and then she saw a small stone bounce off the back of the nearest ox.

"What's going on?" Matthew looked around, and she knew he had been struck by a stone too. A streak of red ran down his cheek.

Something moved behind the fence of a deserted house, and one of the oxen let out a low bellow. Another tossed his horns in a worrisome manner.

"Steady," called Margarette without seeing any noticeable difference in their restless behavior. Though oxen had a reputation for being slow, she knew they could move quickly—with disastrous results—if upset. If whoever was harassing them succeeded in setting the cattle running, the wagon would likely tip over, injuring its occupants and leaving her without a means of getting her family out of Nauvoo. From the corner of her eye, she saw Matthew veer away from the team toward the abandoned house, his newly acquired rifle at the ready. Soren moved up beside her, repeating her command to the nervous animals.

The lead ox seemed to settle down, and Margarette surmised that the animals were accustomed to male voices and would need time to recognize her commands. Though disappointing, this discovery didn't surprise her. The animals had been used to haul freight wagons that were driven by men. She knew from her previous experience with cattle that they were slow to accept change. It had taken many months for Lars's pair of oxen to respond to her commands.

She turned her head to see if she could spot Matthew. She didn't see him, but she saw a figure dart from behind the house and run toward a line of shrubs. A moment later two more shadowy figures left their hiding places to scurry toward the shrubs where the first one hid. All three were shabbily dressed and appeared to be nothing more than overgrown boys.

The sound of hoof beats shifted her attention to the road behind them, where two men were approaching at great speed on horseback. Fearing further attack, she dropped back to assure herself that Anna and the children were safely inside the wagon and out of sight. She glanced toward the abandoned house, wishing Matthew would return.

"Hello, Sister Jorgensen," the first rider called, and she gasped with relief. The men were two of the last Nauvoo Legion soldiers who still patrolled the city. Although without any legal authority, the men, along with a few boys who hadn't already left with their families, still watched for invaders who meant to harm the Saints. Though they were unarmed, their presence alone quelled most troublemakers.

"Mary Johnson's boy said some young thugs were pelting your wagon with rocks," the other rider said. "We were on our way back from accompanying Wilford Woodruff and Orson Hyde to the ferry when the boy alerted us."

"They're over there behind those bushes!" Jens shouted.

Margarette could see that he had hopped back up on the wagon box and was pointing toward the shrubs where the three hoodlums hid. "Sit down!" she admonished him. For him to fall would be all she needed that day. He obeyed reluctantly, and she turned her attention back to the men on horseback.

The lead rider dug his heels into his horse's side and cantered toward the bushes. When he reached the spot, he called back, "There's no one here. They've gone."

"They took off running when they saw me." Matthew approached from the street ahead of them, carrying his rifle. "They'd collected a big pile of rocks behind the house over there. I followed them for a ways but didn't want to get too far from the wagon. Coming back, I discovered several caches of rocks near the road ahead. I tossed them over the fence to make it harder for the rascals to throw them at others using this road."

"Did you recognize any of them?" one of the former soldiers asked.

"No, though the biggest one looks a lot like old Carter Thomas. I saw him a couple of times over in Warsaw."

"That boy's a chip off the old block. He's seventeen, old enough to be working, but he spends his time running around with other idlers like himself, stirring up mischief. His pa thinks he's some kind of hero for heckling Mormons," the first of their rescuers said with disgust.

The men continued to talk as the oxen plodded on, and Margarette returned to her position beside Soren. The animals needed to grow accustomed to her skirts and her voice; Soren was an old man and could not be expected to drive them all the way to the

Rocky Mountains, and Matthew had yet to learn the art of goading the big beasts.

They reached the wharf without further incident and found several other wagons waiting to cross. Margarette was glad to see them, because they meant she and her family wouldn't be alone as they pushed to catch up to the wagons that had already gone ahead. While they waited for their turn to cross the river, Matthew and Soren visited with the other men, but Margarette chose to stay with Anna and the children.

As the other teams and wagons had arrived at the ferry first, they crossed ahead of Margarette's wagon. When it was finally their turn, the children were tired and hungry, and Margarette regretted that she hadn't put a chunk of bread or a piece of boiled potato in her pocket for them. Hearing Annelise cry for milk nearly broke her heart. There had been no milk in their household since Olaf and Katrina departed several months earlier.

It seemed to take forever to get the wagon and oxen loaded on the ferry, though several men standing around volunteered to help. Annelise was still crying when Margarette handed her to Anna to hold during the crossing.

"Mamma! I want Mamma." The little girl held out her arms, begging to remain with her mother.

"Mamma needs to stay with the oxen so they won't be scared." Jens tried to comfort his sister.

"Here, punkin." Matthew popped something in Annelise's mouth. She looked startled, then grinned. He handed something to Jens, too, before hurrying after Margarette and Soren. When he reached Margarette, he put his hand in his pocket and pulled out a single pea pod. "There are volunteer peas, ready for picking in the garden plot behind that abandoned house. I helped myself to a few of them while I was keeping an eye on those rogues who attacked us back there."

"Thank you for thinking of the children," she whispered, touched by his small act of kindness.

"I think that's what papas are supposed to do." He grinned, but she caught a glimpse of sadness in his eyes and knew he was thinking of his own father who had shown him no kindness when he was a small boy. She felt a wave of compassion for the little boy Matthew who'd known only surliness and sharp slaps from his alcoholic father.

The crossing went smoothly, though Margarette was annoyed when the ferry operator charged her more because she had six oxen rather than the two or four that pulled the other wagons. She supposed it was fair, but it left her with few coins should a need for money arise.

The day was damp, and sprinkles of rain made the crossing cold. They could see that darkness would be upon them by the time they cleared the ferry. Soren suggested they travel a mile or so from the river and make camp. He'd spoken with a couple of the other wagon owners who had waited with them to cross the river. They had suggested they form a single camp together to better protect their families and livestock. One who seemed to be the leader had suggested that by traveling a short distance from the river, they might find drier ground and fewer insects. It was Soren's hope that they would be able to catch up to and spend the night with that group.

As the wagon lumbered onto a muddy trail, marked with the signs of those who had gone before them, the oxen's hooves made a sucking sound with each step they took. Margarette's foot came down in the thick ooze, and as she attempted to pull her boot free, she heard the same sound. It had been stormy all of April, and the trail was nothing more than a mud bog. She stumbled on, though Matthew suggested she ride with Anna and the children.

"No, if anyone rides, it should be Soren," she said. "He's tired, and should he catch cold, we'll be in trouble."

Soren refused to climb into the wagon. "It's tough going through this mud even with six fresh oxen. I'll not add to their burden. Besides, the animals aren't yet ready to follow Margarette's commands."

"Teach me the commands," Matthew persisted.

"Not today. Tomorrow you can begin to familiarize yourself with the cattle. They've had enough changes for one day. Until we reach a camping spot, you'd best just observe." The old man plodded on with the thick mud reaching to his pant cuffs in most places.

Margarette had never known a longer mile. Sometimes she walked near the wagon, conversing with Anna and refusing to allow

Jens to climb down and walk beside her. Other times she trudged beside Soren, talking softly to help the animals grow accustomed to her voice. She was glad that earlier, Anna had given the children biscuits left from the previous night's meal, a piece of fruit, and a cup of water. Annelise had finally fallen asleep and been covered with Margarette's shawl. Margarette regretted that she was unable to provide her daughter with the milk she craved and wished that Kraft had been able to find a cow to accompany them on their journey.

As the rainfall grew heavier and the night blacker, Margarette took a lighted lantern and walked some distance ahead of the oxen to be certain they didn't stray from the road they should follow. She was wet and cold, and with her shoes caked in thick mud, they grew heavy, sapping her energy. She found herself praying they would find a safe place to stop for the night where the children could be fed and kept warm. When she spotted five wagons drawn together off the side of the road, she waved the lantern to signal Soren and Matthew. Soren called out "Whoa," to the oxen and tapped the lead ox with the goad.

Matthew hurried ahead of the wagon to stand beside her. His hat brim was pulled low and rain dripped from it. He placed a hand on her shoulder and leaned close to speak over the din of the storm.

"I'll go ahead to make certain they're some of our people," he offered. She nodded her head, and he splashed ahead toward the camp. A few minutes later, he returned to tell her the camp was made up of the people Soren had arranged to meet earlier. Relief filled Margarette, and she offered a silent prayer of gratitude as she walked beside Matthew to inform Soren.

"Walk up!" Soren shouted, and the great animals leaned into their yokes to start the wagon moving again. Several men came toward them as they entered the clearing. One indicated a spot for their wagon. It took several tries to get the wagon in place, but once it was situated to Soren's satisfaction, he showed Matthew how to remove the yokes and chains as he turned the animals loose in the center of the enclosure formed by the wagons.

Seeing a small fire under some sort of shelter near one of the wagons, Margarette walked toward it, hoping someone would give her instructions for lighting a fire and cooking dinner for her family.

"Hello," a woman ten or twelve years older than Margarette reached out to her, drawing her closer to the small amount of heat. "I'm Amy Donaldson. That's my husband, Joe, and our son, Clay, helping your men turn out the oxen. Two more sons are in the wagon. We're glad to have you join us."

"I'm Margarette J—Holmes." She remembered her name had changed. "My husband and I are quite inexperienced at this mode of travel and are grateful to find others to follow."

"None of us have had much experience." Amy laughed a hearty chuckle. She was a large woman with deep laugh lines around her eyes. She wore a heavy wool coat like Margarette had seen on some of the sailors during their crossing from England. "We came from Manchester two years ago and had never ridden a horse or slept under the stars until we reached Nauvoo. Joe was sent up north to the pinery that first winter, and he learned a lot about setting up camp and working with stock. Worked in the textile factories, we did, 'til we heard the gospel. When Brother Brigham said we were to move west we were plumb scared, so Joe studied everything he could about wagon travel most of this past winter. He even took a job in Pennsylvania to earn enough to buy a wagon and four oxen. He just got back with the wagon a week past."

"My husband worked in a factory in London." Margarette shared some of Matthew's background. "He has never even ridden a horse. And just two days ago, he returned from a mission in the South where he and his companion mostly walked or rode in the back of some kind person's wagon. Brother Pedersen, the older brother with us, learned something of animals when he was a young man, and I was taught a bit while living on my first husband's farm, but I know nothing of starting a fire or preparing a meal in this downpour." Margarette looked at the woman, hoping she would offer the information she needed in order to prepare a meal for her family.

Amy laughed again. "My Joe made that iron box while he was in Pennsylvania. He said some of the farmers there use them for heat in their barns and lambing sheds when their critters are birthin' their young. He said it works fine for a smudge pot, too, when frost threatens the buds on orchard trees."

Margarette studied the black box set on three legs. It was a little more than a foot deep, wide, and high. It smoked a lot, but did emit a small amount of heat. One side was open to permit the replenishment of fuel, and there was a hole on the top and several smaller ones on the bottom. A teakettle sat atop the small stovelike object.

"It's near impossible to keep a fire going in this weather, though a piece of canvas set on poles usually keeps the cooking area dry. Folks in the other wagons gave up and crawled inside their wagons to sleep, but Joe said he fancied a cup of tea before turning in. If you've a kettle, I'd be pleased to share the hot water."

Margarette returned to her wagon for a kettle and to explain to Anna that they wouldn't be able to cook anything that night, but they could each have a cup of warm water to go with what remained of the food Anna had cooked the previous night. Annelise whimpered and held out her arms to her mother.

Hesitating to touch the little girl with her cold hands, Margarette backed away. "I'll be right back," she promised, "then I'll hold you."

"How many folks in your wagon?" Amy asked as she poured a generous amount of hot water into Margarette's kettle.

"Six, including two small children," she replied. "My husband and myself and the Pedersens. I'm truly grateful for the hot water as Anna was quite ill on the voyage from England and I shouldn't like for her to take a chill again."

Matthew caught up to her on the way back, taking the heavy kettle from her hand. He passed it up to Soren who sat near the end of the wagon box wrapped in a quilt. They both removed their muddy boots and wet coats, placing the boots near the opening and hanging their coats where they wouldn't drip on the bed.

Once inside the wagon, Margarette carefully poured the precious hot water into six cups. Anna dropped a few dried leaves into each one. She added a teaspoon of sugar to Annelise's cup, and Margarette set the kettle out of the way and picked up her daughter, holding her while she slowly sipped the warm liquid. Anna had lit a lantern, and it spread a gentle glow across the small space that was now their home. From one of the boxes, she withdrew half a loaf of dark brown bread, which she divided. They were in the middle of nowhere, among strangers, with a storm bringing wet and cold, but Margarette's head began to nod. The dim light lent an aura of peace and comfort as her drowsy eyes viewed the faces of those she loved gathered together around their meager repast. Instead of dwelling on the cold and their unknown future, Margarette felt a deep sense of gratitude filling her heart, assuring her that God was watching over them.

"Sleeping quarters will be tight," Soren said. "But you can't roll out bedrolls under the wagon tonight."

"No," Matthew conceded, "but how will we all fit in here?"

Margarette blinked her eyes. She hadn't given a thought to where she would sleep. Margarette estimated that the wagon box was not much more than four feet wide and ten long with the feather-tick covered barrels providing a six-foot bed. The curved supports for the oiled linen added a sense of greater width, but they didn't do anything for the amount of weight-bearing space. She was too tired to think about it. Her head sagged toward her sleeping baby.

"Jens will sleep between us." Anna took charge. "We'll take one end of the feather tick, and you'll have to make do with the other. I expect the little one will cry if her mamma doesn't go right on holding her. If we're careful where we put our feet, we'll be fine."

She was vaguely aware of Matthew pulling her against his chest as he half reclined against the side of the wagon box, and she felt the delicious warmth of the quilt he pulled over them. He murmured something in her ear, but the words didn't make sense.

"Our time will come," she thought she heard him say.

When she awoke to a gray predawn morning, she remembered his words and felt a slow flush on her cheeks. Their marriage began out of necessity, but Matthew had made no secret of his expectation that their marriage would be normal in every way. As she mulled the matter over in her mind, she discovered she wanted that too. Surely friendship and shared faith were a better foundation for marriage than were childish dreams of romance.

16🖎

The day began peacefully, with the sun peeking through the last of the storm's trailing clouds, brightening Margarette's outlook. Enticing aromas from the Donaldsons' breakfast preparations whetted her family's appetites, making preparing a warm breakfast her and Anna's first concern. Anna declared that cooking over a campfire couldn't be a lot different from cooking in a fireplace. The most difficult part would be finding wood that was dry enough to burn.

Jens insisted on helping in the search for wood, and Matthew agreed he was old enough to be a big help. Margarette walked beside them with Annelise riding on her hip. Jens was the first to spot a fallen tree such as Mr. Donaldson had told them to watch for. Matthew stripped off the few branches that remained on it, split it lengthwise, then chopped out the dry inner core. After supplying Anna with the wood she needed, Matthew took the precaution of storing a supply of dry firewood inside the wagon as he'd discovered the Donaldsons had done, which was the reason they'd had a head start preparing breakfast that morning and had managed to heat water the previous night. With that done, he invited the other people, some of whom were just stirring from their wagons, to help themselves to the remainder of the dry wood inside the log.

Anna discovered three unbroken eggs in the hens' cage. The servings of egg were small, even when she added water to make them go farther, but along with salt pork and hot biscuits, they made a satisfying meal.

After breakfast, Anna and Margarette gathered up what was left of the biscuits and pork to save in tin buckets for a cold lunch. It had taken until almost noon for everyone from the six wagons to cook breakfast, clean up, then get their oxen yoked to their wagons. With the late start, the men didn't anticipate stopping until evening, and the women were determined the children wouldn't go hungry again that day as they had on their first day.

They started out well, with the Donaldson wagon in front, as they were the first ones prepared to move out, followed by Margarette's wagon. A big man with a black beard walked beside the third wagon holding the reins to four massive dappled gray horses. A boy in his late teens rode a beautiful roan mare beside the wagon, and a short, plump woman sat on the wagon box.

A swarm of children ran about the fourth wagon, climbing in and out of the wagon and chasing each other. The fifth and sixth wagons had difficulty keeping up, as one was pulled by just two head of cattle that didn't appear well matched, and the other had a problem with the wheels locking up. Margarette heard the big bearded man explain that the problem came about because the axles were cut from green logs that hadn't cured long enough.

A long hill, made slick by two months of rain and hundreds of wagons and teams churning up its muddy sides, proved too much for the slower wagons. Seeing their problem, Soren halted his cattle, and he and Matthew unhooked two of their oxen and drove them back toward the wagon pulled by just two oxen. After some discussion, the oxen were combined to pull the wagon up the hill.

With the additional oxen, the wagon slowly made its way to the top of the hill. Once it was on level ground, they unyoked the oxen and went back for the other wagon. Soren shouted to the lead ox, and all six of the other men and several of the older boys lent their strength to wrestling the stubborn wagon up the hill.

They reached Sugar Creek that evening and were fortunate to find a space large enough for their six wagons. As they drove past haphazardly parked wagons, a large number of tents, and a smattering of shacks that appeared to be constructed of sticks, Margarette was appalled to discover that many of the Saints who had left Nauvoo much earlier were encamped there, most in as precarious condition as those they'd left behind in Nauvoo, and the camp was in serious need of some kind of order.

A number of people appeared to be ill, and Margarette was glad that their group of new arrivals had found space to circle their wagons a little apart from the others. While she and the other women prepared a hot meal for their families, the men, except for Soren, who chose to rest for a bit, wandered through the larger camp, talking to various people. Matthew returned before the others, and she sensed he was upset, though he said nothing and tried to pretend otherwise.

"Come to Papa." He coaxed Annelise away from her hold on Margarette's skirt. "Let's find some more wood while Mamma cooks our supper." With Annelise riding on one arm and Jens grasping his opposite hand, they disappeared into the trees. When they reemerged carrying only a handful of twigs, the stew and biscuits were waiting.

"This area is picked pretty clean of firewood," Matthew commented as he helped Jens place the few sticks in the wagon for cooking the next morning's breakfast. They gathered around the wagon seat that Matthew had lifted down for the women to use as a table. Anna and Soren seated themselves on the wagon tongue, and Matthew found buckets and boxes for the rest of them to use as chairs.

They'd just begun eating when the Donaldson family, carrying their own bowls of stew and small stools, approached.

"Mind if we join you?" Joe asked.

"Happy to have you." Matthew indicated they should seat themselves.

As they ate, Joe expressed concern over what he had seen in the camp. "It seems many of these folks left Nauvoo without following Brigham Young's advice to carry a year's worth of supplies, and now they're trying to acquire provisions for the remainder of their journey. Work is scarce, and few supplies are available for purchase in the surrounding settlements. There are some who could continue on but are hesitant to do so without specific instructions from Brother Brigham, so they're waiting for a courier to arrive with instructions from him."

"I'm one who thinks faith is a fine thing," Amy spoke up. "But while we were doing everything we could think of to make preparations for our journey, I found others who blandly assumed the Lord would provide for them without any effort on their part. I recognized some of those folks as we passed the camp. I don't mean to be selfish, but I don't intend for our supplies to go for the fulfillment of their blind faith"

"I'm concerned on that score too," Joe continued. "If we tarry here, we'll end up depleting our supplies and seeing our children go hungry before we reach the Rocky Mountains."

"While wandering through camp, a powerful feeling came over me that my family will be in danger should we linger here." Matthew's eyes met Margarette's for but a second, but she read the warning there and understood. *The scar-faced man is in camp!* "We're outfitted better than most, due to my wife's sacrifice of some valuable jewels," Matthew went on. "We could spare a barrel of flour to help the poor, but I fear it would only delay the heads of families from seeking the means to go on. I feel it is imperative that we move ahead as quickly as possible to alert Brother Brigham to the plight of those still in Nauvoo and to avoid any danger to my family. With or without you and the others, we'll be pulling out early in the morning."

"I noticed a number of people appeared ill. Do you suppose it is cholera?" Amy cast a worried glance toward her sons.

"Whatever it is," Joe said, "warnings such as Matthew received are not to be ignored. We'll have yokes on our beasts at dawn. We'll breakfast on down the trail. There's no firewood here anyway. After the others have had a chance to eat their supper, I'll call everyone together."

Later that evening, after everyone had been fed and the younger children had been put to bed inside the wagons, the small group who had traveled their first day together gathered around the Donaldsons' fire to discuss their future course.

"I'm for traveling on at daybreak," Joe Donaldson stated. "The Holmes's have indicated they're ready to move on too. If we stay here, we'll use up our supplies before we reach our destination. I've heard winter comes early in the mountains, and if we delay our departure, we may get caught in snow before we reach upper California."

"I'm already short on flour," one of the other men, Bart Davis, admitted. "We didn't have the means to gather all the supplies we should have, but we feared that if we didn't leave at once, we'd be burned out and have nothing. We were the only ones left in our part of town and found it necessary to sit up with a shotgun all night just to keep our family safe. I don't want to start out short on supplies, but I fear matters will only get worse if we wait around here. We'll be ready to leave whenever you say." Margarette looked at Brother Davis's wife and six children ranging from about twelve down to a nursing infant and understood the decision he and his wife had made. It seemed they'd had to choose between two less-than-desirable choices.

"We stayed in Nauvoo longer than we should have, hoping someone would buy the forge and helping others build wagons and make harnesses, but when we couldn't get iron or leather anymore, we thought it best to pull out." A little woman sitting between her large, brawny husband and son spoke up. "We're well-equipped, with four draft horses, a saddle horse, and our barrels are full. We want to go on."

"I don't think we have much choice but to stay here 'til the weather improves," Rufus Finster, who only had two oxen, spoke up. "We weren't sure about coming anyway. All winter we debated between going back to New York and following the Brethren west, but when Joe Donaldson said they were leaving, we decided to follow along. We only had one ox, but our cow is a good-sized one, so we decided to yoke her with the ox. Now I wonder if that was a mistake and we'd be putting ourselves in danger to go on. We're thinking of selling out if we can find anyone to buy our outfit. We'll catch a ferry to St. Louis, then head east."

"My brother is camped here. His saddle horses aren't strong enough to pull their wagon, and one of their oxen died." Rulon Anderson, the last man spoke up. "His wife is expecting a baby any day, and he's been hoping that after it is born, he can get work and sell his horses to resupply and buy oxen. I spoke with him a little while ago, and we decided to travel together from here on. Their wagon is one of the bigger, sturdier ones. Anyway, they have a tent, too. We only have the one boy, and this baby is their first, so there'll be plenty of room. We'll sell what's useable of our wagon for spare parts to buy more supplies to replace the ones we'll use up while waiting. We noticed that quite a few wagons were damaged as we walked through camp, so we should be able to find buyers. We'll use our four oxen to pull his wagon and both be on our way much sooner than either of us could make it alone."

Margarette fingered the leather pouch that hung from the leather thong about her neck. Would it be enough to purchase the Finster's cow? She'd noticed Sister Finster milking it earlier and had longed for some of the milk for Annelise.

"Look." Rufus Finster turned to Rulon Anderson. "We might be able to work out a trade, my outfit for your brother's horses. We'd just take the supplies we'd need to see us to St. Louis, and you'd have the rest of the supplies and the ox your brother is short. With six oxen, you'd be able to manage the hills and mud better."

"I'm sure he'll agree." Rulon sounded excited. "Let's go talk to him right now. With six head of oxen, we'll be able to move right along like Holmes here." He nodded his head toward Matthew. Absorbed in the possibility of making a trade advantageous to both, they rose to their feet and hurried away to discuss the matter with Rulon Anderson's brother.

When they were gone, their wives returned to their wagons. The others sat on, gazing into the fire. Four wagons meant less protection and securing the animals inside the wagon circle at night would be more difficult. Finally Joe spoke. "I noticed a few outfits that looked ready to move out. I'll speak with their owners and invite any that can be ready to join us in the morning."

"I'll go with you," Matthew volunteered. He leaned close to Margarette to whisper, "I'll make certain he doesn't say too much or bring back an unwelcome snoop."

Margarette nodded, grateful for his caution. She rose from the pail she sat on and crossed to her wagon to check on the children. They were both sleeping, seemingly enjoying having the big feather-tick bed to themselves. After assuring herself that they were fine, she returned to the fire, seating herself beside Marissa Davis, who had also sent her large brood of children to their beds.

"Sister Davis," she spoke softly. "You heard my husband. We have more flour than we need. The man who outfitted our wagon put everything on Brother Brigham's list in it, and if he could get extra, he did. We have so many barrels, we're short of space to make a bed for the children. I would be pleased if you would accept one of those barrels of flour."

"We haven't enough funds to pay for a whole barrel of flour, but we would be happy to purchase a few pounds."

"I'm not asking you to buy it. I wish to give it to you." Before the woman could protest, Margarette went on. "My husband received a strong premonition that our family must be gone from here by first light. We do not wish to travel alone or in a party so small that we have no defense against any who might attempt to overpower us. You and your family have impressed me as being compatible with our family and in tune with our Heavenly Father. It is as much to our advantage as yours to help you go on."

"But how can I accept such a valuable gift?" Tears shone in the woman's eyes.

"All summer, I was without a job, and Matthew was away serving a mission. Every night and morning, I pleaded on my knees for a means of feeding my family, and many mornings I found a gift of garden produce on my front stoop and each Sunday night a jug of fresh milk. God answered my prayers, but He did it through dear friends who knew of my plight. He knows your concerns and your children's needs. Let God answer your prayers through me."

"Thank you—oh, I must talk to Bart." Marissa stood, hesitated a moment, then gave Margarette a hug before dashing across the clearing to find her husband.

The blacksmith and his wife, who had introduced themselves as Francis and Lucy Weldon, with their seventeen-year-old son, Collin, bid them good night with an assurance they would be ready to depart before the stars faded. Amy Donaldson continued to sit with Margarette and the Pedersens. Margarette was about to suggest that the Pedersens, who showed signs of weariness, retire for the night, when Matthew and Joe returned.

"We found six, maybe seven, families who want to leave with us in the morning." Joe sounded jubilant. "We warned them that if they're not lined up, ready to move out before daylight, we won't wait for them."

Seeing two dark shapes leave the Davis's wagon and move toward them, Margarette drew Matthew aside.

"I told the Davis's they could have a barrel of flour," she whispered.

"You just gave it to them?" He sounded surprised, but not angry.

"First Olaf, then Hannah, gave me milk and vegetables for months. Without their generosity, my children might have starved. I can do no less for the Davis's children. Besides, with that barrel out of the way, I can make a bed for the children in the back of the wagon."

"You're a good woman, Margarette." He placed an arm around her and drew her to his side. His lips brushed her brow. "And that's another reason we must leave here at once. Were we to stay, your tender heart would give away all your goods to the poor, of whom there are many here."

"Did you really see him?" She ignored his gentle teasing, more concerned for her children's safety.

"Yes, I'm sure he was the same fellow you described. He was making his way from one group to the next inquiring about a Danish woman and her children. I spoke with a woman he had questioned. She said he'd just arrived this morning and was claiming the woman was his runaway wife."

Margarette shuddered.

"Excuse me." Marissa's voice sounded hesitant. "I told Bart what you said."

"The two of us should be able to get that barrel out of our wagon and into yours without any trouble," Matthew said, clapping Bart Davis on the shoulder.

As the two men moved toward the back of the wagon, Marissa asked in a trembling voice, "How shall I ever repay you?"

"Don't even think about repaying me," Margarette told the other woman. "Someday, you'll have something someone else needs more than you do and you'll give it to them. That's the only payment I expect."

"I'll do it, I promise." Marissa wiped her eyes and stumbled after the two men transferring the flour barrel to her wagon.

Margarette hurried to the back of her own wagon. Clambering aboard, she pushed and tugged at the bags and boxes there until they formed an even surface on which she spread blankets and her quilt to form a bed for the children. Matthew joined her and carefully moved Jens without waking him to his new bed. She placed Annelise beside her brother and pulled the quilt securely over them.

"Come." Matthew took her hand and helped her down from the wagon. He picked up a bundle he'd tossed to the ground a few minutes earlier. She watched him spread a canvas ground sheet beneath the wagon and add a thick quilt they'd found in one of the boxes. Kneeling, they crawled beneath the wagon to their makeshift bed. It was the first of many nights that Matthew released her long hair from its braid and combed his fingers through its silky length, marveling as it shimmered in his hands.

"Beautiful," he murmured.

Held in Matthew's arms with the quilt sheltering them from the night air, she'd fallen asleep more quickly than she'd expected. She awoke when Matthew stretched and prepared to leave their cozy cocoon.

"Sleep a few minutes more," he told her. "I can get the yokes on the oxen and bring up their chains myself."

"It'll be quicker if I help." She rose to her knees, then paused. "While we're on our knees, this might be a good time for morning prayers."

He agreed, and though the prayer was short, it seemed a fitting start not only to the day, but also to their life together.

Working together, they soon had their oxen separated from the others and lined up in each oxen's customary place. Soren joined them, and Matthew lifted the heavy yokes across each pair's necks, and then he began attaching the chains that led to the wagon tongue, following the old man's instructions. The sounds of shuffling hooves and the rattle of chains told them the others were hitching up their teams as well.

The stars were growing faint, and a light pink tinged the eastern sky when Joe ordered his oxen to walk up and Soren followed with the same command to their team.

"Hurry, climb into the wagon," Matthew told her. "You and the children need to stay out of sight until we're away from here." Reluctantly, though she saw the wisdom of his words, she moved toward the wagon.

"Sister Holmes." For a moment she didn't realize Rulon Anderson was speaking to her.

"Yes?" She turned to face him. He stood holding a rope. The Finster's big black and white cow stood patiently waiting at the other end of the rope.

"I ain't got no use for a cow, and neither does my brother. And we cain't afford to feed her. We traded them two saddle horses for the

Finster's outfit, so soon as the baby comes, we'll be on our way. I figured with your little ones, you might could take the cow."

"But . . ."

"I heard what you said to Sister Davis last night, so I don't figure there's no way you can say no. You coulda left us back there in the mud, but you didn't. Here." He thrust the rope into her hands and turned to leave. "Better catch up to that wagon," he said before trotting toward his own wagon where five oxen were tethered.

Turning around, she saw the tail end of her wagon disappearing into the trees and a wagon pulled by four horses preparing to follow it. Gathering up her skirts, she ran, the cow trotting after her.

17

Seeing her plight, Collin Weldon leaped from his mare's back to help Margarette climb aboard her wagon and fasten the cow's lead rope to the back of it. She hurriedly whispered, "Thank you," before flopping down beside her children. Annelise went on sleeping, but Jens lifted his head and looked around. In the dim light, he appeared puzzled by his surroundings.

She shifted him to her lap and whispered. "Last night we gave one of the barrels to the Davis family to make room for a little bed for you and Annelise."

"Where are you and Matthew going to sleep?" he asked.

"Last night we slept under the wagon, but when we have enough time, we'll attach a canvas to the side of the wagon to make a tent to sleep in."

"I want to sleep in a tent."

"I'll make sure you get a turn." She hugged him tight, then let her gaze go to the small open circle in the canvas at the rear of the wagon as they came to a stop. There wasn't much to see. The sun wasn't up yet, though the sky was considerably lighter, telling her that sunrise was only minutes away. In the pale light, she caught an occasional glimpse of the cow and felt a swelling of gratitude in her heart for the generous gesture that would mean so much to her small children. She listened to the sounds made by the men and animals as they lined up the wagons. She longed to be outside assisting Matthew and Soren but knew her children's safety might depend on their staying out of sight.

Hearing the unmistakable crack of a bullwhip, Margarette and Jens both jumped. Jens buried his head in his mother's cloak.

"It's all right," she whispered. "Matthew told me Joe has a long whip he cracks in the air to signal his oxen to start up. He doesn't whip them."

"Do you think Pwitty and his family reached that far off place they were going to yet?"

"I hope so, but we might not ever know," she whispered back.

"When I'm grown up, I'm going to find that place and make certain nobody's hurting him."

Soren shouted, "Walk up!" and the wagon began to roll forward again. Before Margarette could breathe a sigh of relief, a commotion broke out behind them. Setting Jens back on his quilt, she crept to the small opening in the back of the wagon cover to peer out. Brilliant rays of light were beginning to light the sky, and far down the line of wagons, she could see a dozen or so men gathered around a figure lying on the ground.

"Thief!" someone shouted. "I caught him sneaking into the back of my wagon."

"My wife was still in her nightclothes and happened to peek out and saw him climb into the Hartwells' wagon," another voice exclaimed.

"Tie him up! I'll turn him over to Bishop Jones," a deep voice exclaimed. "I'm last in line, so I got time."

Margarette sat down abruptly on the bed she'd help make for her children. She suspected the man caught sneaking into the wagon wasn't the usual kind of thief. If Matthew hadn't been prompted to leave before the sun arose . . . If their wagon had been at the back of the line . . . A jumble of thoughts tumbled through her mind. The steady, plodding beat of oxen's and horses' hooves was a joyous sound to her ears.

An hour passed before she mustered enough courage to slip down from the wagon to join Soren and Matthew. Anna insisted she wear a bonnet that completely shaded her face. Matthew frowned when she joined him.

"I'm not sure it's safe yet for you to risk being seen," he said. "There was some commotion as we left, and from what I've been able to piece together, I think the intruder was peering in wagons looking for something specific."

"Or someone." She took several steps before going on. "We're married. Doesn't that make you the children's legal guardian, not a mean old man in another country?"

"Ordinarily, I think American law would uphold our right to the children, but we're close to Missouri, and there are judges there who would send the children back just to spite us because we're Mormons. We can't risk having one of the children grabbed and taken away before we can do anything."

"No, but we can't ride in the wagon all of the time, either. It's not good for the children or the oxen."

"We'll discuss it later. For now, please go back to the wagon."

"All right, but before I do, I wanted to tell you we now have a cow. Rulon Anderson bought the Finster outfit, and since he doesn't need a cow and can't afford to feed one, he gave it to us for the children."

"What! He could have sold that cow for a handsome sum of money." He took her arm and walked her back to the wagon. "Why did he give it away?"

"He said it was because we didn't leave him in the mud yesterday, because we helped him reach camp and his brother." She let him assist her into the wagon, though his eyes were on the cow.

"I hope you know how to milk her, because I don't," he said as he walked away shaking his head.

* * *

The rainy weather wasn't entirely over, but rain fell less frequently and lasted for shorter periods of time as their group moved slowly across Iowa. As they met each day's challenges, everyone grew more adept at caring for their livestock and cooking in the open. Bodies grew leaner and muscles stronger. Learning that several of the Brethren traveled a short distance ahead of them and that they made a practice of stopping early on Saturday and remaining in camp on Sundays, they adopted the same arrangement. Soren arranged a gathering the first Sunday. He preached a short sermon and bore his testimony. The practice continued after that each Sunday, with the different men taking turns telling of their conversions to the gospel and bearing testimony to the others. Their group now included seventeen wagons, all of which were well-equipped with sufficient stock, and as the days grew warmer, their speed increased.

Sometimes they caught up to wagons moving singly or in groups along the trail. Some chose to join their train, others found Joe a hard wagon master and dropped out to travel at their own slower pace. Joe had no patience with those who slept in or took their time getting ready to pull out each morning, and those who remained with him tended to be those who shared his enthusiasm for promptness and order.

When they reached Garden Grove, halfway across the state of Iowa, they found that an effort was being made to bring order to the various camps along the trail and that two hundred people had been assigned to stay at the station to plant crops, build cabins, and make it a place where those following could rest and renew some of their supplies. They stayed two days at Garden Grove to rest the animals and wash their clothes, and then they moved on.

Anna walked beside Margarette one beautiful June morning. They each held one of Annelise's small hands. The little girl's short, pale curls gleamed in the sunlight. Up ahead, Jens walked beside Matthew and Soren. She was surprised at how happy she felt. The past couple of months had been the happiest in her life, though she'd worked as hard as she had on Lars's farm back in Denmark. Matthew helped her keep a careful watch for the stranger who traveled on horseback and without a wagon; their dependence on each other, fresh air, and an abundance of exercise seemed to have strengthened them both. Marissa Davis, Lucy Weldon, and Amy Donaldson had become Margarette's and Anna's close friends, making even the trailside duties far more pleasant than she had expected.

Watching Jens imitating Matthew's long strides brought a smile to her lips. There was a bond between the two that brought joy to her heart. Most of the time, she was too busy to think about it, but sometimes, at quiet moments, she wondered how Matthew felt about her. She was his wife now in the most elemental way, but sometimes she felt guilty lying beside him, because in her need for a man's strength and protection, she had taken advantage of his kindness and compassion. Her life with Matthew was a sharp contrast to the time she'd shared with Jory, just as the two men were complete opposites. Was

Matthew simply making the best of the bargain he'd struck and the circumstances that had thrown them together, or was he truly happy? He was gentle and kind to her, but he never spoke of his feelings. Jory had clung to her and wept, swearing he loved her, but his actions had often been rough and cruel.

"Margarette." Marissa caught up to them, her baby balanced on her hip.

Two little boys raced past them to join Jens. The younger one tripped on a trailing pant leg and tumbled in the dust. Picking himself up, he called, "Wait for me, Peter. Wait for me." He raced on until he reached Peter and Jens.

"The boys are growing so fast, I can't keep up with them." Marissa laughed. "Though I packed a couple extra suits of clothes for each of them, David is now wearing his father's extra pair of britches, Ashton moved up to David's, and Peter is wearing Ashton's. Johnny isn't quite big enough to fit in Peter's, but I can't quite fasten his own on him. If Katherine, who is between Peter and Johnny, had been another boy, passing on clothes would have been simpler."

"Perhaps we should make a trade," Margarette suggested, seeing little Johnny stumble again and noticing that Jens's pants no longer reached all the way to his socks. "Jens and Katherine are about the same size."

When the wagons stopped for a brief nooning, Margarette made the suggestion to Jens, who was pleased at the prospect of wearing Peter's old overalls, so they gathered up his extra suit of clothes and headed for the Davis wagon. Soon, five-year-old Jens was grinning as he viewed himself attired like his six-year-old friend, Peter—in overalls—and three-year-old Johnny danced around demonstrating his new-found agility in Jens's britches.

"Me too!" Annelise snatched a pair of Johnny's outgrown overalls she found hanging over the side of a barrel.

"No, Sweetie," Margarette laughed as she attempted to take the pants from her daughter. "Girls wear dresses, pants are for boys."

"I wear." She plopped herself down on the floor of the Davis's wagon to attempt to pull the pants on.

"She can have them," Marissa said. "They're the ones Johnny outgrew. I don't think anyone out here would fault a little girl for wearing pants to avoid scratches to her legs. Katherine wore a pair of Peter's pants for a few days until she got tired of the trouble they caused every time she needed to answer nature's call."

"Margarette!" Anna was out of breath. She climbed up the step to poke her head in the back of the Davis's wagon. "A man just rode in with a marshal. He's demanding to search the wagons for a woman he says is his wife and who ran away with their children. The marshal ordered all of the men to stay together at the edge of the camp. Soren was bent down checking one of the oxen's hooves, and they didn't see him sneak back to warn me. I told him to lie on the bed and pretend to be napping so they wouldn't know he hadn't been there all along."

Margarette looked around, searching for a place to hide. They'd stopped beside a small stream, but there were few trees and not enough bushes to provide a hiding place.

Marissa looked at Anna, then at Margarette, her expression one of concern and questions.

"It's not true," Margarette whispered. "I did run away with my children, but not from my husband. He's dead. It's my father-in-law who is trying to take my children."

"But Matthew . . ."

"Matthew and I married almost two months ago."

"Matthew is my papa," Jens rushed to Margarette's side and wrapped his arms around her. "I won't leave Mamma and Matthew."

"We'd better move quickly then." A sly expression crept across Marissa's face. She reached for a hairbrush and a jar of molasses she hadn't yet put away after making molasses sandwiches out of soda biscuits and the sticky syrup for her children's lunch. "Get those britches on your little one."

When the scar-faced man stopped beside the Davis's' wagon, he found four dark-haired little boys building a farm in the dirt beside one of the large wagon wheels. A liberal amount of dirt covered each face. A little girl of five or six stirred a kettle hanging from a tripod nearby, and two women, wearing bonnets, scurried about preparing a meal, while a third appeared to be nursing an infant.

"Ladies," the marshal stepped forward. "We won't detain you long. We're looking for a runaway and must be certain she isn't hiding among the Mormons on this wagon train. You only need tell me your names."

"You must be the reason our men are late for lunch," Marissa grumbled. "I'm Marissa Davis, and this is Anna Pedersen. Over there, nursing the wee babe, is me sister, Meg."

The scar-faced man looked unhappy, but the marshal voiced no objection to Marissa speaking for all of them. The man turned abruptly to the boys, "And what are your names?" he demanded.

Peter stood, looking clearly indignant. "Ain't none o' your business." The other boys rose to their feet and stood beside him in stair-step fashion. The littlest one stuck a thumb in his mouth.

"Peter, you need not be rude," Marissa chided him.

"Awright," he continued to look annoyed. "I'm the oldest. I be Peter."

"James," the next boy muttered.

"I, John," the third boy stated proudly and looked to his mother for approval. Margarette caught a glimpse of amusement on the marshal's face.

"And you?" the scar-faced man scowled at the littlest of the foursome."

"Wesa," emerged from behind a well-chewed thumb.

"He's little. He can't say *Wesley,*" the second boy spoke up with a scowl directed at their interrogator.

"Come on, we're wasting our time here," the man turned away. The marshal followed him to the Weldon's wagon.

It was all Margarette could do to stay seated with Marissa's baby in her arms. She wanted to grab her own children and run. She wondered if any of the other women and children might accidentally say something to give away her identity. She wished Matthew would come.

After what seemed an interminable length of time, she heard the sound of horses leaving at a gallop; still, she didn't dare move. Annelise wandered over and sat down nearby. Jens glanced her way, but remained with Peter and Johnny.

"Wesa hold baby?" Annelise asked hopefully.

"Not now, Sweetie," Margarette whispered. "Go play with the boys."

"I boy." She stretched out her legs to admire her overalls.

"Just for today." Margarette smiled, noting that the molasses hair dye was beginning to drip down her daughter's warm face. Annelise scrambled to her feet and hurried back to the boys, who were soon yelling at her for messing up the farm they'd made in the dirt.

"Margarette!" Matthew was at the forefront of a dozen or more men and boys who swept into the clearing, running toward their various wagons. She stood slowly, not wishing to awaken the baby sleeping in her arms. Seeing her, he rushed to her side, and his arms went around her.

"Jens, Annelise, are they safe? Did you have time to hide them?"

"In plain sight." Marissa approached them, mischief dancing in her eyes. "Boys, come introduce yourself to Brother Holmes."

Margarette watched the frightened expression on his face turn to puzzlement, then mirth, as the boys stood.

"I'm Peter," the tallest one said.

"I'm James," the second boy added with a grin.

"Me, John," Johnny added.

"Me, Wesa," Annelise giggled before launching herself into his arms.

"James?" Matthew knelt by Jens, sticky syrup from Annelise's hair smearing its way across his shirt.

"Peter said it wasn't really a lie, 'cause Jens is almost the same as James and the bad man probably knew the boy he was looking for is named Jens."

"Peter is a very smart boy," Matthew said, speaking loudly enough to make certain Peter heard.

"Load up. Let's be on our way." Joe Donaldson stood only a few feet away. "It appears a trip to the creek might be in order, but moving on could be wiser. If your 'boys' don't attract too many flies before we stop for supper, cleaning up will have to wait. I'll watch for a spot by the creek to stop for the night."

18

"I think you should continue using the impromptu names you used that afternoon," Marissa stated her view. "That man who came to our camp was listening for Danish names and accents, I'm sure. Besides, people you meet, who hear your real names, might innocently point you out without knowing the trouble they might cause."

Margarette had just finished explaining to the friends gathered around the campfire the circumstances that had driven her to flee Denmark with her children and the fear that had kept them running from the detectives her former father-in-law had hired.

Margarette looked at the solemn-faced adults she and Matthew had decided needed to know their secret. Telling the Davises, the Donaldsons, and Weldons wasn't really so difficult, and as quick-thinking Marissa had proved, their knowledge of the matter could prove beneficial. Almost two months on the trail had established a bond of trust among the families who had begun the journey together. Her nervousness came from the two gentlemen who sat next to Soren. They had finally caught up to Elders Wilford Woodruff and Orson Hyde at Mt. Pisgah. The two leaders had elected to join their campfire that night.

After a chorus of support from their friends, silence settled around the group. Finally Matthew spoke up, "Elder Woodruff, you performed our marriage two months ago, and, as we hold a great deal of respect for you and Elder Hyde, we would be interested to hear your thoughts on this matter."

"I've been thinking on it," Elder Woodruff stroked his short beard. "The Prophet Joseph always advised that we honor and sustain the law of the land. Yet he did not hold with cruelty to children. He often commented on our Savior's tender regard for children, and he also had strong feelings concerning the bond between a mother and her children. I daresay that in this instance he would have recognized United States laws granting a woman's husband control over her children, but only if doing so was in the children's best interest."

"Then you don't think I was wrong to bring my children to America?" Margarette asked.

"I can't say that taking them from their grandfather was right or wrong; that is between you and the Lord. But it has been my experience that mothers are generally the best judges of what is in their children's best interests, and it would appear that the Holy Spirit has aided you in placing them where they might enjoy the blessings of the restored gospel."

"There are those who claim only men should be given guardianship of minor children, but if I were to depart this world before my wife, I would trust her more than any other to be my children's guardian," Bart Davis spoke up. "My parents are bitter toward the Church, and I would not wish for them to have the raising of our children."

"Brother Brigham, though strong and outspoken," Elder Hyde added, "has often commented on the good sense of women. I think we shall see an adjustment in our new home in the mountains which shall provide women with greater rights and responsibilities than ever before."

"If our men continue to be called away to serve missions, it seems women must be given greater recognition and training, or the men will come home to find their businesses in ruin." Lucy Weldon's voice was sharp.

"And would you be shoein' draft horses if your man be away preachin' the Word?" Joe asked, a smile tilting the corner of his mouth, as he questioned tiny Lucy.

"She'd do it!" Francis grinned. "She's every bit as good at blacksmithin' as the boy and me. Her only shortcoming is that it takes her twice as long, as she has to swing the hammer twice to deliver the blow I do with but one swing." A chorus of laughter spread around the circle, and talk turned to other matters until Joe stood, stretching his arms.

"If we mean to be on our way in the morning, we'd best turn in," he announced.

Matthew rose to his feet too, drawing Margarette with him. "The more distance we put between ourselves and that marshal and his friend, the better I'll like it."

"Perhaps you should wait a bit," Elder Woodruff put in. "A Captain James Allen and a small consignment of soldiers rode into camp late this afternoon. They've asked to address the camp tomorrow morning. They claim that they have arrived to raise a battalion of Mormons to fight in the war against Mexico and that they've come at the urging of Elder Jesse C. Little and Thomas L. Kane. Kane is the son of a prominent federal judge, and Little presides over the Church in the East. They claim that at Brother Brigham's behest, they petitioned President Polk for redress for the perfidy our people have suffered and for financial help in relocating our people."

* * *

The next morning, Margarette and Matthew joined their friends at the impromptu meeting. Soren volunteered to watch the children. The long journey had tired Anna greatly, and Soren thought it a good opportunity for her to rest.

"Army recruiters aren't interested in fellows like me." Soren laughed. "And you'll be able to pay more attention without the little ones drawing your attention away. Besides, it's probably safer if they're not seen with you in a crowd."

The four couples and Collin Weldon stood together near the back of the crowd as Elder Woodruff introduced Captain Allen and encouraged everyone to give the officer a courteous hearing. Even with the subtle admonition, Margarette heard an abundance of grumbling as the speaker explained that the United States had annexed Texas, which angered Mexico, since that country claimed that Texas was a Mexican territory. There had been a skirmish between Mexican and U.S. troops in April, and Congress had declared war on May 12, 1846. They also learned that New Mexico and Upper California were also at stake, as both countries wished to expand their territories into those areas.

"After the way we've been treated, I don't know why the government would think we'd fight for them," Francis complained as they walked back to their wagons some time later.

"I'm not sure we'd be better off under Mexican rule," Joe said. "From what I've heard, the Mexican government is weak and corrupt, with bandits running the country."

"I was hoping we'd go somewhere no one else has claimed, so we'd be free to make our own laws." Bart sighed and wrapped an arm around Marissa's waist. "I don't fancy being uprooted any more once we reach the Rocky Mountains."

"What if it's some kind of trap to lure the young men away from our camps, leaving our wives and children defenseless, then while they're gone, armies like that Missouri bunch come in and find easy pickings?" Matthew expressed his concern.

"I ain't leavin' Lucy to look after herself." Francis put his foot down. "Ain't no tellin' how hard she'd be to get along with if she figured out she can get along just fine without me." This brought a chuckle.

"I don't reckon there's anything to it," Joe said. "Our fine constitution didn't save our people or property, so it's not likely Brother Brigham will be asking us to make any sacrifices to expand the United States."

"Are we moving on today or waiting 'til morning?" Matthew asked. In his opinion, they hadn't put enough distance between them and the man who was hunting Margarette and the children.

"We've lost half a day," Joe said. "But if the women fix a hot meal now, we could keep going until dark, then make do with leftovers for supper."

"Sounds good to me," Bart Davis said, and he was echoed by Francis and Matthew.

"We'd better call everyone together and see who wants to move on with us and who wants to stay here for a time." Matthew volunteered to find the other heads of families, and Francis joined him in the search for the others in their party.

Margarette hurried back to her wagon. She was glad to find that Anna had already started a large kettle of beans and was preparing cornbread to bake in one of the large iron kettles, but she noticed her friend didn't look rested.

"Are you feeling well enough to be doing all this?" she asked.

"I'm fine, just a little tired," Anna answered.

"Where are the children?"

"We're right here!" Jens popped up from behind the wagon. He walked toward her, holding Annelise's hand. "We went with Soren to water the oxen. He said they needed an extra drink because we stayed here longer than we usually stay."

"Mamma, Mamma!" Annelise squirmed away from Jens to run toward her mother. "I gave Flower a drink too. I like Flower the best."

"Flower?" Margarette raised her eyebrows.

"She mixes everything up." Jens looked at his sister in exasperation. "She wanted to hold the cow's rope, so Grandpa Soren let her hold the part that went from his hand down to the ground. Then she wanted to know the cow's name. Grandpa said the Finsters called the cow Buttercup, then she wanted to know what a buttercup is, and he said it's a yellow flower. I thought that was funny because the cow is black and white, but Annelise has been calling the cow Flower instead of Buttercup all morning."

"I'm sure Buttercup doesn't mind being called Flower." She swung Annelise up into her arms to give her a hug. "I think whoever named the cow Buttercup was probably thinking of the pretty yellow butter made from her milk that's just the color of buttercups. But talking about changing names reminds me of something we need to talk about. Let's climb in the wagon to talk."

She boosted Annelise inside the wagon, then followed her son. When they were settled on the large bed, she reminded Jens of the frightening experience they'd had with the man who was searching for them.

"I've been thinking it might be harder for that man to find us and take us back to Denmark if we have different names."

"That's what Peter said, so we've been pretending my name is James."

"Would James Holmes be hard for you to get used to?" she asked.

"I kind of like it," Jens admitted. "It sounds like Matthew is really my papa."

"Matthew *is* your papa. When we get to the place where Brother Brigham said we shall build a new city, we'll build a new temple, too, and if you and Annelise would like to go there with Matthew and me, you shall become Matthew's son forever. Do you think you would want that, Jens?"

"I'm not Jens anymore, Mamma," he grinned. "You have to call me James Holmes."

"All right, James Holmes." She laughed, and James giggled with delight.

"What about Annelise? She won't remember it if we give her another name." James's brow wrinkled with concern for his sister.

"She can't pronounce Annelise anyway," Margarette said. "She calls herself 'Wesa.' If we begin calling her Lisa, I think that will be enough change. And I'll be Meg Holmes. Do you think you can remember that?"

James nodded his head, and she suspected he really would remember. The ugly cruelty of his first three years had not entirely left his memory, and he longed to ally himself as closely as possible with Matthew. She drew him onto her lap and gave him a hug. Not to be left out, Annelise dropped the small rocks she'd found into her pocket and threw her arms around her mother too.

"I'm getting too big to sit on your lap," James protested at last and squirmed to be free. Laughing, Margarette let him go.

"Mine!" Lisa had found the leather thong and small pouch Meg wore about her neck. The child's little fingers pried it open and reached inside. She pulled out a tiny twig that Meg had broken from the thick shrubbery that had hidden the cabin and kept her family safe in Nauvoo. Next she pulled out a sliver of limestone that had somehow found its way inside her shoe the night she and Matthew were wed in the Nauvoo temple. There was also a seed from the last squash Hannah had left on their doorstep and three seeds from the apple Matthew had given Jens aboard the *Carolina,* a shriveled berry from their first campsite, and a tiny, fluffy feather that had dropped from the chickens' cage.

Lisa's fingers closed around another object, and she squealed with delight when she brought the large green emerald to light. "My pwitty." She stroked the gem and brought it to her cheek in a motion like that of a caress. It took all of Meg's powers of persuasion to convince Lisa to put the items back in the little bag. Only the promise of a visit with the cow, whose name suddenly changed again from Flower to Buttercup, was convincing enough.

Leaving Mount Pisgah, Meg was impressed by the fields of growing crops they passed. She learned that a leader at that camp, a man by the name of Ezra T. Benson, had been appointed to enclose and plant thousands of acres of crops for the Saints who would pass through later. These crops were to sustain them through another winter and to replenish their supplies as they moved west.

Only ten wagons departed from Mount Pisgah that afternoon. Traveling with them were Elders Woodruff and Hyde, who expressed an interest in traveling as quickly as possible in order to reach Council Bluffs, where the other Apostles were waiting. An added incentive for hurrying was their eagerness to warn Brigham Young about the military officer headed toward his encampment. Though Captain Allen insisted that the recruitment of an all-Mormon brigade was in response to an arrangement worked out by Elder Little and President Polk, Elder Woodruff and most of the leaders at Mount Pisgah had their doubts.

The wagon train moved at a rapid pace, but the next two weeks still had a pleasant quality to them. Grass for their animals was plentiful, and the storms seemed to be at an end, leaving a dry track for the wagons to follow. Buttercup provided enough milk for both the Holmes and Davis children. On occasion, Meg even churned enough butter to share with the Donaldsons and Weldons. Each time that the hens appeared to no longer be laying and she would threaten to turn them into stew, another egg or two would appear. Soren had become as sturdy and strong as many of the younger men. The children were healthy and seldom complained about the miles they walked each day. James particularly occupied himself playing with the Davis children, and when Lisa grew tired, Meg insisted that she nap inside the wagon with Anna beside her to make certain she didn't climb out. This also provided an excuse to make certain Anna rested for a time each day as well.

On this leg of their journey, Matthew began collecting all of the boys, from Collin down to James, each evening for an hour's schooling while the women prepared dinner. As soon as the wagons were drawn into a circle, the boys hurried to fetch wood and water the stock before gathering around Matthew. Without slates and only possessing a few books, the boys usually copied their letters in the dirt.

After a few days, Elder Woodruff selected a few young men with fast horses and sent them ahead to warn Brigham Young that Captain Allen was on his way. It was apparent that the wagons could not stay ahead of the military contingent. Collin was excited to be chosen, though he was a year or two younger than the other two young men. Lucy fussed with packing more food than he needed in his saddlebag and sent him off with a teary farewell, though she expected to catch up to him in little more than a week.

On their last night on the trail before reaching Council Bluffs, Meg lay beside Matthew beneath their wagon. Canvas awnings had been erected to form a sort of tent, affording them privacy and warding off any sudden weather changes. She was tired, but sleep eluded her. Though the wagon partially blocked the view, she could see a wide swath of sky sprinkled with a million stars. The air was warm, and from nearby she could hear the quiet snuffling of the horses and cattle. Occasionally, a snore from inside a wagon or tent reached her ears. Her fingers touched the small bag that had become a sort of talisman reminding her of the journey she'd undertaken when she'd fled her father-in-law's farm and the hope she carried in her heart for a real home and an opportunity for her children to grow up among people who accepted the gospel.

Beside her, Matthew stirred, shifting closer, though his breathing continued its steady, rhythmic pattern. Insomnia was a problem she wrestled with frequently. Since childhood she'd often awakened in the night feeling lost and alone. Early in her first marriage, she'd found herself frequently lying awake late into the night. Though physically exhausted, her mind wouldn't allow her to sleep.

She'd often regretted her brief marriage to Jory. Had she not been so alone and afraid . . . Had she not been so young and just lost her mother, would everything have worked out differently? There had been too much pressure then, and Jory had seemed to be her only means of having a home and someone to care for her. He said he loved her, and she'd believed him, even believed she loved him.

There was one similarity between her two marriages. She'd been afraid and had rushed into both marriages as a means of finding help and security. She'd known almost at once that her marriage to Jory was a mistake, but after almost three months of marriage to Matthew, he was still an enigma in many ways.

His hand lightly touched her waist, and she felt a pleasant little shiver. He treated her with deference and kindness, he showered her children with attention and laughter, he was ever her friend, and sometimes, in the night, he stirred a passion inside her that brought a blush to her cheeks all the next day. She suspected he'd married her out of the same loneliness and desperation that had pushed her to marry twice. And were these feelings any different from those Isaac had felt for her? Isaac was a good man, yet she'd hesitated to accept his offer.

Surely the fact that Matthew had lacked the means to travel west on his own had played a part in his decision to wed her, as had the compassion he felt for two elderly people and a single woman with two small children, who were setting out on a long and dangerous journey alone. Occasionally, she wondered if he might feel more than friendship and compassion toward her. When that question entered her mind, it was quickly followed by a question concerning her feelings for him, which she hurriedly brushed aside. Friendship was enough for her. Hadn't she learned a long time ago that love was merely a sad illusion?

While she'd lain awake watching the stars and asking unanswerable questions, Matthew had snuggled closer. His hand covered hers where she held the tiny leather pouch he'd given her after their wedding.

"Does your heart ache with regret? Do you wish you hadn't married me? Is that why you lie awake so many nights?" His voice was soft in her ear, yet it held a note of hurt that saddened her.

She was startled to discover he was awake and knew of her sleepless nights. Not for anything would she wish to hurt him. "N-n-no. I've always had nights when I couldn't sleep."

"Even when you were a child?"

"Not so often then, but sometimes after Far had been home, then had gone away again."

"Did your mother know you couldn't sleep?"

"I think she did. I remember she used to hold me. She'd sit in a big wooden rocking chair, slowly rocking back and forth with me until I fell asleep."

Matthew gathered her close, his hand slowly stroking her long hair, freeing it from its restricting braid. "Did she sing to you?"

Warmth filled her as she remembered her mother singing, the same way Meg sang to Lisa, when the little girl was restless. "Yes," she admitted.

"Something like this? 'Hush, my pretty darling, don't you cry,'" he crooned in her ear. Soft, silly words followed, and Meg felt warm and happy, just as when her mother had sung to her long ago.

* * *

They arrived at Council Bluffs to learn that Captain Allen had arrived the day before and that Elder Woodruff's messengers had arrived two days earlier. Collin came striding toward them with the news before they'd circled their wagons. Elders Woodruff and Hyde left immediately to meet with the other Apostles, and as soon as their camp was arranged, most of the adults from the ten wagons gathered around Collin and the other young men who had ridden ahead to hear a report of their ride and of Captain Allen's arrival.

"It's not the way we thought it was," one of the young men spoke up. "Most of our people are going to have to winter over here on the Missouri, but we're short on food and supplies, and this land belongs to the Indians. Brother Brigham says if five hundred men enlist, it will mean the difference between starvation and survival for our people."

"The government will let us stay on Indian land for the winter if we raise a battalion, and the pay the recruits will receive will be enough to outfit our families to go on next spring. It's already the first of July, and we've run out of time to cross the mountains before the passes are filled with snow," the second young man said, picking up the story.

"Brother Brigham says we should look on this as an opportunity and a blessing," Collin said. He cast an apologetic look at his mother. "I've already signed up. Captain Allen said they're going to need men like me who know how to properly shoe a horse or mule."

Lucy screamed and fainted dead away. While her husband and son fussed over her, the others returned to their own wagons, and a strange silence hung over their camp. Most of the men drifted away later that evening to hear more of what Captain Allen and Brother Brigham had to say.

Over the next two weeks, the camp was abuzz with talk about the battalion being formed. Brigham Young sent Heber C. Kimball and Willard Richards east to camps strung across Iowa to talk up joining the battalion, and each day more recruits were added to the roster. Matthew became withdrawn, and Meg could tell he was torn between staying with her and answering the call to arms. If he hadn't taken on the burden of her and her children, he'd be free to join the battalion. Her heart ached as her suspicion that he regretted their hasty marriage grew.

One night, he sat on the wagon tongue beside her watching the children play. Just as she started to rise to call them to get ready for bed, Matthew took her arm.

"Meg, it has been a hard decision, and I've spent much time on my knees, but I believe it is the Lord's will that I should join the battalion," he said the words slowly, as if he didn't quite wish to say them. "Brother Brigham is right. Our people are going to starve if we don't find a means to buy needed supplies."

"I could give Brother Brigham the sapphire Kraft Rundell returned to me. It would buy many barrels of flour."

"There's no one out here with money to buy an expensive jewel." He waited a moment then asked, "Do you feel that it is the Lord's desire that you donate the gem?"

"No, I have prayed about it many times, but the only answer I have received is a sense that I should give it to the Pedersens to help them build a home when we reach the place God has prepared for us."

"Unless God tells you otherwise, you should continue to hold the jewels in reserve. The battalion, I believe, is God's answer for now."

She looked across the camp, seeing cabins under construction, the river in the background, a huge herd of horses and cattle grazing in a meadow, and the children playing. At first, she didn't know what to say. She felt anger, betrayal, then acceptance. If the Lord wanted Matthew to be a soldier, then that was what he should do. But she wanted Matthew too. How could she let him go? She lowered her eyes, watching her hands twist slowly in her lap.

"I haven't signed the papers yet," he said. "I'll not go if you are against my joining the army."

She knew she was behaving selfishly. One of the things she admired about Matthew was his generosity. His decision to join the army was based on his desire to see not only her, the Pedersens, and her children have adequate supplies, but he would want all of the children from Council Bluff back to Nauvoo to have food to fill their stomachs. She thought of their supplies. Hers was one of the few wagons with sufficient supplies to go on, but her flour and meal were dwindling fast. It was impossible, not only for Matthew, but for her as well, to see others going hungry and not share.

She lifted her eyes, seeing Matthew's dark locks curling against his collar, his clear, blue eyes watching her in waiting somberness, and felt a catch in her chest. From the day she'd fled Lars's farm in Denmark, she had tried to be obedient to God. And though Brigham Young had made a strong argument for the need for funds to replenish the Saints' supplies and she could see with her own eyes the desperate plight of many of the pioneers, barrels of flour or even obedience to God's will were not uppermost in her mind. It was her heart that cried against separation from Matthew.

"Armies need laundresses. Tomorrow, I shall enlist too." She surprised herself as much as Matthew with her announcement.

19

Anna sat on a campstool fanning herself. The relentless heat of the sultry July day had sapped the energy of almost everyone in camp. Meg sat down beside her, noting that the older woman's skin had taken on a grayish tone. She hoped the dear woman hadn't caught the fever that had struck a number of people in camp, including one of Joe and Amy's sons.

"Anna, this is difficult to say."

Anna turned to face her friend.

"Matthew has decided to join the battalion. Not wishing to be separated from him, I volunteered to be a laundress, and my offer has been accepted." Before Anna could respond, Meg hurried on. "We're trading wagons and teams with the Weldons, as Matthew and Soren think the horses and smaller wagon will be easier for me to handle. There will be plenty of room for you and Soren to stay with the Weldons and share our wagon."

"My dear child." Anna placed an arm around Meg. "I've been expecting Matthew would choose to join the battalion, but I shall miss you greatly. For forty years, Soren and I wondered why we hadn't been blessed with children, but you and Matthew, along with James and Lisa, have removed that ache from our hearts. We couldn't love you more if you were our children."

"I feel you are our parents. I don't know how I would have managed if God hadn't placed my children and me near you on the voyage from Denmark and helped us to stay together all this time."

The two women sat with their arms entwined for some time, and then Meg drew the sapphire from her pocket where she had placed it earlier. Pressing it into Anna's hand, she said, "Last night Matthew and I prayed about what to do with the two remaining jewels. We both feel we should leave the sapphire with you. If the need should arise for you to buy supplies or to build a home in the mountains, it is yours to do with as you feel prompted."

"Oh, but I can't accept—"

"You must." She closed Anna's fingers around the stone. "You, yourself, told me I should trust God to tell me what to do with the jewels, and I am certain it is His will that I give the stone to you."

Anna wiped at her tears with her free hand. "Thank you," she whispered. "When Soren is too old to get work, perhaps we shall have need of it. I shall go at once and place it in our trunk for safe-keeping." She rose to her feet. Her steps were slow, and Meg walked beside her to the wagon where she assisted the older woman inside.

"Meg!"

She turned to see Matthew and Joe stumbling toward her, carrying Soren. "What happened?" She ran toward them. Behind her, she heard Anna cry out. Gently, the men placed Soren on a blanket that Meg fetched and spread out in the shade of the wagon. Anna knelt beside her husband, crying and patting his face.

"Where are you hurt?" she asked.

Seeing no wound, Meg turned a questioning look toward Matthew.

"He was helping those of us who are leaving tomorrow to separate the stock, when he suddenly collapsed."

"It was the heat," Anna exclaimed. "I told him that an old man who has lived all of his life in a north country shouldn't work so hard in this heat."

Amy arrived with a bucket of water. She thrust her way to Soren's side, where she knelt to bathe his face. Anna tore off her apron, dipped it in the water, and joined in Amy's attempt to revive Soren. After a few minutes, he coughed, then opened his eyes. He turned his head and was violently ill.

When Soren stopped puking, he leaned back and was soon asleep. All evening, Anna, Amy, and Meg took turns cooling his fevered skin as he drifted between sleep and wakefulness. The children returned from a walk with Marissa and her children and were instantly subdued when they learned Soren was ill.

Brother Brigham was called, and he arrived to give the stricken man a blessing in which Soren was promised an abundance of peace and joy along with the righteous desires of his heart. Feeling somewhat comforted, Anna hovered over her husband as he was moved inside the wagon where the Weldons would join them the following day.

Meg and Matthew slept under their wagon one last time that night to be near Soren, though their belongings had already been transferred to the Weldons' wagon. When morning arrived, they hurried to check on Soren and then brought their children to bid the Pedersens farewell.

Soren pulled himself up on one elbow. "Be kind to each other," he cautioned the children in a shaky voice. "And have faith that God will bring us together again." He lay back down, seemingly exhausted. Anna bid them a tearful farewell, then turned to Meg, unable to speak. They held each other and cried unashamed tears.

Bidding Marissa, Amy, and Lucy farewell brought more tears.

"Look after Collin for me," Lucy begged.

"I will," Meg agreed. "And take care of Soren and Anna. They are dear beyond words to me and my family."

* * *

On the morning of July twenty-first, Meg maneuvered her wagon into position midway in the lineup driven mostly by the women who were accompanying the battalion. She blinked to hold back tears that threatened to fall. Bidding the Pedersens and the friends they'd made over the past few months farewell had been difficult. She could still hear Lisa's sobs coming from the back of the wagon. The little girl had no memory of a time when the Pedersens had not been a part of their family and was heartbroken by the pending separation. Meg wondered if she would see her dear friends again in this life. It was painful to see Soren stricken and feeble when he had been her strength for so long. They were both weighed down with years, and Anna had seemed short of breath and fatigued of late.

James sat beside her on the wagon seat. A cloud of dust a short distance ahead marked the beginning of the long march for Matthew,

Joe and Clay Donaldson, and Collin Weldon. Olaf was there too, she'd learned, but assigned to a different company.

The wagons began to move, and she slapped the reins across the broad backs of Frank Weldon's horses, signaling for them to move ahead. She'd left the chickens with Lucy and the cow with Marissa. The Davises promised to care for Buttercup until they met again somewhere beyond the Rocky Mountains. Lisa had bid the cow a tearful farewell.

Spotting Amy Donaldson in the crowd gathered to see them off, Meg waved. Since Joe had been selected to be an officer, Amy could have joined the thirty-five women making the trek had not her youngest son, Jeremiah, fallen ill. After a great deal of prayer and turmoil, the couple had decided it would be best for their son if Amy and her son David stayed behind to winter over at the encampment on the banks of the Missouri. David, who would be sixteen in a month's time, was charged with looking after his mother and younger brother.

"Good-bye, Peter! Good-bye, Johnny!" James rose to his feet to call to his friends who stood beside their parents, waving frantically. Meg waved too. She would miss Marissa, Lucy, and Amy; they had become the sisters she'd always longed for. She'd miss Anna most of all.

She spotted Olaf's Katrina and waved to her. Swollen with their first child, she stood beside her aunt and uncle, waving her handkerchief toward the troops long after they had passed out of sight.

For a time, Meg was occupied with managing the horses, but it soon became apparent that the well-trained animals needed little in the way of direction when they only needed to follow the wagon ahead of them. James crawled inside the wagon to play with his sister, and Meg fingered the leather thong at her throat and let her mind wander. Just that morning, as she'd folded Lisa's quilt, she'd found a long silver hair, left there unwittingly by Anna. She'd coiled it on a finger and placed it inside the little bag with the other small mementos she'd collected. What a strange journey her life had become.

Even her name was different. She found it difficult to think of herself as Meg and to introduce herself by the new name. She wasn't the only one who had trouble with the new name. Matthew sometimes forgot and occasionally called her Margarette. Shortening Annelise's name to Lisa wasn't so difficult, and it was becoming easier to call Jens James, but she stumbled over the shortened version of her own name.

Captain Allen proved to be a considerate officer who marched the new soldiers two hundred miles down the east side of the Missouri River and allowed the married men who had wives in the company to join their families after supper each night. He treated the men with courtesy, and most were content with their lot, though those who were separated from their loved ones missed their families and spent their evenings listening to a fiddle player or composing letters that they hoped would be carried back to their families once the recruits reached Fort Leavenworth.

Having the sole responsibility of her children, working with the other women, and caring for the wagon and horses left Meg exhausted each night, but when she lay beside Matthew, feeling his warmth and hearing him breathe, she didn't doubt they'd made the right decision to undertake this journey together. On the nights that Matthew stood watch, Meg found sleep difficult and wondered about her dependence on him. Those were the times when she had to remind herself that their marriage was an arrangement between friends. Still, she found herself recounting the stories she'd heard of husbands and wives who had grown to love each other after they were wed.

Two weeks later, they crossed the river and entered Fort Leavenworth, Kansas. Meg welcomed a respite from the constant traveling. She pitched in with the other women to wash the clothing and uniforms of the more than five hundred battalion members while James and Lisa got acquainted with the other children traveling with the battalion. Matthew drew his clothing allowance and sent half of it back to Soren and Anna, then added another five dollars to assist the poor Saints who needed help getting out of Nauvoo. He kept little for himself, as the Army furnished most of their supplies.

Meg saw little of Matthew as he and Joe were kept busy supervising the loading of the baggage wagons, attending meetings, and drilling their men. Joe had been selected to serve as a captain, and he'd chosen Matthew for his lieutenant. One evening, after settling the children in bed, Meg returned to the fire to wait, hoping that Matthew would be allowed to join her.

"Sister Holmes." She looked up to see Olaf coming toward her. She arose, extending her hands in greeting.

"Just because Matthew and I are now wed, there is no need for formality."

"I saw Matthew a short time ago. He said I should not use your first name because of the detective who is pursuing you."

"You can call me Meg." She motioned for him to sit on a camp-stool. "We missed you when you left, and we often wondered if you and Katrina were well."

"At first, it was hard because of the poor weather, and we were all so unfamiliar with the tasks that needed doing, but we persevered. Katrina's aunt and uncle have been kind to us, but we are anxious to have a home of our own."

"Yes, we are anxious to have a home too, but if the Pedersens wish to live with us, we shall welcome them."

"I wanted to tell you," Olaf appeared nervous. "Brigham Young sent a rider to take letters and money back to our families in Winter Quarters. He brought word that attacks on the poor saints in Nauvoo have escalated, and many of those who remain have suffered greatly. Even those Nauvoo citizens who are not members have been attacked by the unruly mobs. Kraft Rundell is one who lost his life when he was attacked and his business burned to the ground."

Tears formed in her eyes. "But for him, we wouldn't have been able to escape. He was a man with many faults, but there was good in him, too, and I cannot but mourn for him."

"Sister Holmes! Sister Holmes!" Two young men dashed into the firelight. "We saw . . ." Their voices trailed off, and they saluted sharply.

"Sergeant Kjelstrom!" Clay and Collin spoke in unison. Olaf looked uncomfortable.

Laughing, Meg told her visitors, "Around my fire, there are no ranks, just friends."

"We stopped by to tell you," Collin looked hesitantly at Olaf before turning his attention back to Meg, "that we met some soldiers who recently arrived here from St. Louis, where they said some foreigner had posted a reward for information concerning Margarette, Jens, and Annelise Jorgensen. He was passing out posters to the soldiers headed west and to the Oregon-bound wagon trains. The soldiers brought one of the posters with them."

"We saw it, ma'am. It has a pretty good likeness of you on it," Clay added, looking apologetic.

Meg sat down heavily on the wagon tongue. Her hands covered her face, and her shoulders shook. Coming on top of the news about Kraft Rundell, it seemed more than she could bear. "What am I going to do? Why won't that wicked man leave us alone?"

Olaf crouched before her. "You have friends, and we'll not let you down. I heard a rumor of what your young friends came to tell you, and warning you is part of the reason I came tonight. Some of the regular soldiers are planning to stroll through our camp tomorrow looking for the woman on the poster. Katrina is on my mind a lot, and I remember a threat she made to cut her hair, claiming she was tired of the heavy braids she wears atop her head and that she wished to look like other women. It is true her thick, yellow braids, like yours, reveal you are Scandinavian. Perhaps if you cut—"

"Cut my hair?" It was almost a scream.

"Remember how Sister Davis put molasses in Jens . . . uh, James's and Lisa's hair?" Clay asked with a grin.

"We have something better than molasses," Clay added. "Pa and Matthew told us to bring their supplies back here, and they were both issued shoe blacking."

Meg looked at the three eager faces gathered around her. They meant well, but her hair? Lisa whimpered in her sleep, and Meg knew the young men were right. She'd do anything to keep her children safe.

"It won't be so bad," Collin said, looking apologetic. "I've been trimming horses' manes and tails, then giving them a shine with boot polish most of my life."

She swallowed and brushed a hand across her damp eyes. "All right, but it might be best to use my mending scissors rather than the clippers I've seen you use on the horses."

Collin insisted she sit on the stool before the fire. It felt strange, almost indecent, to remove the wooden pins from her hair and run her fingers through the long strands that reached almost to the ground. Few men, only Jory, Soren, and Matthew, had ever viewed her hair completely unbound. For just a moment, she wondered if she should wait for Matthew to return and cut her hair for her. But she knew it couldn't wait. She didn't even know if he would make it back to their wagon before dawn.

"Be quick about it," she whispered.

The first long lock fell to her lap, and her fingers curled around it. A tear leaked its way down her cheek, dropping to her hands. The next long tress landed at her feet. She saw Olaf reach for it, a look of pain etched on his face, and she knew he was picturing Katrina's long golden hair. He flung the lock into the fire. It was quickly followed by another and another.

When Collin finished, Meg lifted her hands to touch what was left of her hair. It fell to just below her shoulders, leaving her head feeling strangely light. When she turned her head, she felt it brush against her cheeks.

"Now to change the color." Collin lifted the bottle of boot blacking.

"Wait." Meg held up her hand to stop the application of black polish. "I'd like to try something else. I fear boot polish will look strange. My mother used to dye cloth with mixtures of plants or roots seeped in boiling water. I want to see if one of her recipes will work on hair. Tea has seeped in that pot all day." She pointed to a teakettle hanging over the cook fire.

She reached for the pot. Then taking the long lock she'd held in her lap, she dipped one end into the strong mixture. After a few minutes, she drew it out to reveal that it had turned a light brown.

"But won't it wash right out?" Clay asked.

"Not if it's rinsed with vinegar," Collin pointed out.

When the young men finished with her hair, Meg bid them good night, then returned to the stool beside the fire to brush it dry. It dried more quickly than her long hair had, but she continued to sit, watching the line of red beneath the edge of a half-burned log. She made no move to stir up the fire. It was August, and the nights didn't seem to cool much from the blistering daytime heat, but she shivered as though touched by a chill wind.

Hearing a sound behind her, she turned to see Matthew staring at her.

"Meg? Is that you?" His voice was tentative.

"Yes, Matthew."

"Is something wrong? You should be sleeping." He walked toward her, concern in his voice. He stopped, then reached out a hand to touch her hair. "What have you done?" There was a catch in his voice.

"Oh, Matthew." Suddenly she was in his arms, sobbing out the story.

"I shall miss your golden crown," he whispered against her ear. "But the safety of you and the children is of far more importance to me."

"I should have waited until you came."

"It was likely best that I was not here." With his arm around her shoulders, he led her to the wagon and helped her climb inside. Most of the men slept in small tents, six men to a tent, but Captain Allen permitted those officers whose wives were present to join them at night, and now Matthew sank down beside his wife on the mattress. On the prairie they would have slept beneath the wagon to catch the evening breezes, but inside the fort it was considered safer for the women and children to sleep inside their wagons. He seemed distracted, and she wondered if he were upset about her hair.

Once they were settled, he cleared his throat several times, then spoke in the straightforward way he addressed most issues. "Joe received a letter from Amy when the courier arrived today." He hesitated, and his voice was tinged with sadness. "Soren never recovered from the heatstroke. He died four days after the battalion left camp. His death was too much for Anna. She collapsed at his graveside and was buried beside him the next day."

"No!" Meg couldn't believe it. "I should have been there to help them." She began to cry.

"They wouldn't want you to feel guilty because you weren't there. Soren told me they left their home and all they knew in Denmark because they wanted to be sealed in the temple so they would be together for eternity. They achieved that goal, he said, and more. Being needed by you and your children, he said, brought them the greatest joy they'd ever known."

"They never wished to be apart. If they had to leave this life, I'm glad they didn't have to wait years to be together again. But I shall sorely miss them."

Matthew held her close, whispering soothing words until she fell asleep. Just before sleep claimed her, she heard him whisper, "Sleep well, my love."

When she awoke, she was alone, and she wondered if she'd dreamed those words. Still, she held that softly whispered phrase close to her heart and found herself taking comfort from it during the difficult days ahead as she mourned the loss of Anna and Soren.

* * *

Matthew stood before Meg one morning a few days later, one foot resting on the wagon tongue. He leaned forward to daub boot black on his boots. "Captain Hunt said he'd be more comfortable with a regular officer leading the battalion, but Joe and I feel he'll do fine until Captain Allen catches up to us. Most of the men feel good about Captain Hunt leading us."

"Wouldn't it be better to wait a few days until the captain can travel?" she asked.

"No, Captain Allen is adamant that we obey orders."

Those orders were to advance at once to join the regiment ahead of them headed by General Stephen W. Kearney. The battalion would leave Fort Leavenworth for Santa Fe at dawn on the morrow. The men were eager to be on their way, believing their two weeks of training had aided a great deal in shaping farm boys and factory workers into some semblance of an army, though they were aware that they were in no way seasoned soldiers. Anxious to be with their families again, they wished to complete their military service as quickly as possible.

Many of the men were ill from the terrible heat and the fevers they'd contracted during their sojourn along the Missouri River. Most expected they would feel better as they moved away from the sultry heat around Fort Leavenworth. Besides, with the addition of baggage wagons, the men expected to no longer be quite as encumbered as they had been by their gear, making their march easier. Unfortunately, Captain Allen was one of those laid low by the fever.

Matthew picked up a soft cloth to buff his boots while he explained the preparations that were being made.

"Prepare porridge tonight," he told Meg. "In the morning, it can be sliced and eaten cold, which will speed preparations." He set the cloth inside the wagon and stopped beside her. He stretched out a hand to brush a strand of her now light brown hair behind her ear. "Don't wait up for me." He kissed her cheek and hurried away to join Joe and the other officers in making final preparations for their departure.

They left the fort the next morning under the command of Jefferson Hunt, a Mormon captain appointed by the Church's leaders. Meg awoke to find Lisa listless and whiney. With little time to give her the attention the little girl wanted, Meg worked quickly to harness the horses and pull her wagon into position while shouting instructions to James for looking after his sister. She silently prayed that her daughter hadn't contracted the fever that had laid so many soldiers low and necessitated that Captain Allen be left behind.

She put off telling them about the Pedersens. Lisa was too young to understand anyway, but she would need to find the right moment to tell James.

"Mamma, Lisa wants a drink," James called as the wagon approached the gates of the fort.

"I can't reach the water barrel right now. See if she'll drink cider." The cider jug was still sitting on the floor from the night Collin had used the cider in place of vinegar to set the color in her hair.

"Uh oh."

Meg cringed. "What's wrong?" She didn't dare turn to look, as the gate sentries were stopping each wagon to peer inside and she had her hands full managing the horses.

"Lisa puked."

"Oh dear, clean her up the best you can," she instructed. "Whoa!" She pulled back on the reins, keeping a tight grip on the well-rested animals that were now frisky and anxious to move out.

One sentry looked up at her as though memorizing her features, while two others went to the back of the wagon to peer inside. Hoping her light brown hair drawn in a chignon at the back of her neck was an adequate disguise, she tried to appear relaxed and unconcerned.

"Whew!" one sentry shouted from the back of the wagon. "There's just a couple of sick kids back here."

"Them Mormons are in for a rotten time with so many sick folks," the other soldier said.

"Those kids got straw-colored hair?" The sentry at the front of the wagon asked, and Meg's heart skipped a beat. Stopping all of the wagons to peer inside was just a ruse to search for her and the children. What would the sentry do when he saw James and Lisa's pale hair?

"Naw! Looks dark to me," he called back, and Meg barely resisted turning her head to look at her children. She couldn't do more than wonder why the children's hair appeared dark. The lead pair of horses tossed their heads and stamped their hooves, impatient at the delay.

"You may go," the sentry said, and Meg lost no time slapping the reins across the backs of the eager animals, urging them forward.

They traveled some distance before she dared call to James. "Is Lisa any better?"

"She made a really big mess, but she's sleeping now."

"Can you hear her sleeping?" Meg considered pulling aside to check on her daughter.

James climbed onto the wagon seat beside Meg. "She's making that whistling noise."

Meg's hunched shoulders relaxed. She was familiar with the sound Lisa made when she fell asleep with two fingers in her mouth. She glanced down at her son to discover he was wet and his hair really was dark. He also smelled strongly of cider. He sat with hunched shoulders, not meeting her eyes. A dark red circle showed on the back of his hand.

"What happened?"

"I tried to pour Lisa a cup of cider like you said, but she wanted to help and the jug fell. I got it really fast, but it splashed all over us. There was a cloth hanging on a nail. I wiped off my hair, then used it to dry Lisa's hair, but it turned her hair black, and the black got all over my hands and on your quilt."

Meg's puzzlement turned to understanding as she remembered seeing Matthew polish his boots then hang the cloth he'd used to buff them on a nail inside the wagon the night before.

"I'm sorry, Mamma. I tried to help, but Lisa doesn't mind me so good." He paused and she saw him manfully square his shoulders. "She bit me because I wouldn't let her pour the cider."

"It's all right, son." She put an arm around his forlorn shoulders. "I think Lisa isn't terribly sick, and we can clean up the mess when we stop for lunch. I also think that Lisa's illness and the boot dye in her hair were part of Heavenly Father's plan to keep us safe. Those soldiers back at the gate were looking for children with pale hair. When they saw you and Lisa with boot dye in your hair and smelled how bad our wagon stinks, they let us go."

* * *

A rider approached camp a few days later. Expecting Captain Allen to be rejoining them, the men were disappointed to learn that he had died. An air of uncertainty hung over the battalion for several days. A petition was sent to President Polk requesting that Captain Hunt remain their leader, but they learned that First Lieutenant A. J. Smith of the regular army was already en route to assume command.

At first, Joe and Matthew were pleased to learn that Lieutenant Smith was a stickler for order and punctuality. They told Meg that some of the men were lacking in discipline and held up the battalion with their tardiness and casual attention to orderliness—shortcomings Captain Hunt had been unable to correct.

In a few days, a swell of grumbling had grown against the lieutenant. Determined to meet up with General Kearny in Santa Fe, he began each day's march earlier and ended it later. Appearing to hold the battalion in contempt, he ignored the Mormon officers' pleas for consideration of their men and animals. Meg took to keeping the children inside the sweltering wagon and wearing a scarf tied about her face to ward off the dust as the soldiers and the baggage wagons left the wives and laundresses' wagons to bring up the rear in a thick cloud of roiling dust that hid the ruts and rocks that threatened to disable their wagons.

One morning, as Meg struggled to see her lead pair through the dust, she thought she heard someone call her name. Tilting her head to hear over the rumble of wagons, squeaking leather, and the jangle of harnesses, she heard the call again, then saw two figures stumbling out of the dust cloud toward her. Pulling the reins to guide the horses off the track, she gave up her position in the line of wagons.

"Sister Holmes, you got to help Collin. He's real sick." Clay staggered forward with his shoulder beneath his friend's arm. Collin appeared only semiconscious, with his head hanging limply, almost to his chest.

20

Clay helped Collin into the wagon, then turned to leave.

"I've got to catch up to my unit before Lieutenant Smith learns I left or I'll be in big trouble," he hastily explained before disappearing back into the cloud of dust. Meg stared helplessly after him.

After a moment's hesitation, she climbed down from the wagon seat to place a few dippers of water in a bucket. This she handed to James.

"Set aside a dipper of water for Collin to drink if he's thirsty. Then wring out a cloth and wash his face," she told her son. "Keep washing him until the water is gone. Let Lisa help."

Meg climbed on the wagon, looked back once to see her children with wet cloths on either side of poor Collin, and hoped their ministrations would do more good than harm. She shook out the reins, and the horses plodded on.

When they made camp that night, she found Collin able to sit up. He drank a few sips of broth, then fell asleep.

Matthew arrived, looking tired and disheveled, with a rim of red marking his eyes where they looked out from his grimy face. On finding Collin in their wagon and Meg upset over Clay's abrupt abandonment of him, he tried to explain.

"When Lieutenant Smith arrived, he brought several aides and an army doctor."

"A doctor?" Meg interrupted. "Then we should call him to see to Collin. The boy is dreadfully ill with the fever."

"The doctor is the problem," Matthew spoke slowly, as though hesitant to go on. "It seems he's quite opposed to Mormons. He accuses the soldiers who are sick of malingering to get out of performing their duties. Unless a soldier passes out and is left beside the trail for the sick wagon to pick up, he refuses all medical exemptions from duty. The sick men must march, carrying all their gear, no matter how ill they are."

"But that is cruel. Collin is so sick, he can barely sit up. He certainly can't march."

When morning came, Meg heard a series of notes sounded by the bugler and was appalled to see Collin climb from the wagon and stagger toward the sound. A wagon driven by a soldier stopped to pick him up, and she could see it was already filled with men who appeared gravely ill.

"You can't—" She started toward him, intent on bringing him back.

"He has to go." Matthew caught her arm, checking her movement.

"But I promised Lucy I'd look after him." She tried to free herself.

"You mustn't interfere," Matthew warned. "Dr. Sanderson could have him flogged for failure to appear for roll call. By reporting to sick call, he'll be given medicine."

Collin hadn't returned by the time the column moved out, and Meg spent all day worrying about him and wondering if he was one of the poor men bouncing over the rutted trail in the sick wagon. When Matthew arrived at the wagon late that night, she bombarded him with questions, only to learn that the boy had thrown up repeatedly after receiving Dr. Sanderson's medicine and had been carried to the sick wagon, where he'd lain in a stupor under the blazing sun all day. Under the cover of darkness, Matthew and Joe had moved him to his tent, where Clay had promised to watch over him through the night.

A few hours into the next day's march, Matthew climbed onto the wagon seat beside her.

"Clay and Joe are bringing Collin," he told her. "He didn't take the doctor's medicine this morning. He learned from one of the other ill men that the medicine the doctor is passing out is made up of calomel and arsenic, which makes the men puke. So Clay helped him bury the dose he was given in his cup and has been carrying both his gear and Collin's while Collin has attempted to keep up with his unit. Collin fainted. Fortunately Joe saw him go down."

"What should I do?" Meg gasped.

"Should I wash him again?" Meg and Matthew both turned to see that James had climbed up behind them and had been listening.

"Yes," Matthew told him. "And get him to drink as much water as you can."

The days that followed saw Collin shrink to a skeletal shadow of the husky young man who began the journey. By only pretending to take his medication, he became strong enough to begin the march each day, but by mid-morning, he would creep inside Meg's wagon to lie exhausted until shortly before Lieutenant Smith called a halt for the night.

After a time, the long days and forced marches began to run together. James and Lisa became cranky, and Lisa frequently whined and cried. There was no time to visit or share tasks with the other women, though Meg began to suspect that she wasn't the only one harboring an ailing soldier in her wagon. Collin took a turn for the worse, and from the bits of gossip that came her way, she learned that the doctor had discovered that the ill Mormons were burying their medicine instead of swallowing it, so using one rusty spoon for all of the sick men, he went down the line of those who were sick, forcing them each to take the medicine in his presence, one after another.

On a still, hot September day, the company came to a halt near the Arkansas River and began setting up camp. Stragglers who had been unable to keep up the pace continued to trickle into camp for several hours.

A ripple of excitement spread through camp when a sentry announced the approach of a group of travelers headed east. A shout went up, and someone summoned Captain Hunt, who issued a hearty greeting when he learned the group led by John Brown was a group of Mormon men from Mississippi and other southern states. Lieutenant Smith invited the travelers to join the officers for a discussion of trail conditions and of any savages who might be in the area.

On hearing that the visitors were from the Southern States, Matthew hurried to meet them and was delighted to encounter old friends, whom he invited back to his wagon to meet his wife and children, while Lieutenant Smith and Captain Hunt entertained the leaders of the group.

"Your pa's a fine man." One of the visitors spoke to James, shaking his hand as though he were an adult. "I had a hard time accepting the gospel 'fore he come along and explained things slow and easy, so's I could study it out keerful. Your pa's a mighty fine teacher."

James nodded his head in agreement.

Meg listened as the men talked with Matthew, and she felt a measure of pride occasioned by the respect they showed him. Talk of missionary experiences shifted to an account of the group's travels.

"We left Monroe County, Mississippi, on the eighth April," a tall, thin man explained. "There were twenty-four men in our group; most had wives and a passel of children. When we reached Independence, we met up with the Crowe family who were planning to meet the Nauvoo Saints somewhere along the trail, same as we were. We decided to travel together, figuring a train with sixty adults would provide some protection against Indians."

"Not wanting to be left behind," another brother picked up the story, "we set a right smart pace and reached the Platte River by mid-June. We waited around for two weeks, not knowing if we were ahead or behind the Nauvoo bunch. When no one showed up, we figured we were behind and followed the Oregon Trail to Fort Laramie. There, we learned there weren't any Mormons ahead of us or, as far as anyone knew, behind us either."

"We was right perplexed about what to do," the man who credited Matthew with aiding in his conversion said, "'til some of the trappers invited us to winter over with them at Pueblo, near Bent's Fort. We arrived there on the seventh of August. It's a fine place in a sheltered valley with water and trees. We set right in building cabins, and some of the men traded work for supplies at the fort, and some of the trappers offered us meat in exchange for building cabins for them."

"Brigham Young and the folks from Nauvoo are planning to winter over in Iowa," Matthew said. "They ran out of supplies early on." He went on to explain about the battalion and ended by asking, "With a good place to settle down for the winter and with access to supplies, why are you heading back east?"

"Most of us still have family and friends in Mississippi. We're headed back there to lead them out here," the first man answered.

After the men returned to their own camp, Matthew was quiet, and Meg feared that he regretted leaving the South to hurry back to Nauvoo. If he'd stayed with John Brown and the others, he'd be looking forward to reaching their destination in the spring instead of being married to her and enlisting in the battalion, with its endless marching.

When they retired to the wagon and lay side-by-side, Matthew took her hand. "Lieutenant Smith is up to something. It's not like him to be so gracious to Mormons, and he was practically falling all over John Brown."

"He can't conscript them, can he?"

"I don't think so, but he means to use the information they gave him some way."

* * *

Morning brought more than the usual amount of confusion. The wagon she usually followed was not in its place, and the teams were left standing idle long after they should have been underway. The children were cranky and begged to sit on the wagon seat beside her. She finally relented with the warning that they would have to climb back into the wagon as soon as the march began.

"I don't care if it's dusty. I'm tired of playing with Lisa in the wagon," James complained. "She bites, and I saw some boys I could play with a little while ago."

"Lisa hasn't bitten you for three days, and those boys' ma will make them stay inside their wagon too as soon as we start moving."

"Why can't I march with Papa? I can march fast." He continued to search for an excuse to avoid being cooped up in the wagon another day.

The wagon Meg found herself behind was pulled by four mules that balked, demonstrating their objection to the change in the lineup. Not trusting their unpredictable antics, Meg took care to keep a little more distance than usual between her horses and the wagon in front of her.

Matthew dropped back to speak to her an hour after they got underway. He swung aboard the moving wagon and spoke quickly. "Lieutenant Smith sent some of the men who are ill back to the settlement the Mississippi men told us about last night. He sent their wives and children, too. Captain Nelson Higgins and his men were assigned as escort. Collin was one of those sent to Pueblo."

"Collin? But I promised Lucy . . ."

"Perhaps he'll get the care he needs now." Bitterness tinged Matthew's voice. "At least Dr. Sanderson won't be able to continue poisoning him."

"But who will look after him? He's just a boy, only turned eighteen two months past."

"Once he reaches the settlement at Pueblo, the sisters will look after him. They're good women. It's the battalion I fear for. He was our only blacksmith. Besides, we were promised that our group would not be broken up." Matthew slipped off of the wagon box to disappear into the cloud of dust ahead of Meg.

The nights grew cooler, and with the beginnings of fall weather, Lieutenant Smith demanded the troops move faster. The faster pace wore heavily on the men, but it placed a greater strain on the women, children, animals, and wagons. When the mule carts heaped with baggage began to break down, the men were ordered to carry their own bedrolls, food, cooking pans, tents, and clothing, as well as their weapons, ammunition, and canteens. Many of the heavily burdened soldiers, especially those who were ill, often crept into camp so far behind their units, they scarcely had time to roll out their bedrolls before the bugle called them to resume their march.

More men fell ill, and those who were already ill failed to recover. Most denied they were ill until they collapsed, as Doctor Sanderson and his poisonous medicine were a strong deterrent to seeking help. The women who were official laundresses often found their wagons filled with soldiers attempting to evade the sick wagon and the doctor's ministrations. Joe and a number of officers repeatedly petitioned Lieutenant Smith to intercede on the sick men's behalf, but he refused to do so.

October arrived and with it a rider from Santa Fe with orders to rendezvous at that town in less than a week. Lieutenant Smith picked the healthiest of the men and stock to race forward, unhampered by wagons or those who were too ill to comply with the order, and the rest of the battalion followed as quickly as they could.

Being one of the few men whose family was with him, Matthew stayed behind while Joe, his son, Clay, and Olaf were chosen for the advance party. Two days later, Meg regretted that Matthew had remained behind.

He didn't appear at their wagon that evening to eat supper with her. She fed the children and encouraged them to run races and play with children from the other wagons until bedtime. The battalion had been slowly climbing for some time, and at the higher altitude, the nights were cold. A chill wind swept across the campground. Meg had just placed the few remaining chunks of wood she'd managed to gather onto the fire when two men entered the circle of light around her campfire. They were carrying Matthew.

"Sister Holmes." The older of the two men spoke. "Lieutenant Holmes was knocked down this morning by a mule he was harnessing. The fool critter stepped on his leg. Dr. Sanderson says it's busted."

"Matthew!" Meg rushed to his side, then seeing he was unconscious, motioned for the men to place him inside the wagon on the mattress. "Why did you wait so long to bring him to me?"

"Doc set his leg, then gave him some of his medicine afore ordering two aides to put him in the sick wagon. Barnes—he's one of our mates what's been sick a lot—was in the wagon, and when we went to get him tonight and take him to our tent, he said the lieutenant was conscious and mad as a hornet to start with, and then he started puking. After awhile he told Barnes his name and said he wanted to be taken to his wife's wagon. As the day wore on he started mumbling things Barnes couldn't understand, then he passed out. We promised Barnes we'd bring him here."

"Thank you," Meg told them. "Place him in the wagon, and I'll care for him from here on."

They did as she asked, then hurried away.

She crawled into the wagon and knelt beside Matthew. By leaving the rear wagon flap open, she could just see his face, which appeared pinched and drained. She positioned him as comfortably as possible, noticing how thin he'd become during the long march. His skin felt hot, so she fetched a bucket of water and clean rags. Carefully, she wiped away the grime covering his face and stroked his temples with the cooling cloth.

"Matthew," she whispered over and over as she fought unsuccessfully to reduce his fever. Sometime during the long night, her words changed to prayer, and she pleaded with God to spare Matthew and make him well.

James awoke. He climbed out of his bed and crawled across the mattress to kneel beside Meg. He watched Matthew for several minutes before turning to his mother to ask, "Is Papa going to die?"

"No," Meg answered, her voice fierce. "Brother Brigham promised the officers that if they would be faithful and remember their prayers, they would be safe."

"If Grandpa Pedersen were here, he'd bless Papa to get better."

Meg didn't see her son slip from the back of the wagon, and she didn't notice he was gone until he returned with two men she remembered from brief services held on the Sundays before Lieutenant Smith had taken over command of the battalion.

"Sister Holmes, your son says your husband is in need of a blessing." She turned to see a man she barely recognized. He climbed into the wagon, taking care not to step on Lisa. He was followed by the second man. They worked their way forward until they knelt beside Matthew.

"Do you wish us to give your husband a blessing?" one asked. She nodded her head and moved a little distance away to allow them more room. Peace and hope filled Meg's heart as they prayed. She felt James's small hand grip hers, and she squeezed it back. When the two elders finished, the older one shook her hand and whispered, "Don't lose faith. He'll come around."

The younger one also clasped her hand before leaving. "Don't let the doc give him any more medicine," he whispered. "Brigham Young counseled us before we left Iowa not to accept any chemical potions for our ills, and I've noticed that those men the doctor has treated have only grown more ill."

After they left, she resumed bathing Matthew's face and chest. She was aware of her son watching.

"Go back to bed," she whispered. "Tomorrow I shall have to drive the wagon, and it will be up to you to care for Papa. You must rest now so you can help when you're needed."

"All right, Mamma." He crawled slowly to the foot of the mattress and dropped to his bed on the floor.

She continued wringing out the rag in cool water, and then drawing it slowly across Matthew's fevered brow. After a time, her ministrations paid off. She heard him mumble a few words, then speak her name.

"Margarette." He spoke in the faintest of whispers.

"I'm here," she whispered back. His breathing changed, becoming slow and even. She sensed that he was no longer unconscious, but sleeping. She continued her attempt to bring down his fever, but gradually her hand slowed, her head drooped, and the next thing she knew, she awoke curled at Matthew's side. Her eyes flew open, and she was staring into Matthew's wide blue eyes.

"Matthew! You're awake."

"I am, but I fear we've overslept."

She sat up abruptly as she recognized the unmistakable notes of roll call coming from a distant bugle. When Matthew attempted to sit up, she shoved him back down none too gently.

"Don't you dare try to stand on that leg," she hissed.

"I have to—"

"No, you don't. Not even a sadist can expect an unconscious man with a broken leg to appear for roll call."

"But I'm not unconscious."

"You *will* be when Sanderson and his aides come looking for you, even if I have to hit you over the head with a skillet!" She clambered to her feet.

"James." She awoke her son. "Look after Papa and Lisa while I harness the horses."

She paused only long enough to stir up the fire and set a kettle of water to boil before fetching the horses. The worn animals plodded obediently to their positions on either side of the wagon tongue, and with practiced skill, Meg hooked up the traces.

When she finished with the horses, she stirred a handful of oats into the hot water and filled three mugs with the watery porridge. She quickly swallowed hers, then refilled it. Minutes later, she passed the mugs up to James.

"If anyone asks, that mug is mine," she pointed to the tin cup she'd refilled. "But I would be very happy to share it with Papa. Get dressed and help Lisa fasten her gown. You'll both have to visit the bushes quickly before we start moving."

When the doctor appeared alongside her wagon, shortly after the march began, he deigned to crawl inside the moving wagon.

"Lieutenant Smith's orders are to move forward without delay," Meg shouted from her perch on the wagon seat, indicating she had no intention of halting the wagon.

"Your husband needs to be treated," the doctor called back.

"He was unconscious when he was brought here last night!" she snapped back.

"That leg will fester, and he'll get an infection without treatment."

"I won't force anything down his throat while he's unable to move for fear he'll choke!" She slapped the reins across the horses' backs, encouraging a faster pace.

"Give him this when he awakes." The doctor passed a twisted paper to one of his aides who set it on the seat beside Meg. "I'll be by to check on him when we halt tonight." He spurred his horse and galloped away, his aides following.

Meg left the tonic-filled paper where it had been set. Occasionally she glanced toward it. Was it possible the potion might help Matthew? She remembered the elder's advice. If Brother Brigham had cautioned against the use of medicines, then she'd make certain none was forced on Matthew. It wasn't long before the wagon lurched over an unseen rock and the paper fell to the ground to be run over and trampled into the dirt.

When the doctor returned that evening, he checked the splint he'd placed on Matthew's leg the day before. Matthew groaned in response to the doctor's pushing and poking. The sound brought Lisa scooting across the bed to hold Papa's hand. When the doctor attempted to force his spoon between his patient's clenched teeth, Lisa sank her teeth into the hand holding the vile medicine.

"Stop that this minute!" the doctor shouted, jerking his hand back. The medicine spilled across his patient's shirt. Grasping Lisa, the doctor stepped down from the wagon.

Seeing his sister squirming and screaming in the doctor's grasp, James delivered a swift kick to the man's shins.

"Let my sister go!" he shouted.

Meg, who had been standing beside the wagon unsure of what action to take, reached for her daughter. "Apologize at once," she ordered James.

"He was hurting Lisa." James scowled at the doctor.

"I didn't hurt your sister," the doctor defended himself. "She bit my hand and spilled her father's medicine."

"Lisa!" Meg scolded. "You know biting isn't allowed. Now apologize. Both of you."

"I'm sorry," James mumbled.

"Saw-wee." Lisa smiled a brilliant smile and batted her long lashes. When the doctor turned to walk away, she stuck out her tongue, and Meg couldn't bring herself to reprimand her for doing what she herself felt like doing.

21

Matthew's condition became a constant source of concern for Meg. His face twisted in pain with each movement of the wagon, and his skin felt warm to her touch, though not so heated as poor Collin's had been. She squeezed water from a cloth each time the march stopped, letting the excess water run back into the bucket, then gently bathed Matthew's face and chest. Though James was much too young for so much responsibility, she sometimes left him on the wagon seat to hold the reins while she tended to Matthew. Other times, she left Matthew's care to her young children while she drove the wagon across a landscape more austere and strange than any she had ever imagined.

Sometimes, as she stared across the bleak, rocky terrain, she thought about Collin and grew even more scared. Had Collin made it to Pueblo? He'd been nearly delirious with fever and unable to feed himself or drink without assistance when the Higgins party began their trek to meet up with the Southern Saints. How could she face Francis and Lucy if their son died? And what would she and her children do if they lost Matthew?

For a couple of days, Meg kept up a stubborn tug-of-war with the doctor. His examinations were cursory, and he kept a distance from his patient—and from Lisa. Sometimes he sent one of the assistants he'd brought with him from Fort Leavenworth, and Meg found them surly and rude. Each day he left medicine, and each day Meg buried it or allowed it to be trampled underfoot by the horses and run over by the wagon. Then, on the ninth of October, the battalion arrived in Santa Fe.

Colonel Alexander Doniphan, who knew many of the men from when he'd sided with them in Missouri, ordered a one-hundred-gun salute to honor the Mormon Battalion. Lisa clapped her hands over her ears and began to cry as the cannon fire boomed across the desert, but James danced in glee. Matthew tried to sit up but groaned and collapsed back on his bed. Meg was simply pleased to know that the men and animals would have a few days to rest before moving on. It was her hope that Matthew might begin to heal without the jostling of the past week and the doctor's harassment.

Seeing the doctor and Lieutenant Smith ride away from their campground in their dress uniforms, Meg relaxed and spent the day coaxing Matthew to eat and allowing the children to run about freely.

Joe and Clay, then later Olaf, stopped by and were horrified to learn of Matthew's condition. Joe climbed to the wagon seat and then turned to face Matthew where he lay on the mattress.

"We reached here by the deadline General Kearney set. He has moved on and left orders for Lieutenant Colonel Philip St. George Cooke to replace Smith at this point," Joe said. "The men at the garrison who have served under Cooke report he's a firm officer, but fair. He has twenty years of experience in the West, which should prove invaluable."

"It will be weeks before I can march. Do you suppose he will leave me here?" There was deep concern in Matthew's voice. Meg hadn't considered that Matthew might be left behind. Fear filled her heart as she considered the possibility of being left, nearly penniless, far from the other Saints. Between worrying about Matthew and concern for their family's support should they be left behind, she slept little at night. She awoke each morning wondering if this was the reason she'd felt impressed not to sell the emerald. Would she need it now for their support? She wondered, too, what kind of price she could get for a valuable jewel in a military outpost filled with penniless soldiers or in the village composed mostly of Mexican peasants.

Only a few days passed before they learned that Colonel Cooke intended to lighten the battalion considerably by leaving behind what he considered an excessive number of women and sick soldiers. It was with mixed feelings that she learned a detachment of ninety-two men, nineteen women, and ten children would be escorted by Captain

James Brown to Pueblo. She and her family were among those ordered back to the settlement there.

Matthew seemed to rest more easily, knowing they would soon be among the Southern Saints where he had friends, but other families took the news hard. It did no good to remind the regular army officers of the promise made at the time of their enlistment that families would be able to stay together and that the battalion wouldn't be broken up. Those men who were able-bodied would move on to blaze a wagon trail to California, while their wives and children were to be sent to the settlement of Saints waiting out the winter to continue their journey over the Rocky Mountains. Meg recognized how hard it was for those men to leave wives, who were beginning to run low on supplies, among strangers.

Most of the battalion's mules and horses were needed by those men who were continuing on to California, so the morning that the Santa Fe Detachment, or Sick Detachment, as it became known, departed for Pueblo, Meg found herself with four additional passengers and a queasy stomach. Fortunately, the horses were rested again and didn't object to carrying the additional weight, and her slight nausea lifted once they were on the trail.

Olaf saw them off with tears in his eyes. "If you see Katrina before I do, tell her I'm thinking of her. And the baby—I think the baby is a girl—should be here by now. Give her this." He thrust a cloth doll with a carved wooden head toward Meg. The doll was about ten inches long with a bright red and yellow dress. "I bought it at the Mexican market."

"I'll tell her," she promised and gave him an impulsive hug.

Joe Donaldson bid them a hasty farewell. He needed to get back to his men. He peeked inside the back of the wagon to say, "I wish you were going on with us, Matt. I had to choose another lieutenant. Billy McBride will do fine, but I'll miss your steady influence among the men."

"We'll meet again," Matthew tried to say.

The high desert and strange mountains and formations made travel difficult, leaving Meg both light-headed and wary of damage to the horses and wagon. Concentrating on driving was difficult when her mind strayed continually to Matthew and the children.

Lisa was frightened of the strange men in their wagon and wanted them to go away when they first set out. Both James and Matthew worked hard to entertain her, and under Matthew's direction, James attempted to sponge the ill men's faces and give them a small amount of comfort. After becoming accustomed to the men who shared their wagon, Lisa got over her fear and attempted to mother them all. The men who were conscious enough to be aware of her efforts to cool their faces and give them sips of water became enthralled with their pint-sized ministering angel.

After the second day, Meg found there were advantages to having additional passengers. One of the young men was sitting up by the third day and able to spell her off in driving the team for short periods of time. She took advantage of those short periods to check on Matthew and the other three men, then climb down to walk for short distances with the children. One of the other men seemed to be showing improvement too, and Meg credited the two men's improved health to no longer being forced to take Doctor Sanderson's poisonous medicine.

The Sick Detachment moved along at a good pace, though not as quickly as the battalion had traveled. The cooler autumn temperatures seemed to revive the travelers and their teams, bringing a general air of good cheer. Those men who were well enough assisted in the care of their comrades and gave the women breaks from the constant driving. Some of the younger men seemed to draw strength from playing with the few children in the party. Except for her constant concern for Matthew and fleeting bouts of nausea that brought a fear that she might be next to succumb to the fever, the days were almost pleasant. Captain Brown's escort handled the heavier tasks and kept an eye out for Indians.

As long as the battalion had been together, there had been little threat from Indians, but the smaller detachment was more vulnerable, and even the sickest of the men kept their rifles close. Even after they reached the grasslands, which at first glance appeared empty and free of threats, the men who were now seasoned travelers kept a careful watch.

About mid-morning one day in early November, Captain Brown signaled for the detachment to halt. With nervous dread, Meg scanned the endless miles of brown grass and was mystified by a darker brown stain spreading across the prairie toward them.

"Buffalo!" someone shouted.

Captain Brown pointed toward a hill and led a charge toward the higher ground, where he ordered the wagons to form a double circle. Every man who could crawl out of the wagons with his gun crouched behind a wheel. Meg stood near the heads of her lead horses, gripping their cheek straps in an attempt to control the frightened animals as they jerked their heads and stomped their hooves, displaying their displeasure with the approaching horde of animals. Her own nervousness was apparent in the frequent glances she made inside the wagon to check on Matthew and the children. Matthew leaned with his back against the wagon box. Lisa sat on his good knee, hugging his chest while James sat close with an arm around her.

The great shaggy beasts raced toward them. The ground trembled, and men and women fought to control the frightened horses and mules. When it seemed they would certainly run them over and trample them underfoot, the massive heard split like the Red Sea divided by Moses, leaving the hill high and dry. Meg watched in awe as the buffalo flowed like water around them. It seemed to take hours for them to pass by.

When the great herd at last disappeared like a shadow receding in the distance, Captain Brown and his second-in-command stood together, looking back in the direction from which the animals had come. Curious to see what they were watching, Meg stood on the wagon seat for a better view. Several miles out on the prairie, she saw something move. At first, it appeared to be only a dark line. But after a few minutes of careful watching, she could make out a line of horses.

"There's a hunting party following those buffalo." It was the first she was aware of the young soldier who had climbed up on the wagon seat beside her. He didn't need to add that the hunting party was composed of Indians. A tremor of fear seemed to run through the party, even though the detachment clearly outnumbered the savages.

"Moving out!" Captain Brown called.

Meg sat abruptly and reached to release the brake. Simon, the young soldier beside her, beat her to it. Captain Brown set a course that would not bisect the Indians' path, though everyone knew the hunting party could not have missed seeing them. That night, he called on some of the more fit men to double the watch. Each shadow and rustle of grass evoked fear of an Indian attack.

That night when they made camp, she prepared a hearty stew and, with Simon's help, she spooned the rich broth into the mouths of the two men who lay sweating with fever and shaking with chills. Their companion, still too weak to eat or drink anything, drifted in and out of consciousness.

After the sick men were moved to their own tent for the night, Matthew led Meg and the children in a prayer of gratitude for their escape from the buffalo and appealed for divine help in reaching their destination safely.

The following morning only three men returned to the Holmes's wagon, and Meg learned that the man who had awakened only a few times since their journey began had died during the night. Simon and Meg gathered beside the grave that Captain Brown's men dug for the man, but there was no time to linger. After a short eulogy and a brief prayer by the captain, the grave was filled in and a call was issued to move on.

An air of somberness hung over the detachment all day, and when night came, they ate their meal in silence.

"Tomorrow," Matthew told James before Meg tucked the boy in bed, "we shall start your lessons again. It is time you learned to read and do sums." Meg suspected the lessons were a means of distracting her son from his fear of an Indian attack.

When Meg lay down beside Matthew, he tugged her closer to his side, the way he'd held her before his injury. "It's time I pulled my own weight again," he told her. The low-grade fever which had concerned her over the several weeks since the accident appeared to be gone, and she welcomed his attempt to return to normality.

Matthew appeared to be much better after that and insisted on sitting up to feed himself and to help Lisa with her dinner. Climbing in and out of the wagon was a challenge he wasn't up to yet, and he chafed at sitting inside the wagon while Meg dealt with the horses and prepared meals. With the help of Simon and little James, he took over the care of the two soldiers, freeing her of that task. And he began tutoring James as he had promised. Lisa insisted on being included in the lessons, and Meg noticed that Simon showed more than a passing interest in being schooled too.

The days took on an even sameness, and the men who had been so terribly ill began to show small signs of improvement. A high range of mountains paralleled their route to their left. Captain Brown announced his estimation that they were more than halfway to their destination, and a general rise in spirits seemed to take place. Meg ignored the uneasiness she'd first experienced on seeing the captain stand each morning and evening at the camp's edge, peering out as though watching something far out on the sea of grass.

As the days passed and there was no further sighting of the Indians, Meg began to relax. A number of the sick men were regaining their strength and were helping with camp chores, which gave her more time to spend with the children. Between Matthew's lessons and being free to walk for short stretches, the children were happier and quarreled less. With a little assistance, Matthew could now make his way from the wagon to sit with her in the evenings beside the fire. Lisa became Papa's shadow, running to fetch items he needed and curling up at his side when he rested. Sometimes Meg envied their little naps. The long journey had lately begun to leave her feeling greatly fatigued.

One day, they passed by a dry streambed, beside which grew a few forlorn trees. In hopes of finding firewood, Meg and James hurried to search the long grass that grew along its banks. Spotting two slender trees that were almost symmetrical in size, Matthew persuaded Simon to chop them down for him and strip off the few scrawny branches while he took over driving the wagon. Lisa pulled herself up beside him on the wagon box and clung to his trouser leg.

That evening, the two men fashioned a pair of crutches for Matthew's use. After that, he was able to move about more freely, so long as someone was available to help him in or out of the wagon.

Some days, a chill wind swept from the north, and the peaks of the distant mountains turned white, warning them that winter was approaching, but most days remained warm, with only the nights being cold. Firewood became scarce, and Meg soon discovered that knots of dry prairie grass burned too quickly to be practical for cooking fires. Some of the older children and the women who had been relieved from driving their wagons by the recuperating soldiers, spread out on either side of the wagons to search for bits of wood each day. Often they were forced to burn buffalo chips in their cook fires.

James wore a second shirt, refusing to wear his coat, as he and Meg walked away from their wagon to hunt for wood one morning. She looked back once to see Matthew on the wagon seat, his injured leg stretched out before him, and Lisa leaning against his shoulder. She waved, and Lisa waved back.

The sun beat down on them as they walked, and Meg regretted the impulse that had made her grab her shawl. Knotting it around her shoulders to keep it from sliding away, she stooped to gather a small, dry tree branch. Mountains at the edge of the plain likely bore trees, but no trees were nearby. She knew the mountains appeared closer than they actually were. She wondered how far the wind had carried the small branches she found and what kind of terrible storm could carry the bits of wood so far out onto the prairie.

"Mamma!" There was excitement in James's voice. She looked up to see that he had wandered some distance ahead. He was looking at something near his feet and urging her to hurry.

When she reached him, he was pointing to a jagged cut in the earth carved, she assumed, by fast moving water from a long-ago storm. At the bottom of the wash, a skeletal tree, bleached almost white by months, possibly years, in the fierce summer sun, lay on its side.

"What a find! You are the best wood hunter in the detachment." She ruffled her son's wind-blown hair, noting that she needed to darken it again. It gleamed gold in the bright sunlight. She'd been so busy caring for Matthew, the children, and the sick soldiers assigned to her wagon that she'd forgotten the tea rinses that dulled their pale locks to brown.

The tree was a marvelous find that would keep a dozen campfires burning until they reached a more wooded area. She glanced around, searching for other wood gatherers, but seeing none, she took James's hand to work their way down the steep sides of the small ravine. They would carry as much of the wood as they could back to the wagons. When she stood beside the tree, she wondered if she'd made a mistake. It would likely have been better to return to the detachment for a couple of men with axes.

Seeing her son picking up loose pieces of wood and chips that lay on the ground to fill the sack he carried, she pitched in to help. After a few minutes, she discovered she could break off larger pieces from the ends of the tree's branches by exerting pressure on them with one foot and her hands. When both the bag and her apron were filled, they found a large limb a short distance from the tree.

"We could drag it to the top," James proposed.

"But I need one hand to hold my apron."

"You could take your apron off and tie it with the strings, then loop it over your head and shoulders like my bag."

When they were both satisfied that their burdens of smaller pieces of the wood were secure, they clasped the small log by the broken limbs that extended from it in several places and began their torturous climb out of the wash. James took the lead, leaving Meg the greater portion of the branch's weight. Loose dirt fell on her, and sometimes she slid back a few steps. Her hair slipped free of the bun she'd secured at the back of her neck that morning, and the strands brushed across her face, nearly obscuring her vision. As they neared the top, Meg could hear the rush of wind and noticed that the bright sun no longer beat against her back. The log suddenly seemed heavier, as though James had lost his grip on it. She staggered to maintain her hold and to prevent their prize from crashing back into the ravine.

"James, perhaps we should leave—" She lifted her eyes. James was no longer in front of her, and his end of the log rested against the lip of the wash. All she could see was the long, brown prairie grass thrashing about in the wind a few feet above her head.

Shoving the log with as much strength as she could muster to keep it from sliding back into the ravine, she left it precariously balanced on the edge of the wash and scrambled the remainder of the way up. Sweeping her hair back with her hands, she looked about, seeing nothing but the waving grass. There was no sign of James, and the detachment had completely disappeared.

"James!" she opened her mouth to call his name. A heavy hand descended over her face, cutting off her cry.

22 ௸

Her struggles were to no avail, and she soon found herself draped across the rear end of a horse, headed north. At least she was headed in the right direction. No matter how hard she tried to turn her head, she could see nothing but the legs of the horse she was tied to and the prairie grass beneath its hooves. A thick rope cut across her throat, and again across her mouth, eliminating any possibility of calling out to James. She found herself praying that he had somehow escaped her captors and was hurrying back to the Sick Detachment to alert Captain Brown.

At first, she was mortified by her undignified position, but before long, she began to fear she would pass out or die as her blood ran to her head and she became lightheaded and disoriented. Another fear invaded her mind. Of late, she had begun to suspect it wasn't the fever that was causing her frequent bouts of mild nausea. If her suspicions were correct, the rough uncomfortable ride could cause terrible harm. She strained to lift her head, but as she did, the rope around her throat tightened painfully. The world receded to a dark, cold blur, and she was scarcely aware they had stopped until she felt rough hands drag her from the horse and felt herself slump against the ground.

"Mamma!" A small figure dropped beside her, and she struggled to reach out to him. By the time her vision cleared enough to see clearly, James was gone. Through eyes narrowed against the pounding pain in her head, she searched her surroundings, learning she was in one of the narrow washes that riddled this part of the plain. A handful of saplings and several squat, leafless shrubs surrounded her. Farther out, she could see where the wash ended in a ripple of grass swaying before the wind. A low fire burned in the middle of what was probably a streambed in the spring. A man wearing mismatched pieces of an army uniform knelt beside the fire. Beyond him, she found James leaning against one of the stunted trees, his hands thrust behind him and a gag in his mouth. He was twisting his head as though trying to spit out the cloth, but he wasn't choking or gasping for breath.

James was alive. That knowledge gave her hope.

As sensation returned to her feet, she had to bite her lip to keep from crying out from the pain. Her arms were still bound behind her back, but the choke rope that had circled her neck was gone, as was the thick rope that had cut her mouth, leaving it bruised and swollen. She didn't know how much time had passed. The sun was no longer bright, and twilight seemed to be upon them.

"You're awake."

The man was standing over her. There was something familiar about him. It took several minutes for her mind to register that she was looking at one of the army regulars from Fort Leavenworth who had arrived with Lieutenant Smith. Meg began to suspect that he had learned her identity and that he was looking to collect the reward for turning her and James over to the detective Lars had hired.

"Why did you wait?" The words came out thick and garbled, but her captor understood them.

"I didn't know until we reached Santa Fe and I noticed your hair had gotten lighter. Even then I wasn't sure 'til I heard the doctor's assistants laughing about your husband mumbling another woman's name—Margarette, not Meg—while he was unconscious."

"You've been following us since we left Santa Fe?"

"I'm a patient man. I knew I'd find you alone sooner or later."

"They'll come looking for us."

"Ain't nobody going to look for you. The captain won't leave all those sick folks to fend for themselves, and your husband's a cripple. 'Sides, they'll figure the Comanches took ya to sell south, and they won't even bother to look north. Now git up. You ought to have your senses back by now. I ain't had a decent meal for nigh on a month." He kicked her shoe, urging her to her feet.

"I can't cook with my hands tied."

He pulled a wicked looking knife from his belt and cut her hands free.

Shaking her hands and rubbing them to restore circulation, she stumbled toward the fire. In spite of the man's insistence that no one would search for them, she felt certain Matthew would sound an alarm and demand that Captain Brown send out a search party when she didn't return to the wagon. She added more wood to the fire—wood she discovered came from James's bag—in hopes a larger blaze would produce smoke that would guide searchers to them. To her disappointment, the sun-bleached wood produced an almost smokeless fire.

"My son . . ." she began.

"The brat is staying tied up." She noticed a circle of red teeth marks on the man's hand and a long scratch down his cheek. She almost smiled.

The burly soldier pointed to a few items he'd dumped on the ground near the fire. She bent to pick up a skillet and wondered if she might use it as a weapon, but the man's close scrutiny of her actions made her hesitate. Even if she managed to hurt the man, she couldn't hit him hard enough to render him unconscious so she could free James. She would have no chance against someone so much larger. He was also armed.

While mixing biscuits and turning the odds and ends she found in a bag near the skillet into a meal, she cast frequent glances toward her son. She was relieved to see he was conscious and that his eyes were following her movements.

When the meal was ready, she set a plate before the man, then filled a tin bowl and began walking toward James. Behind him she could see roiling black clouds tumbling over each other, hiding the mountains and foothills to the west. Thunder rumbled in the distance.

"Get back here!" the man shouted at her.

"James is just a little boy. Surely you don't mean to starve him," she countered, growing braver as she realized that she and her son would be useless to their captor if he killed them. "You won't collect a reward for turning us over to that detective if he isn't well enough to travel."

"All right, feed him, but if you make a move to untie him, I'll hit you both over the head to make certain you behave yourselves."

"Are you all right?" she whispered as she knelt to remove the filthy rag covering James mouth and release his hands, in spite of their captor's threat, so he could feed himself. She didn't dare loosen the rope that held his feet and secured him to the tree.

"Yes." Tears sparkled in his eyes. "Matthew is going to be mad. I promised Papa I would look after you."

"It's all right." She attempted to comfort him. "We must pray—"

"No talking," the man ordered. "Woman, get back over here and fill my plate up agin."

"Mamma!"

She saw James's eyes grow round as they looked beyond her to something only he could see.

Fearing the rebel soldier was about to attack her, she turned in time to see an Indian with a raised club leap toward the former soldier. She screamed.

"I'm not falling for that trick—" The man crumpled beside the fire, a gaping wound in his head.

The Indian released a shout, and half a dozen more Indians sprang from the grass to advance toward her. She took a step closer to James in a vain effort to conceal him.

A fist grasped her hair, jerking her backward with enough force to bring tears to her eyes.

"Leave my Mamma alone!" James, who had freed his legs or been cut free by one of the savages, lurched toward the Indian who held her. His small fists pummeled the brave until one of the other Indians grabbed him from behind and tossed him in the air. She screamed, fearing he would be killed if he fell to the ground.

It became a game, the Indians tossing the boy from one to another. Furious at the treatment given her son, she struggled to escape by clawing and kicking at the person holding her, delivering several kicks to the Indian's bare shins eliciting yelps of surprise and, she hoped, pain. Their tormenters shouted in apparent glee.

When they tired of the game, they set the boy on his feet where he stood defiantly glaring at them. Her captor released his grip on her hair, and she stumbled to her son's side. The Indians formed a circle around them, pointing and speaking in animated excitement as one after another, they reached out their hands to touch her hair or

James's. She suspected that they had never seen hair of the pale, golden shade she and her children shared.

A sick sensation filled her. They would be killed, and their hair would hang from the savages' belts as trophies. She didn't want to die, but she would willingly trade her life for James's if she could. Only that choice was not hers.

She stepped forward, placing a protective arm around James, her brave small son. Her mind whirled with the prospect of imminent death. Lisa would be all right. Matthew would care for her. Matthew! She could not bear to part from him. She had been foolish all these months not to admit that what she felt for him went far beyond friendship. She loved him. And though he'd never said the words, his actions had shouted his love for her almost from the beginning. His love for the gospel had been evident since the day they first met on the *Carolina*. How had she let Jory's shortcomings blind her until she didn't recognize the meaning behind Matthew's commitment and tenderness toward her and her children?

One hand slipped to the small mound just beginning to show at her waist. She must live. Matthew's child deserved a chance at life, and James had endured too much for her to give up now. Her hand drifted to the thong that held the leather pouch Matthew had given her. A strong prompting came to her. Did the savages know the value of the emerald the bag held? Could she trade it for their freedom? Or seeing it, would they just take it from her?

She tightened her grip on James's shoulder. He didn't change his angry stance but stood with his feet spread and his hands on his hips. Her other hand tugged on the thong, drawing the bag from beneath her bodice. A couple of the Indians watched her, showing both curiosity and a readiness to pounce should she produce a weapon. When she withdrew her hand from James's shoulders to lift the thong from around her neck and place the bag on the flat of one hand, the watching Indians jumped back, startled expressions on their faces. With excited gestures, they pointed toward her and the small leather bag. They took another step back, wariness in the lines of their bronzed faces.

One by one, she began to draw the simple items from the pouch. First came the feather. The wind caught it, sending it soaring into the sky. Each dark head bobbed as though expressing approval. The same reaction followed as the twig and berry were removed. Their brown fingers reached for the squash and apple seeds. Broad smiles appeared on the dark faces as the items were passed from hand to hand around the circle. Admiring glances met the curl of wood that had fallen from Matthew's knife when he'd fashioned his crutches. A small gasp greeted Anna's long silver hair. Each man touched it with something resembling reverence. She shook the last two objects onto her palm— the sliver of white limestone from the Nauvoo Temple and the brilliant green emerald.

An uneasy murmur rippled through the half-clad natives. As one, they took a step backward, widening the circle. A sudden flash of lightning shot downward, followed almost immediately by a tremendous clap of thunder. Caught in the quick burst of light, the stones in Meg's hand took on an eerie glow. Static electricity set James's hair on end, making it stand out from his head, giving him a crazed look. A skeletal tree on the edge of the shallow ravine burst into flame as a second tongue of lighting flashed downward. Terror was etched on the Indians' faces.

A low rumble shook the ground, and the Indians scattered, racing up the sides of the wash to disappear into the long grass. In seconds they were gone. The soldier's terrified horse pulled free of its tether and followed.

"Mamma, what's happening?" James clutched at her arm.

"I don't know." She dumped the items resting on her hand back into the small bag and, clasping her son's hand, began running. "But this is likely our best chance to escape."

She dashed down the narrow wash toward the prairie just visible in the distance, but as the rumble behind them grew louder, she remembered the buffalo herd and wondered if they were in the path of that massive sea of animals. "Hurry!" she screamed, dragging James toward the steep sides of the wash. They needed to seek the highest point they could find.

James released his grip on her hand to better grasp the rocks and roots on the side of the steep slope. Meg's skirt caught on a bramble. Instinct or perhaps the whispering of the Spirit told her there was no time to work it free. Giving the fabric a jerk, she left at least a yard of her skirt behind.

Rain streamed from the sky without a spattering preamble, turning the slope to slippery mud. James lost his footing and plunged backward. Meg barely managed to catch his sliding figure with one hand. Together, they stood teetering, searching for anything to anchor them in place. Her hand grasped a fistful of sturdy roots. With all of the strength she could muster, she thrust James ahead of her. Clawing with both hands, he pulled himself out of the wash to lie winded in the tall grass. Meg clambered after him to lie beside him, gasping and wheezing.

The roar coming from behind her reminded her that there was no time to rest. The deafening noise drowned out the beat of the downpour that had descended upon them. Struggling to her feet, she reached for James's hand, pulling him upright. Behind him, she caught sight of a powerful wall of water pouring down the gully and spilling over its sides. Great chunks of dirt and grass were ripping free from the sides of the wash to be sucked into the water's greedy grasp.

"Run!" she screamed, jerking her son after her, endeavoring to put as much space as she possibly could between them and the cascade of water filling the wash and overflowing its banks. It didn't take long to discover that James couldn't match her long strides. She swept him into her arms and ran on until his weight caused her to stumble and stagger. The rain fell in torrents, blinding her, and the slippery grass brought her lurching to her knees. Twisting to look behind her, she could see little for the blinding rain and dark clouds that brought an illusion of early nightfall.

A flash of lightning illuminated their surroundings for a brief second, but it was enough to assure her they weren't being pursued by floodwaters or buffalo. James flung himself into her arms, and she sat cradling him while the rain beat relentlessly against them and their breathing gradually slowed to normal.

She tried to think, to form a plan. They needed to travel north to reach Pueblo, but she had no idea whether the detachment was ahead or behind them. They were safe from the man who planned to turn them over to the detective. If he hadn't died from the blow to his head, he must surely have been swept away by the flash flood. The Indians were another matter. They could be anywhere.

Lightning flashed again, and the thunder seemed to roll all around them. She felt an urgency to keep moving, but she remembered that Soren had once said a person should avoid being the tallest object in a lightning storm.

"We need to keep moving," she spoke against James's ear, "but Grandpa Pedersen said we shouldn't stand when there is lightning around us."

"We can crawl." James slid off her lap, landing on all fours.

Meg soon discovered that her long skirts weren't meant for crawling. She bunched them about her waist, but her movement was slow and messy. James moved more easily and stayed ahead of her, pausing occasionally to wait for her to catch up.

"Ouch!"

"What is it? Are you all right?" She closed the space between them.

"Rocks. I bumped into a rock, but I'm not hurt."

Lightning soon revealed that they had stumbled onto one of the raised, rocky islands that now, along with washes and dried streams, appeared more frequently as they neared the mountains. Creeping to the sheltered side of the large rock, Meg decided they should stay there until the storm ended. Seating herself, she pulled her son close against her to provide him with as much warmth and comfort as possible. They huddled together and waited.

With the cessation of movement, Meg became aware of the drop in temperature. Their wet clothing added to their discomfort, and she felt James's small body shiver. She reached for her shawl, but it was gone, lost, as was her apron. Fear grew in her heart. They were stranded somewhere on the Great Plains with no food or fire in a cold November rain which might turn to snow.

"When you said I should pray, I didn't have time," James said. "Will Heavenly Father help us anyway?"

"I think He already has, but we need more help. We could pray right now, asking Him to keep helping us." She knew God could help them—but if it were their appointed time to die . . .

"Papa said when we pray, we have to have faith. You better say the prayer because I don't know if my faith is big enough." Any other time, his earnest admission would have brought a smile to her lips. Now she wondered if *her* faith was big enough.

Her teeth chattered as she began to pray. Opening her heart, she pleaded to be shown the way she and James should go, asked for protection from the cold, and begged for her children's lives to be spared. She asked for strength and faith and finished with a request for peace and comfort for Matthew and Lisa. When she finished, she felt James's small, chilled hand against her cheek.

"Papa will find us." He spoke with confidence. "My faith is little, but Papa's is big."

She held him close and thought of Matthew. Even if she and James perished, the long journey they'd taken from Lars's farm to this rocky ridge had been a journey worth taking. "The gospel is worth all we have endured," she whispered against her son's drenched hair.

The rain stopped as abruptly as it had begun. Far in the distance, a pink light began to emerge through the clouds, revealing mountaintops. That way was west.

Together they stood. Meg bent to wring water from her tattered, muddy skirts. Straightening, she squeezed the excess water from her hair. The glow from the setting sun revealed James's hair plastered against his head, a jagged tear in his pants, and scratches on his face and hands.

"Which way should we go?" James was gazing around, a look of puzzlement on his face. He scrambled up the side of the rock where they had taken shelter. "The mountains are that way." He pointed. "And that's the way the rain went." He pointed to the black clouds that were now moving away from them to the east. "And there's a big river that way."

Meg looked in the direction her son pointed and saw that they hadn't traveled far from the ravine where they'd barely managed to escape with their lives. It was filled with a churning torrent that spilled from the large gulley to spread across the prairie, forming a large lake. Taking James's hand, they began to walk in what she estimated was a northeastern direction, hoping they would eventually meet the track the detachment was following.

The light was almost gone when Meg caught sight of movement far ahead of them. Crouching low in the tall, wet grass with James beside her, she watched the object slowly move closer. After what seemed a long time, she became convinced a horse or some other large animal was coming their way. She thought of the soldier's horse. If she could catch it . . .

The animal moved closer, and though the light disappeared, she could make out a figure on its back. Hope that they were about to be rescued warred with the fear that one of the Indians had caught the soldier's horse and was now looking for them.

Continuing to hide and watch, she was startled when James jumped to his feet and began to run toward the approaching horse.

"James, no. Wait." She ran after him.

The horse sprang forward as though urged by its rider to run.

"Margarette!" A shout carried to her ears.

"Papa! Papa!" Her son's words drifted back to her. Matthew had come for them. Before she reached him, she recognized the draft horse he rode and the set of his shoulders. But how could he be riding a horse? He still had difficulty climbing out of their wagon.

She saw Matthew reach a hand down to James and pull him up to sit before him on the big horse's back. Then she was beside him, clinging to his good leg and sobbing.

He placed one hand on her shoulder and leaned toward her.

"Meg." There was a catch in his voice. "Meg, my darling, Margarette, I was afraid I'd lost you."

"What are you doing on a horse?" She leaned her cheek against his thigh and closed her eyes. Tears streamed from beneath her lowered lashes. "I'm so happy to see you, but I'll never forgive myself if riding this horse makes your injury permanent."

"I couldn't wait in the wagon while others searched for you. You're my wife, my love, my forever. I had to come."

"But your leg . . ."

"We'll discuss it later. You and James are cold and wet. I've got to get you back to camp, but I can't get off to help you mount. Do you think you can grab my belt and pull yourself up?"

It took several attempts, but she finally managed to mount the horse's broad back. As she did, she realized there was no saddle on the horse. Matthew had somehow climbed aboard a draft animal and with only a bridle to guide the big horse had come searching for her and James. She scooted close to his back, wrapping her arms around his waist and pressing her face into his shirt.

He urged the horse back the way he'd come. "I knew you'd come," she heard James say, and then she heard Matthew tell him how the two riders Captain Brown sent out had found her apron, then her shawl, which caught on some roots miles down the wash from where the apron was found. They'd been convinced that the two of them had drowned in the flash flood that had roared out of the mountains.

"I couldn't believe it. If it were true, somehow I would have known it," Matthew's voice broke. "Simon helped me in removing my leg splints and in mounting the only horse available. He promised to take care of Lisa until I returned with you."

She hugged him tighter. "I love you," she whispered.

"I have loved you since the day I first saw you aboard the *Carolina,*" he whispered back in a choked voice. She leaned her face against his wet shirt and felt the warmth of his skin.

James told him about finding the tree and about the man who carried them away. Matthew's back stiffened. James started to tell about the Indians, but his voice dwindled away, and Meg knew her little boy had fallen asleep, safe in his papa's arms.

She felt sleep stealing closer and fought to remain awake, fearing she might fall beneath the horse's feet if she gave in to the fatigue that pulled at her eyelids. She was only semi-aware of the two riders who rode out to meet them, of someone taking James from Matthew's arms, then loosening her hold on Matthew's belt and drawing her from the horse's back. Simon and Captain Brown carried her inside the wagon, then went back for Matthew. Simon stayed only long enough to strip off James's wet clothing, pull his nightshirt over his head, and tuck the sleeping child in his bed.

Matthew helped her free herself of her sodden clothing and buttoned her nightdress in a crooked line. He pulled her close beneath the quilt she'd brought all the way from Denmark, and she drifted to sleep, dreaming of a house in a valley with children playing in a lovely sunlit garden. Only James and Lisa had hair the color of spun gold. The others had dark curls just like Matthew's.

She awoke to the jostling motion of two small children climbing from their bed onto hers. They threw themselves upon her with shouts of laughter. Matthew parted the canvas between the wagon seat and their bed to smile down at her, filling her heart with gladness.

* * *

Three days later, they arrived at the settlement near Old Fort Bent to a joyful reunion with the families who had first been rerouted to Pueblo. Some were still ill, but many, including Collin, were much recovered. The Southern Saints were excited to see Matthew and lost no time constructing a simple cabin for him and his family. Matthew and Meg invited Collin to move in with them, much to the delight of James and Lisa.

Several of the Southern families formed a committee to invite Matthew to teach their children through the winter. Meg was pleased to see the satisfaction Matthew derived from being a schoolmaster.

The winter months passed quickly. Though Meg was anxious to move on and establish a permanent home, the waiting in Pueblo was a pleasant time, allowing her and Matthew to draw closer as they openly shared their feelings for each other. Sometimes they talked about Meg and James's frightful experience.

"I've thought about it," Meg told Matthew. "The Indians seemed to be afraid of the emerald, but I don't believe it has the mystical powers that saved us. I think God knew of their superstition and prompted me to show it to them. Then He sent the storm."

With the arrival of spring, the Crowe family grew impatient and set out for Laramie to meet the Pioneer Company. The other three hundred members of John Brown's company and the Sick Detachments were eager to be on their way as well. Meg grew fearful that they would leave before her baby arrived, but early on the morning of May third, she awoke Matthew to tell him her time had come.

After sending Collin to fetch a woman who had delivered several other babies since their arrival in Pueblo, Matthew dressed the children and took them next door, then hurried back to alternate pacing the floor and kneeling at her side.

Watching Matthew's uneven gait as he walked back and forth across the cabin's floor, Meg could only love him more and marvel that he loved her. She'd waited as long as she dared to call for a midwife to spare him worry, and now she almost hated for their brief time alone to end.

The midwife arrived, and a short time later, without a great deal of fuss, Meg gave birth to her third child. Matthew never left her side, and when the midwife placed the baby in her arms, he pulled back a corner of the flannel blanket she'd wrapped around the infant. After watching the grimaces and yawns his son made, he asked, "What shall we call him? I was thinking of Wilford, or maybe Brigham."

"He already has a name. That day on the prairie when you rescued us, I named him for the two men I love most. His name is Matthew Soren Holmes."

Lisa was delighted with her new brother, but James was a little uncertain about Little Matt until his papa assured him with both words and actions that the baby hadn't replaced James in Matthew's heart.

Three weeks later, they once again set out for the valley in the mountains. Matthew and Collin took over driving and caring for the team, allowing Meg to rest much of each day. They crossed the Platte River, and followed it, and then the Sweetwater, to Devil's Gate, where the soldiers celebrated the end of their enlistment.

Most of the soldiers were young and had recovered from their illnesses. They far outnumbered the women and children in their group. Most were anxious to rejoin the families they hadn't seen for more than a year. They needed no prompting to begin their journey early each morning. The entire group was composed of seasoned travelers, which helped to make the journey go much more smoothly. They almost caught up to the vanguard company, but knowing they had the worst of the mountains yet to cross, they stopped to shoe their animals and to make repairs on their wagons.

On July twenty-eighth, excitement rippled through the Brown Company, as their combined group had come to be called, when they caught the first tantalizing glimpse of their destination. Drawing the wagon to a halt, Matthew called to Meg.

"Come. You and the children must see and remember this all your lives." They stood on the wagon seat, and Matthew lifted James, then Lisa to see the valley beyond the trees and mountains.

Matthew and Collin joined the men of their regiment the next day as they approached the valley, and Meg drove the last stretch. The men had decided to make a grand, military parade entry into the valley, but a sudden violent thunderstorm disrupted both their plans and the plans of Brigham Young, Wilford Woodruff, and the group of brethren who rode to the mouth of the canyon to meet them.

Meg couldn't help smiling as she saw Matthew with his odd gait hurrying toward her in the rain. In two-and-a-half years, she'd seen him just this way many times, coming toward her, out of the clouds and rain, to make her life better and shower her with love. He caught the side of the wagon and heaved himself to the seat beside her.

"Get in the back where it's dry," he told her.

"I'm fine." She scooted closer to him. "We've waited a long time to reach this place, and I want to enter the valley at your side."

He smiled that boyish grin she loved and clucked to the horses to move on. Her fingers went to the medicine bag at her throat. Through the soft leather, she touched the emerald, her talisman of new beginnings.